Chapter 1

December 25, 1817, Pemberley

I t is Christmas night, and I have been looking forward to this moment all day. My mind has been racing, and my fingers have been itching to pick up my pen and *write*. That, I suppose, is why Fitzwilliam has given me such a gift. He knows me and my imaginings so well, and I hope that I do him as a great a service when I select presents for him.

We awoke early and celebrated the day as we have done every year since we were married. Small gifts were exchanged in the dim light of the winter morning, and then he made love to me—although, given my size and condition, the second part of our tradition was more difficult to achieve than it has been in previous years. It was, nonetheless, both successful and enjoyable. Do I shock you? I confess that I have half shocked myself. And yet I shall continue, for it is my resolution that this is *my book* and shall be a faithful account of matters relating to me.

For all that I have worried about inflicting my entire family on Fitzwilliam at Christmas, the day passed well and largely without incident. After he departed, Hannah helped me into my day gown. Her poor face creased with worry and concentration as she tried to squeeze me into it, pulling the fabric this way and that and tugging on the hem. She looked up at me in exasperation.

"I do not think I can take this one out any further, madam. I will have to put another panel in. While I am at it, I will put one in your blue and your green if that is agreeable. Those are good, warm gowns for the season.

Would you like me to alter any of your evening gowns?"

"No, Hannah, that will not be necessary. We shall not be going anywhere before the baby is born. But maybe add a panel to my red gown as well? Mr. Darcy likes that one."

I turned to the side and considered my reflection in the glass.

"Goodness, Hannah. I look like a ship! Great naval fortunes have been made with smaller cargoes than this belly. How can it be that I still have two months to go?"

When Hannah smiled, she showed all of her teeth and looked every bit as pretty as my sister Jane.

"You are full large, madam, but the midwife is happy, is she not? In any case, a larger belly might be a good thing."

"What do you mean? Do you think it might mean that it is a boy?"

"Well maybe, madam. Mrs. Reynolds says that if you carry high then it is a boy but I have seen women carry girls so high that you could hardly see their bosoms, so maybe it is best not to torture ourselves with speculation…"

"That is easier said than done. I have looked at it from all directions, poked and prodded the poor babe, and even tried talking to it. I have prayed on the subject. If I knew some manner of magic that would assure Mr. Darcy of a son to join his two daughters, then I would do it."

"I am sure that all will be well, madam. You are young, and you gave birth to Miss Anne and Miss Emma with ease, so you should not be worrying yourself about this matter. I am sure that Mr. Darcy would not approve."

"No, indeed, he would not approve. He has said nothing about it, for I believe that he fears worrying me. But it is useless, Hannah, for I am worried already! I *must* give him a son."

She placed a pretty shawl across my shoulders and, giving one last tug of the skirt over the swell of my belly, said, "And so, I am sure you shall."

As is my custom, I visited Anne and Emma in the day nursery the moment I was dressed. From the corridor, I heard shrieks, laughter, and the happy sounds of their morning, and I knew that all was well. As I peeked around the door, they cried, "Mama," at great volume as if I did not visit them thus every morning. They each flung their little bodies at me for cuddles, and Christmas greetings were exchanged. Anne, I notice, looks more like Fitz-william every day. Nanny said that they had each eaten a good breakfast and were just engaged in a game of imaginary carriages. I was about to ask them to tell me where they were going in their carriages when I heard the unmistakable sound of my own mama shrieking below stairs. In my mind, I was transported back to Longbourn, and it took me a moment to recall that I was a married woman with my own household who did not have to do as my mother bade me do. I kissed the girls and made my way to the source of the commotion.

"Mr. Darcy, I simply do not believe it! What a notion. I cannot think that she would be doing such a thing. It is quite unconscionable!"

I hastened down the great staircase, Mama's volume and agitation growing as I neared. As she caught sight of me, she changed tack.

"Ah, Lizzy, there you are. I am glad that you are come, but do not hurry so down those stairs, girl; it is too much for me. Now what on earth is this nonsense about your accompanying us to church? I am sure that Mr. Darcy must be mistaken, for what manner of madness would it be for a woman in your condition to undertake that great carriage ride up hill and down dale, over ice and heaven knows what, when there is a chapel here at Pemberley that you can pray in if you must. You had much better stay here with the children. No, it simply cannot be that you would take such risks. I—"

"Mama, Mama, calm yourself. There is nothing to worry about. There is a chapel at Pemberley, but I explained to you before that on Christmas Day we always attend church in the village. It is where most of Mr. Darcy's tenants worship, and they expect to see us there. Today is not icy, and the roads shall be clear. It is not far, and the carriage is comfortable."

"But Lizzy—"

"In any case, I have my husband, my parents, and *all of my sisters* to watch over me, do I not?"

With this, I turned to see that it was quite literally true, for they were all present in their Christmas Day best, their eyes trained upon Mama and her histrionics. Jane, from her posture, I believe had been trying to quieten our mother before my arrival, and she was now putting on her bonnet and straightening her skirts.

"Of course you do, Lizzy," she said. "Now, who is going in which carriage? Charles and I can take at least two—maybe three if they do not mind being cosy. How about Mama and Papa and Lydia come with us?"

I shot her a look to thank her for this characteristic act of generosity, for the two people most likely to irritate Fitzwilliam were undoubtedly Mama and Lydia, and the only person who could really subdue either was Jane.

"Mary and Mr. Lander, would you like to travel with Fitzwilliam and me? Kitty and Reverend Braithwaite can travel in the spare with Georgiana, and we shall all meet there. Is everyone content with those arrangements?"

They each nodded, bonnets were tied and cloaks fixed, the chill of the morning remarked upon, and we were away. I had volunteered to escort Mary and her husband Mr. Lander not out of any great wish for their company but in order that Georgiana may travel with Kitty, of whom she is fond. Mr. Lander is a gentleman of Cambridgeshire who was brought into contact with our family when he visited his aunt in Meryton last year. He has a small estate and lives modestly. However, he is respectable and it was, as Mama had pronounced loudly at the time, a "blessing" that a man had at last appreciated Mary's virtues. It was less of a blessing that my husband was confined upon Christmas morning in a cold carriage with him.

"Mr. Darcy, do you have an opinion on the history of the levellers[1]?" asked he as if it were a perfectly normal question to ask of a gentleman whom he had met on only two occasions. Mr. Lander, we were given to understand, fancied himself an academic and was forever researching some new subject with which to enlighten his acquaintances.

"Erm, I cannot say that I do, Mr. Lander. I assume that you do, sir?"

"Yes, I do; indeed, I do. I have been reading extensively on the subject, sir. Or rather, I should say that I have been reading as extensively as the subject allows, for it is one that is served ill by existing studies. There is a great need, Mr. Darcy, for more to be written on them—for they were in my view, Mr. Darcy, a most significant group of people. I am, I hope you know, Mr. Darcy, no revolutionary myself, but I sincerely believe that there is a group of men who shall come to be regarded as *important* in later generations."

Fitzwilliam nodded politely and inserted the occasional "I see" and "indeed" into Mr. Lander's speech. Thus, we proceeded out of Pemberley and into the village for our Christmas Day service. My sister Mary sat straight

---

1 A political movement originating in 1645-46 among radical supporters of Parliament during the English Civil War that demanded that real sovereignty should be transferred to the House of Commons (the exclusion of kings and lords); a redistribution of seats, and an annual or biennial sessions of Parliament making the legislative body truly representative; and that all government should be decentralized to local communities—all of which were expressed in the manifesto "Agreement of the People." By 1650, they were no longer a serious threat to the established order. —Editor's note.

across the carriage from me, her hands clasped in her lap and a smile of utter contentment and admiration directed towards her husband. Did they discuss the levellers when they were in bed, I wondered?

Cumbersome as my swollen body is and uncomfortable as the journey was, it was a thrill to alight into the chill air outside the church as the bells rang out and all of the local families swarmed to the service like ants. I was glad that I had come, in spite of Fitzwilliam saying that nobody would mind if I had decided to stay at Pemberley. He offered me his arm, and as we walked in, we exchanged greetings with no less than twenty people. I knew that Mama and Lydia were pouting and strutting behind me and that Mr. Lander continued his monologue on the levellers, this time to poor Kitty, but I resolved not to care. I had caught Fitzwilliam smiling a laughing smile as he handed me out of the carriage, and I knew that he was taking the events of the morning in good humour.

We were spared the ruminations of Mr. Lander on our journey home and were joined by my sister Kitty and her husband, Reverend Braithwaite. Absent the influence of our sister Lydia and happily married to a kind and amiable man, Kitty has become a pleasant girl who is sensible of others and easy company. Fitzwilliam can hardly believe the change in her from when he first knew us all in Hertfordshire, and I saw briefly the relief that spread across his face when he saw me take *her* arm and lead her to our carriage outside the church. Fitzwilliam helped me into the carriage, and Kitty sat beside me, looking at my face in a searching manner.

"Are you sure that you are comfortable, Lizzy? Can I get you another cushion? You can have mine. How about that?"

"I am fine, Kitty. There is no need. Just sit down beside me and tell me of your parsonage. You must be well settled now."

"Yes, we are, Lizzy, very well settled, although Mama has been most scathing of my colour choices. I fear that she would have chosen differently, and I shall never hear the end of it! Oh, Lizzy"—she looked around to be sure we were alone and then, in an excited whisper redolent of her old self, asked—"May I?"

I nodded, and she placed her delicate hands on my great belly, stroking it and inclining her head in amazement.

"I am afraid that I cannot guarantee that the babe will move for you. If you are lucky, you may get a kick or a nudge. He or she may be asleep."

"It is so exciting, Lizzy. Another niece or nephew. I am building up quite a collection. I so hope that I may have a child of my own."

"I am sure your time will come, Kitty."

She saw the men readying to join us and quickly moved her hands away.

It seemed hardly any time at all before we were back at Pemberley—hats, bonnets, and cloaks removed, and warming our chilly selves before the fire in the drawing room. Mrs. Reynolds and various servants hurried about readying nuncheon and tidying in the wake of my family. Fitzwilliam and I brought Anne and Emma down from the day nursery, and everyone remarked on how tall they were and how dark their hair was.

"That is a Darcy face if ever I saw one!" pronounced Mama noisily, leaning into poor Anne and nodding in Mr. Darcy's direction. "As for you, Miss Emma, I am not sure. You have the look of your Aunt Georgiana about you."

"I believe that Emma looks a lot like the late Mrs. Darcy, Mama," I offered. It was one of the first things that Fitzwilliam had said to me when Emma was born, and I could see now from comparing my daughter's face and his mama's portrait on the stairs that he was right. It amazes me how strong a likeness can be even in an infant face.

"Neither of them looks anything like you, Lizzy!" said my sister Lydia, laughing between sips of her tea. "How very vexing that must be, to go through all the discomfort and pain, and then they are not even a likeness to one! If I ever have a child, I should wish for a girl who looks exactly like me. Would not that be droll?"

She giggled and did not notice that Fitzwilliam and Papa had turned to look out of the window, and Mr. Bingley had begun stoking the fire unnecessarily.

"Of course, no doubt, dear Wickham would wish for a son in his own image, and I suppose that would not be so bad, for my husband *is* devilish handsome!" She clonked her cup and saucer down upon the table with more force than was warranted before continuing. "Oh, how I miss him, Mama. What a great shame that he cannot be here with us. I know that he would love it so to be with all of our family in the place where he grew up."

Mama nodded sympathetically and reached for Lydia's hand.

"Yes, my child, what a pleasure it would have been to have dear Wickham here. He is always remarking upon his fondness for Pemberley!"

At this, Fitzwilliam raked his fingers through his dark hair and exhaled slightly. I felt agitation rising within me like a pot bubbling on the stove. My fear of the manner in which my family would embarrass me, I knew well. My husband's having to bribe Wickham to marry Lydia came back to me in a flash. The ingrate had attempted to seduce Mr. Darcy's sister and injured him greatly, he had eloped with Lydia, and then my husband had intervened to save her reputation and mine. It had cost him I know not what in money and mortification, and in that moment, it returned to me as though it were yesterday. That he was now confined in his own drawing room while Wickham was praised and his knowledge of Pemberley remarked upon was too much, and I knew that I had to stop it.

"Mama, you must be hungry. Did I tell you that we have venison for nuncheon? I told Mrs. Reynolds that it was your favourite, and Cook has tried a new recipe, so I hope that you are ready to feast!"

Her eyes danced between Lydia and me and she seemed to grasp that I was asking her to help me redirect the conversation. "You treat me, Lizzy!"

Our nuncheon passed perfectly well and conversation flowed freely even between Mr. Lander and Fitzwilliam. Mama was a credit to me and did not mention the absent Mr. Wickham again. She did express in strident terms, after some little wine, her wish to visit the Darcy estate in Ireland.

"Rothchapel! What name that is for the imaginings!"

"It is called Rosschapel, Mama, and it is a most arduous journey, not to be undertaken easily. I have never travelled there, and Mr. Darcy has only been once, is that not so?"

He nodded and put down his fork. "Yes, I went with my father when I was fifteen. I recall that we were beset by gales on the journey, even in July. I am afraid, Mrs. Bennet, that you would find it a difficult passage and may not like it when you arrived. It is not a long distance from Dublin, but Dublin is nothing to London I am afraid, and the roads are rather poor. Our house at Rosschapel is not at all like Pemberley. It is about the same size as Longbourn but nowhere near as comfortable."

Mama blushed and giggled quietly at this compliment, and I resolved to tease my husband later for his forwardness. "I should like to know more of it, Mr. Darcy."

"Rosschapel? At present, it is let to a Scottish gentleman and his family. The whole estate there is managed by my Irish steward, and so I am fortunate that there is no call for me to visit. If I should ever need to travel there, I shall bear you in mind, Mrs. Bennet."

Everyone smiled at this, and inwardly I laughed to think of Mama and Fitzwilliam making such a journey with only each other for company.

Later, I awoke fully clothed and lying on my bed. My legs and feet were covered with a light blanket, and the heavy curtains in my chamber had been drawn shut. I moved with a start to see my husband in the chair beside me, squinting in the dim light to read his book.

"Fitzwilliam! What is the time? How long have I been asleep? I hope it is not nighttime!"

"Calm yourself, Elizabeth. It is not late. It is almost five o'clock. You have been sleeping for nearly two hours, as well you might. Everybody is presently resting or preparing for dinner, and you are not to worry about them."

I recalled that, after nuncheon, I could hardly get up from my seat for fatigue, and Jane had taken me above stairs for a rest. I had gone only reluctantly, concerned at what may assail Fitzwilliam in my absence.

"How have our guests been while I have been up here? Has everything passed reasonably?"

"They have been fine, and of course, everything has passed happily. Your mama and Lydia have spent most of the afternoon admiring the house. Mrs. Bennet ceased her requests to visit Rosschapel when I told her that our carriage lost a wheel to a crater in the road on my last visit there. Mr. Bennet barricaded himself in the library the moment it was politic to do so. Mary has been playing duets with Georgiana, and Jane and Katherine have been amusing the children. Reverend Braithwaite joined Bingley and me for a game of billiards, and Mr. Lander, to my complete astonishment, found a book in the library that includes a chapter on the levellers. Fortunately, he has been reading it rather than talking about it for most of the afternoon. Nothing unpleasant has occurred."

He kissed my forehead and closed his book.

"Then why are you taking refuge here, Fitzwilliam?"

"Because I wanted to sit with you." He leant over and kissed me again, seeming to stifle a laugh. "There is nothing more to it than that, and you really must cease this worrying, Elizabeth. Do not fret about your family. I am perfectly capable of coping with their exuberance and...well...if Wickham is mentioned occasionally, then I can cope with that as well. It is only to be expected that Lydia will speak of her husband from time to time, and

Georgiana has said that she does not mind."

"I know Fitzwilliam. But…well it is still mortifying even if it is to be expected."

I thought, not for the first time, how fortunate we were that Mr. Wickham was kept away from home by his duties. When Fitzwilliam had paid off Mr. Wickham's debts and corralled him into marrying my sister, he had also purchased for him a commission in a regiment in Newcastle. Much to our surprise, he has not only remained there but has seemingly prospered and is currently away on campaign with his regiment. He is, we are told, doing admirably well. He and Lydia seem to live quite happily together, no doubt due to his extended absences. It struck me, not for the first time, that I had had two, nearly three, babies and Lydia none although she had been married the longest. Is it just that they have not been blessed? Or is there something *deliberate*?

"Well, try not to be mortified, Elizabeth. You will not change it. Would you like to sit?"

I nodded, and he slid his arms under my back and head, planting a kiss on the rise of my bosom as he brought me up. He ran his hand over my belly and looked at me in a most serious way.

"You must also stop worrying about the babe being a boy."

"I—"

"No, do not argue with me. Your mind is stuck on it. I know, and you must stop. It is not good for you."

I looked away from him and spoke into the dimly lit, shadowy space of my chamber.

"But you need a son."

"Stop it, Elizabeth. I will not say it again. I need a healthy child and a happy, healthy wife. The babe will be whatever it is, and we will have more children. So cease distressing yourself. Cease asking Mrs. Reynolds whether she thinks that your belly *looks* like a boy or a girl—"

"What a snake in the grass that woman is! I did not think she was so little to be trusted!"

"She only told me because she thought you were worrying too much and that I would reassure you, which is what I am doing, I hope."

I was by no means convinced, but I knew that he would like to think that I was, so I lifted both of his strong hands to my belly, kissed him on the lips, and said, "You are. Thank you.

"I was quite an attraction at church this morning, Fitzwilliam. I think the villagers were surprised to see me sailing in. If I were any larger, I would need my own pew."

"Well, there was not a great deal of space for me, Elizabeth. It is a good thing that we have our own, although it is maybe unfortunate for those seated behind that your place is right at the front."

I struck him on the leg for this insult, and he laughed.

"I noticed that some of the servants were at church this morning, and they all sat at the same pew. Is that a rule?"

"Yes, of a sort. It is the servants' pew, just as they have in the chapel at Pemberley. Of course, it is hardly used these days, but in my grandparents' time, the Darcys and all of their servants worshipped here and hardly ever went into the village. It was my parents who started the tradition of our attending the village church for high days and holidays. They thought the tenants would like it, and they were probably right. It was only quite recently that the chapel at Pemberley stopped having regular services."

"I know. Hannah told me that, when she was a young girl, it was every Sunday, so the servants hardly ever left the estate! Did you know that there is a secret box under a pew in the Pemberley chapel? The servants used to hide things in it, and it was a great joke amongst them apparently."

"No, I did not. Did Hannah tell you that as well? Sometimes I think she knows this house better than I do. Anyway, you should be pleased that the chapel is used so little, Elizabeth. It is very draughty, and its pews even narrower than those in the village. In your current condition, it would serve you very ill." He leaned forward and softly planted a smiling kiss on my forehead. "Thank you for coming this morning. Everybody appreciated it."

Everybody, I thought, except Mama, but I knew my husband too well to mention her at that moment.

"Well, good. What is the use of being such a sight if I am not occasionally put on display, Mr. Darcy?"

Chapter 2

T o me, to me. No! That's enough. Back a bit. Back a bit. That's the ticket. *Evie, watch the cat!*"

A sharp meow accompanied a blur of ginger fur sweeping by their ankles.

"Sorry, Uncle John. I can't see very well. Can we just stop for a moment?"

Evie Pemberton brushed her hair off her forehead with one hand and, holding her end of the ten-foot canvass with the other, wondered how they were ever going to get it out of her uncle's house, never mind all the way to Cork Street. Despite its wooden frame, it billowed about like a sheet of tracing paper. It was her largest and most impressive piece, given to Uncle John and Auntie Betty to thank them for all of their help with Clemmie after everything that had happened. She had also given it to them to say, "I love you," which she did. It had been up in their living room in Putney ever since, and no visitor to the house was allowed to escape without hearing about their marvellous niece, the up and coming artist. It made her heart ache to think of how they must have exaggerated. Now she had, for the first time, an exclusive show of her work in a proper gallery in town, and Uncle John and Auntie Betty were loaning it for display.

"It's not for sale, mind," Auntie Betty had said and winked when Evie came around to ask the previous month. Back in the present, her uncle spoke, his voice slightly muffled by the painting between them.

"Are you ready to try again, love?"

"Yes, Uncle John. Let's get this party started." She tried to look as cheerful as possible and not let on that her mind was reeling with the difficulty of the two of them hauling such a thing through the streets of West London and onto the Number 22 bus all the way to Piccadilly.

"Wilco. Right, all set? Down a bit. Down a bit. Now, easy does it around that corner. That's the job. We'll be there in no time; you see if we're not! Might even drum up some interest along the way. It isn't every day that you see a ten-foot troupe of ballerinas making their way down Putney High Street!"

"You never know, Uncle John, maybe we will. People will certainly remember it at any rate."

She wanted to say that she hoped to God it didn't rain and it wasn't windy, but she knew it didn't do to be gloomy. They had got the thing down the stairs, along the corridor, and out into the tiny, front garden when Auntie Betty had a suggestion.

"Right, you two. I propose a cuppa and a piece of cake before you're on your way. You need to keep your strength up." They sat on the low, red brick wall in the warm air of the August morning sipping from unmatched cups and nibbling Auntie Betty's homemade fruitcake. Evie's ballerinas were propped up against the house, bathed in unfamiliar sunshine.

"This is lovely, Auntie Bet."

"Thank you, darling, have another piece. I won't give it to you now, as you can't carry it with that great picture to cart about, but I'll have John pop some around to you in the week. Clemmie should have some too. She's always liked a bit of cake."

"She'll enjoy that. Thank you. Right. I think we had better be off."

And they were. Uncle and niece made wobbly progress past row on row of terraced houses and polished front doors, turning left onto the bustling High Street. It was a risk trying to do it by bus, but Evie really didn't have the money to hire a courier, and she had convinced Uncle John that, in the mid-morning during the week, the Number 22 would not be that busy and the double door would be big enough to get the canvas in. It was, just about, and they made a comical journey through London with old ladies nodding an interest and children on scooters swerving to avoid them.

"It was worth it just to see that bus driver's face!" remarked Uncle John as they winched the thing off onto the pavement outside the Royal Academy for the last leg of the journey to Cork Street.

When they rested it against the main wall inside the gallery with other much smaller canvases piled around, Evie felt that she could finally breathe. She was meeting the guys who would install the collection in a couple of hours, but it wouldn't hurt to just look through it all again—make sure the catalogue was exactly right.

"Thank you, Uncle John. You are a complete star."

"You're welcome, lovey. It's no problem. What's family for if not lugging bloody, great paintings through Central London, eh? Anyway, I'd better be getting home. I suppose I'll see you at the exhibition?"

"Yes, I suppose so. Thanks for coming. It will be full of awful arty types. I'll be glad of you and Auntie Betty."

"I better not mention that to her. She'll be wanting a new dress for the occasion. Speaking of which: Have you got yourself something nice to wear? I mean, we want to make sure everyone knows you are the centre of attention, don't we?"

He winked, and Evie looked down at her faded jeans and paint-spattered Converse trainers.

"Are you suggesting that I won't do as I am?" She laughed and reminded him instantly of her mother.

"I hadn't actually thought about it, but now that you say it, I'll see what I can find in the wardrobe."

He went to speak, but she stopped him short. "And before you say it— yes, I promise it will have a skirt! I might even buy something new. You never know."

"There's a good girl. Well, I'll better be wending my way."

She exhaled and gave him her broadest smile. When he hugged her, he squeezed her shoulders as if she were a little girl. At the door, he turned back and took her by surprise.

"Evie…"

"Yes?"

"Well done, darling. We're very proud of you."

She was embarrassed to think of how little there really was to be proud of, and the soft humble look on his face made her tummy flip. When he was gone, she sat down on a box by the gallery door and looked around her, hardly believing that this was finally happening.

In another part of the city, the clock ticked on the wall of Haywood Enquiry Agents. It was a small office, stylish and simple. Charlie Haywood sat back in his big leather chair, feet up on the desk, enjoying a moment of calm before he had to meet another stranger about a subject that probably didn't matter. He could hear the tap of Maureen's keyboard through the wall and was briefly irritated. Why did she have to bash it so? Was it because she was old? Was it because she learned to be a secretary in the days before touch screens and swiping apps? A younger girl would be very different, he thought. That led him to ponder the sort of trouble that he would get into and the lack of work he would do if his secretary were not old enough to be his mother. Then he remembered why Maureen was so good for him. He reminded himself also that he liked and trusted her. With that, he buzzed her.

"Okay, Mau, let her in!"

Maureen's chair made a gentle motion on the thick pile of the carpet as she stood.

"Miss Carter? Mr. Haywood will see you now. Would you like tea or coffee?"

The woman who had been plumped down on the sofa in the waiting room for no more than ten minutes seemed startled. Her half read copy of *Country Life* was slipped back onto the low table in front of her. She asked for a coffee, stood, and straightening her slightly too-tight skirt, followed Maureen into the room. When she saw Charlie Haywood for the first time, her eyes widened as she took him in. He was quite used to this reaction and did not demur from it. He looked at her for a beat too long but then relaxed and was as friendly and professional as he knew how to be. He didn't want to make the woman uncomfortable. She was paying, after all. Added to which, her expression led him to think she didn't need to be encouraged.

"Come in, Miss Carter. Please, take a seat. I am sorry to have kept you waiting."

"Oh, thank you," she replied, almost surprised.

"Pleasant journey, I hope? You have come from Shropshire, I think?"

"Yes, yes, I have."

"Well, do come in and sit down. Maureen will fetch you a drink, and we can have a chat about your case. I believe that you spoke to my colleague, Simon, when you rang before?"

She nodded. Charlie thought briefly of Simon, his would-be prodigy.

Simon, who was currently on the tail of the trophy wife of a Lebanese businessman, whose taste for men who were not her husband had made her the talk of Chelsea and had brought yet another remunerative brief to the door of Haywood Enquiry Agents. He knew Simon to be following her that afternoon and hoped that he wasn't being too obvious about it. Suddenly remembering that he needed to concentrate, he fixed his gaze on the lady in front of him and put all ideas of Simon aside.

"I understand that you are considering mounting a legal challenge to a trust of which you are a beneficiary and that there is a historical element involved. You have come to the right place, Miss Carter. I would not say this to all of my clients, but I have a special interest in enquiries that involve a bit of history. I hope we can help. I am fairly sure that if we can't help you then nobody can."

"You did come very highly recommended, Mr. Haywood." She smiled, and for a moment, he felt sick. She was, he would estimate, in her late twenties, and she was by no means unattractive. Still, there was something about her that made him want to turn away.

"Well, that is always gratifying. I hope we will not disappoint. Ah, here is Maureen. Thanks, Maureen."

There was a brief interlude in which sugar lumps were dropped in hot coffee and silver teaspoons tinkled around china.

"Maybe it would be best, Miss Carter, if you just told me your story in your own words. Then I can tell you what I think, and we can go from there?"

"No problem. I can do that. Let's start from the beginning. It's like this. My family on Mummy's side is terribly grand, Mr. Haywood. Our branch of the family is one of the less well-off ones unfortunately, but there are landed estates and aristocrats if you look back—the whole damned shooting match. Don't really see much of them all now of course, but families are like that, aren't they? I am sure that I am related to all sorts of impressive people. Anyway, when I was eighteen, I started receiving money from something called the Darcy Trust. Mummy does too and my cousin on her side, Jennifer. It turns out that all of the women in Mummy's family get money from it. Mummy has been getting it ever since she was eighteen. It is a pretty penny too, I can tell you. Over the years…well…it has paid for quite a lot."

She blinked, and he knew that she had wanted to say more but thought better of it. Running her manicured hand along the groove at the edge of his desk, she continued.

"Anyway, until very recently, I didn't know all that much about it. I just got the money, and I was bloody glad of it. Then Mummy said that her Aunt Mary was on her last legs with cancer, and she really wanted to see her before she died. Now, I hadn't seen Aunt Mary since I was a child, but a trip to Scotland didn't sound too shabby, and Mummy really wanted some company, so along I went. I suppose that it was a bit grim at times, but it wasn't too bad. Aunt Mary's place was lovely—really gorgeous—and my bedroom had a super view. Anyway, it was pretty obvious that she was very ill, and we spent a few days with her talking about the old days and family history and all of that, you know?"

He nodded, but of course, he didn't know. Miss Carter crossed her legs and leaned towards him, sipping awkwardly from her cup.

"She was really into it—family history, I mean. She seemed to know all sorts—more than me, and I know a bit. Told us all about the war and other times as well, much further back. She was amazing, really, when you think of her age and her health. It was one morning just after breakfast. Mummy was having a potter around the garden, and I had just made myself a coffee. I didn't have anything else to do, so I sat with Aunt Mary and asked her if she'd like some help with her crossword. She looked me squarely in the face and said, 'Victoria Darcy wasn't his daughter you know. Nobody was allowed to say, but it was the truth.' I was completely foxed, but she looked as if she was saying something important. So, I put down my coffee, took her frail old hand, and said, 'Come again, Aunt Mary?' It was then that she told me about the Darcy Trust. It turns out that it was started by some long-dead relation of ours, Fitzwilliam Darcy. He had five daughters and set up a trust to benefit his female descendants. Only that's just the thing. One of the daughters, this Victoria, *wasn't his daughter at all.* Born on the wrong side of the bed sheets, and somehow his wife passed it off. Did the dirty and got away with it. Apparently, according to Aunt Mary, there has always been talk about it in the family, but nobody ever actually did any- thing about it, but people knew."

"Do you know when this was, Miss Carter?"

"Sure. Victoria Darcy was born in 1821."

"1821?"

"Yes. I did a bit of research. I hope you're impressed, Mr. Haywood?"

He resisted the temptation to laugh but smiled at her instead.

"Charlie, please."

"Charlie." She seemed to pass the word around in her mouth. "Anyway, the upshot is that this *Victoria* and all of her daughters and granddaughters and so on are not real Darcys. If they are getting money from the trust, then they bloody well shouldn't be. That's what I'm here about."

So she was a greedy one. There were the greedy ones, the resentful ones, the mad ones, the campaigning ones, and the ones who had too much money and not enough to do. She was definitely a greedy one.

"So, this Fitzwilliam Darcy—he was married?"

"Yes, he was married."

"Do you know anything else about him or his wife?"

"No, that is why I have come to you."

She looked suddenly aggressive, and Charlie reflected that she didn't have much of a "middle gear" when it came to being aggravated.

"And do you know whether or not Victoria Darcy has any living female descendants? People who are alive and receiving money from the trust?"

"Yes. Well, Aunt Mary actually told me that. She said that the only people left in Victoria's line were the "Pemberton girls." I didn't know that I had any relations called Pemberton, but there you are. Anyway, these people, whoever they are, are getting money that they shouldn't be getting."

"Have you seen a lawyer about this, Miss Carter?"

"Cressida, please."

She leaned further towards him and fiddled with her watch. He noticed that she was too thin and wondered how hard she worked at it.

"Have you seen a lawyer about this, Cressida?"

"Yes, I have. I went straight to our family solicitor in Shropshire. He has been great actually. He dug out the trust document, and we looked at it together. He advised me that if Victoria Darcy were not really the daughter of Fitzwilliam Darcy then she and her descendants definitely should not be getting any money. He said that we would be able to challenge it and get them excluded. More buns for the rest of us. Only problem he said was that we need to prove it, and that is why I've come to you."

Charlie took a deep breath and put the lid back on his fountain pen without writing anything down. He considered noting "Victoria Darcy, born 1821" on his pad but couldn't see the point. He had been sent on some wild goose chases in his time. More often than not, he had to listen to a crazy story or two from his clients. He had been through people's bins and hidden behind moss-cloaked garden walls. He had hacked into people's voice mails and followed their cars to their lovers' houses down country lanes and sodium-lit streets. He had dredged through the contents of stolen laptops, dragging his tired eyes over file upon file of holiday snaps and letters and nonsense. He had read through thousands of pages of bank statements, telephone transcripts, and court documents. He was good—really good. If a secret was there, Charlie Haywood would find it. But he had never been asked to bust somebody for adultery nearly two hundred years after it had occurred.

"Right. Thanks. That is an amazing story, Cressida. You probably don't need me to tell you that it is rather unusual. I am going to need to go away and do a bit of background research because, well, I'm sure you realise that what you are asking me to look at is a long way in the past. Paternity disputes are a different thing these days, of course. We have DNA testing and so on. And when people are still alive, somebody always knows, somebody will always talk. Do you know what I mean?"

She nodded, but he was not at all sure she was following him.

"But when it comes to this Victoria Darcy—well you are talking about a woman who was born nearly two hundred years ago. I am going to need to do some serious rooting around just to work out the basics of who she was and who her family were. I am going to want to see that trust document and learn all about this Fitzwilliam Darcy and his family. Once I have done that, we can think about how we might go about uncovering the truth of Victoria's paternity. I'm afraid there aren't any guarantees here. This is a tricky one. The plain hard truth is that it might be impossible to prove that Victoria wasn't his daughter. You might spend a lot of money and get nowhere. Do you understand that, Cressida?"

"Yes, I understand."

"And you will take the risk?"

"Yeah, I'll take the risk." She tilted her head and smiled. "I reckon it's going to pay off."

Later, when Cressida Carter left the office, Charlie closed the heavy door behind her and turned to Maureen, who did not look up from her typing.

"Where do we find them, Mau?"

"Well, they find us usually, Mr. Haywood, which is better than them *not* finding us."

He smiled, knowing she was right. Maureen had refused to let go of "Mr. Haywood" despite repeated requests, and eventually, Charlie had let it be.

"Well, I suppose it keeps us off the streets. Speaking of which, I had better run."

"Off somewhere nice, Mr. Haywood?"

"Just meeting my cousin Peter for a drink and a catch up. He has a new girlfriend he's bringing along. *Ballerina* apparently."

He said it almost as if he didn't believe it to be true. It amazed Charlie that his cousin Peter was able to attract a woman, let alone a professional dancer who was presumably young and fit and…well, *sexy*. He was trying to think of a way to share this reflection with Maureen when Simon came crashing through the door, all geniality and clutching a Starbucks hot chocolate with all the add-ons.

"Evening, boss. Evening, Maureen. Passed a skinny woman on the stairs. Looked like she had just won the lottery. She one of yours?"

"I hope not, at least not in the way you mean, Simon. *That* was the famous Miss Carter."

"Oh, *that* was Miss Carter! Was she as barmy in real life as she sounded on the phone?"

Chapter 3

May 22, 1860
Pemberley

Galbraith,

Thank you for coming to Pemberley. I am sorry not to be more in your company but hope that my son and his wife looked after you. I am afraid that my days of dining into the night and besting my friends at billiards are behind me.

We discussed the Rosschapel matter when you were here, and maybe I was too short with you on the subject. I have since given it some thought. As you know, Victoria (who is now Mrs. Montague) does not know the truth. I do not know whether she would be able to cope with knowing the truth, and she has lived, happily, in ignorance all her life. You mentioned Mr. Montague. He is, as you know, a man whom I respect as well as Victoria's husband. Having considered the matter, however, I can see no real purpose in reporting to him the truth of Victoria's position. Whatever would he do with this information, and how could it ever benefit anyone, least of all her?

I hardly need add, therefore, that when I am dead, you will be the only living soul who knows the truth. I can see no reason why you should ever need to tell anyone else, and it is my instruction that you should not do so.

Yours,
Darcy

Chapter 4

I have missed writing this past week but so much has happened, and my mind has been so full that I hardly know where I would have found the words. It is now a full week since we learned the news, but I still cannot comprehend it. We had dined, and I was playing the pianoforte, Fitzwilliam listening with his eyes closed, his whiskey glistening in the candlelight. I believe that I heard the commotion at the main door before he did and looked up from the keyboard in alarm. A horse whinnied, far-off voices mumbled, and heels clicked on polished floors. By the time James knocked on the door of the music room and entered, it was plain that something was amiss.

"An express has come for you, sir."

Fitzwilliam started then stood. He gestured to me to be seated on the stool, took the weather-beaten letter from James's tray, and turning his back to the room, began to read. I thought of my parents and my sister Mary who is expecting her first child. I could not keep silent.

"Fitzwilliam, what is it? Please, tell me. Is it bad news?"

He turned steadily, his profile against the yellow of the wall and moved his hands in a way that told me he was formulating a response. He gestured to James to leave the room, and we were alone.

"Yes, Elizabeth, it is bad news. It is from the colonel of George Wickham's regiment. I am afraid that Mr. Wickham has died on return from duties in Spain. He took a fever and perished, as did a number of his fellow officers." He turned the soggy letter over in his hands. "It says precious little else, I am afraid. I assume that he wrote to me as he knows that I paid for his commission."

I could not but gasp to hear such news. My hand flew to my mouth, and my breath grew short. My stays seemed suddenly tight, and my whole person discomforted. Images flew through my mind—images of George Wickham as I had first known him, bowing deeply in the market place at Meryton, the smartest coat he could not afford upon his back, then later, in shining regimentals and a sword at his side. I recalled our dancing in the home of my aunt Philips in the days when I thought him handsome, agreeable, *and* honourable. I had come to understand that he was not what I had first thought him. He had been a man of many faults, and he had wronged Fitzwilliam and Georgiana. The last time I had seen him had been before I was married when he and Lydia visited Longbourn after their marriage. By then, I knew the truth of his character although I did not know at that time that Fitzwilliam had had to bribe the man to marry my sister. George Wickham, the reluctantly married man, standing by the fire in my mama's parlour, smiling and calling me "sister," had seemed such a diminished creature. Now, knowing that he was dead, I felt a pang of regret that I could not account for. A young man I danced with departed, my youngest sister a widow. I pondered, not for the first time, the tiny silver hairs at Fitzwilliam's temple, and I suppose I felt rather old.

Fitzwilliam's face darkened, and I knew that he had caught my expression. I took a breath and brought myself to.

"Poor, Lydia! Does the letter say whether she knows?"

"No, it does not, but she must, Elizabeth. He would not have written to me without also having written to her."

A strange, stilted silence settled between us. I wanted to run to him but felt pinned to the floor.

"Yes, of course. I did not think. I am sure you are right. I shall write to her in the morning and Mama as well. I expect they shall both be in quite a state."

Fitzwilliam looked at me, but he only grunted his assent.

"Shall I tell Georgiana?" I ventured. I had thought that this would be worrying him, but he looked completely surprised by the question.

"Erm, yes, Elizabeth. You tell Georgiana. When are you next visiting her?"

Georgiana lives but ten miles from Pemberley with her husband, Lord Avery, on a small but beautiful estate overlooking Padley Gorge. With my own sisters settled farther away, it has been my pleasure to visit her often since her marriage.

"I had planned to visit her at Broughton Park on Wednesday. I usually take the girls, but I will leave them behind so that I can talk to her alone." I searched his blank face for some emotion but found none. "If you think it appropriate, that is?"

"Yes, of course," he barked. "Why would it not be appropriate?"

"Well, I thought that you may wish to approach her yourself or with me. And, do I need to talk to her alone and only her? What if Lord Avery is there? What do I say to him?"

"Nothing. He knows nothing of the…business between Wickham and Georgiana. I considered telling him when he asked for Georgiana's hand but decided there was no need. He certainly does not need to know now…"

He creased his face, ran his fingers through his hair, and turned away from me. I blinked in astonishment. What has happened here? A part of my life that I did not know was brittle has fractured. I smiled, but it did not seem to touch him.

"I understand. In that case, I shall ensure that we are alone. I am sure she will be shocked, but I hope not excessively affected. After all, it was a long time ago, and Georgiana is a married woman with a baby."

I did not say a "baby boy." My mind flew to a vision of Georgiana in bed nine months after her marriage, cradling little Archibald and beaming up at me, declaiming, "What a size he is, Lizzy! I know not how I produced such a son!" I thought of our three daughters sleeping above our heads, and I could not bear to mention that our sister had produced an heir for her husband on the first attempt. Did Fitzwilliam think this too? Now, there is a scowl upon his face, but is it for me?

With few further pleasantries, he went to his study to pen a response for the colonel and, I believe, to write to his cousin Colonel Fitzwilliam. I sat at the instrument to play, thinking that it may soothe me but could not make my fingers work. I thought of my poor sister whose precarious existence was now in even greater jeopardy. Would being George Wickham's widow be even less desirable than being his wife? Would Lydia marry again? She was forward enough to attract attention but too forward to be an attractive prospect for most sensible men. Would she return to Longbourn? I thought of my poor Papa in Hertfordshire with only an aging Mama and a heartbroken Lydia for company. I consoled myself that at least she did not have any children to worry for and resolved to retire before I became unmanageably maudlin.

In bed, alone, I could not turn my mind to sleep. I was a riot of restlessness and odd, undefined discomforts. The fire in my chamber died down to an amber glow. My dressing table and stool and the mirrors and brushes and boxes of my personal space seemed to form strange shapes and dance in the darkness. How could George Wickham, of all men, be dead? Did he not have the luck of the devil? Was he not a man to always fall upon his feet however undeserved? I drank some of my water and pushed the counterpane down on the bed, for it was unseasonably warm. I could not make out the clock face now that the fire was almost out, but I knew that it was late. Apart from my confinement or illness—or when he had been away from Pemberley—Fitzwilliam had shared my bed every night of our marriage. Except this one. I tried not to think upon it. I closed my eyes, curled my body tightly, and worked to persuade my frantic mind into slumber.

When he did come, I felt rather than saw him approach. It seemed to be not quite as dark, and a creeping light was breaking through the pitch of the room. He saw me stir, and his voice came in a whisper.

"Elizabeth, may I join you?"

"Yes, of course." I pushed the covers back and was suddenly chilly, for I wore only a summer nightgown.

He smiled nervously in the half-light and covered me as well as himself. He lay on his side and looked at my face, not touching.

"You do not have to ask me. What time is it?"

"It is about four in the morning."

Had I slept? I was not sure.

"But…"

"I find that I cannot sleep without you, Elizabeth."

I reached my hand out from beneath the cover and touched it to his face, which felt slightly rough. He moved closer. His nearness made me quiver as if I were a girl of one and twenty.

"Then do not try."

Later we woke, and I knew that it was late in the morning. I had a recollection of Hannah having come to my side of the bed, but I had indicated to her that we would remain. She would no doubt have been told by Fitzwilliam's valet that his own bed had also been slept in, and so she would know that we had had a disturbed night. Tiredness was writ upon his handsome face, even in sleep, and I did not want him awakened. I curled myself in his embrace and enjoyed his warmth and smell. After some time, I felt a light kiss upon my temple.

"Good morning, Elizabeth. If morning it still is?"

"It is still the morning. Just a little later than you are accustomed to waking."

He stretched and fixed his gaze on the canopy above.

"When I have been confined with the girls, or unwell, have you passed those nights without sleep, you poor man?"

He smiled and turned to me, his hand resting heavily on the side of my belly.

"No. I did not sleep well on those nights, but I did sleep a little. Last night was different. I went to my own bed, not out of consideration for you, Elizabeth, but to indulge my own pride. And, I suppose, because I was fighting against a fact I know to be true: that whatever ails me and whatever has occurred, you are the best person for my comfort."

His candour confused me in an instant, but I did not want to lose the intimacy between us. I grasped his hand in mine.

"Is it Wickham? Are you grieved? I would not be surprised if you were, Fitzwilliam. You have known him all your life. And even though unpleasant things have happened, he is part of your story. It is not a wonder that you should be shocked by his early death. It is not disloyalty to Georgiana or unkindness to her. It is quite to be expected."

My speech complete, I kissed his arm and listened to the silence. After a moment, he broke it.

"I am grieved, much more grieved than I ever would have thought. There was a time when I actually wished death on George Wickham but…well, it was a long time ago. I find that my anger has quite gone. The fact is that Georgiana is married to a suitable and respectable man and is happy. Apart from the unhappiness that was occasioned to her by Wickham's attempt to inveigle himself with her, there were no real consequences. No. I am surprised to learn that I am less affected by that history than I might have been just last year or the year before."

"Then what is it?"

He opened his mouth but spoke not. I rolled against his side, my bosom pressed against his hard, lean chest and my face close to his.

"What is it, Fitzwilliam?"

"It is you, Elizabeth. I saw how you looked when you learned he was dead and…I'm sorry, but it has tormented me."

"How I looked? I…I was shocked, Fitzwilliam. Wickham was my sister's husband, and he was young. She is young. Surely…"

"I know, but I also know that, when you and I first knew each other in Hertfordshire, you…well, you favoured him, Elizabeth. You favoured him above me."

"But that was when I did not really know you. No woman, no *person*, knowing you properly could prefer him to you, you know that."

"Yes, I do know that, but…well you must allow me my feelings, Elizabeth. Seeing you cry out to learn that he was dead, it took me back to a time that I wanted you and you did not want me. I could not bear it, and so I pushed you away. I know it was foolish, and I am sorry."

I blinked and paused, the light in the room seeming suddenly too bright for comfort.

"I am sorry if I have not made you certain enough of me. But surely… surely, you do not doubt my love for you? We have been happy, have we not, these six years? How can you think that I—"

"Shh, Elizabeth. Do not distress yourself. I am not criticising you. It is with me that the fault lies. I am prideful, and well, sometimes, I am less secure in your love for me than I ought to be."

His attempt to quieten me was not successful, for now I was cross as well as upset.

"Sometimes? What other times have you felt this, sir?" I thought of our three daughters, no doubt up by this hour, dressed, and breakfasted. "I love you completely and utterly, Fitzwilliam. How could you think that I do not or that I give you less than I should?"

With this, I stopped short, for I had not yet given him a son. Was that the heart of the matter? If I could give him an heir, would he stop doubting me? I burned with the injustice of it. As if he knew, he touched his hand to my forehead.

"Shh. That is not what I think. I know that you love me, and I love you. But…you are a sparkling person, Elizabeth. You are bright and amusing and beautiful and you charm the world. People—men—who meet you, admire you. I know they do. Sometimes, just sometimes, it wounds me. I did not expect to be revisited by the jealously that I once felt towards George

Wickham, but last night, I was. I am sorry."

My heart softened to see his earnest expression, and I could not be angry.

"Do not be sorry, sir." I kissed his nose, and he laughed.

"I should write to Lydia and Mama directly I am dressed. But then I shall be at liberty, and the weather is fine. Are you too jealous and prideful to accompany your wife on a walk?"

"No, I would like that."

"Should you like just me, or shall we take Anne and Emma? Frances shall be sleeping, and I leave her with Nanny, but Anne and Emma love to join me." I smiled at the recollection of their running around me like puppies as I walk, their little legs carrying them many multiples of my own journey.

"Yes, let us take them with us."

Thus, it was decided.

Chapter 5

Charlie had taken the Tube to Piccadilly Circus and regretted it. It was steaming hot at this time of year and stuffed to bursting with tired, sweaty office workers. He could have hailed a taxi, of course, but this way, he got a bit of a walk. Glancing at his watch, he was glad to note that it was already nearly half past seven. That was good. It didn't do to be too early. He wanted to get a look at her—see what he was dealing with. He did not want to be the first person there and be forced into conversation with the woman. He knew about art; it wasn't that. Art had come into quite a few of the cases he had worked on, and he could pretend he knew what he was talking about. No, he was not worried that he would be caught out. Nobody, particularly somebody who was not doing anything wrong, ever thought they had a private investigator on their tail. It simply wasn't the kind of thing that occurred to people. For a moment, he struggled to justify why he was going there at all. What did he expect to find? What would she even know? He could not really answer those questions, which for him was unusual. Still, his instinct compelled him on. He just wanted to get a glimpse of her, see the lie of the land, and get the measure of the situation.

It was Simon who had found out about the exhibition, and as soon as he said it, Charlie knew he would be going. Poor, old Simon had been at it all day searching databases and online records to build up the Darcy family tree. It had been pretty easy to find the so-called "Pemberton sisters," Evangeline and Clementine. Charlie rolled their names around on his tongue.

He noticed, when looking at the fruit of Simon's research, that their parents, David and Nora Pemberton, had both died on the same day five years previously and wondered what the story was behind that. He could ask Simon to find out, but did it really matter? It was the living Darcy descendants he was interested in.

"I just can't find anything about this Clementine Pemberton, boss," Simon had said that morning as Charlie arrived at the office. "There is just nothing. No Facebook. No Twitter. No nothing. It is like she doesn't really exist. Maybe she is a nun in a silent order?" He laughed at his own joke, but Charlie could tell that he felt defeated by the search.

"Okay. Well, what about the other one?"

"Evangeline. Ah, well, now you're talking. I found her easily enough. *Artist*, if you don't mind. Studied at the Camberwell School of Art. Did a stint at art school in Paris. And guess what? She has only got an exhibition on in Cork Street this week! I couldn't believe the luck of it. It runs for three days. Today is the first day. The gallery is open all day, but if you go along in the evening, they do drinkies. So can't be bad, can it, boss?" He gestured his hand as if holding a glass of wine and smiled one of his "Simon" smiles.

"Great. I'll go tonight."

And so, there he was, pacing down Cork Street in the hazy heat of a London summer evening, wondering what he would find. The double doors of the gallery were open, and the pavement outside was crowded with men in chinos and young fashionable women, laughing and smoking. A girl in a red dress paused and appraised him as he approached, for which he smiled a polite smile but did not break step. There was a buzz of many voices coming from inside and permeating the street. There were a lot of people here. Some were serious men in tweed jackets and heavy framed spectacles. They furrowed their brows and said little, and Charlie thought they must be buyers. Then there were the hipsters in their low-slung jeans, their hair arranged in peculiar montages of colour and style. A couple of stragglers roamed around: women in suits and ballet flats, their smart heels sticking out of their handbags; an oldish couple in their Sunday best who shuffled around the room looking out of place; a guy wearing a trilby and looking overheated.

Later, Charlie reflected that he could never have been prepared for the first moment he saw her. A huge painting of ballerinas in unlikely colours formed the backdrop, and there she was. Her right toe tapped the wooden floor, and he noticed a tiny, gold chain around her left ankle. Her hair, which was the colour of acacia honey, was so thick he thought she might need a spoon to brush it. It was already half out of its ponytail, and he noticed that she moved her head around a lot when she talked. She was the right age, and everyone seemed to be addressing her. He *knew* that this was the girl. The gallery lights bounced off her creamy skin, and he felt a tightening in his throat. Unused to being disconcerted by another person's appearance, Charlie got himself a glass of wine and did a circle of the room before approaching her.

There were a number of people surging around her, babbling and pecking one another on the cheek between hugs. Charlie decided that his only option was to abuse his height and move closer, gazing up at the ballerinas then over the top of her acolytes and down at her honey-blonde head.

"Miss Pemberton, I assume?"

"You assume right, but it's Evie, please."

He shook the hand she held out to him and was momentarily shocked by the soft silk of her skin against his. She looked at him expectantly, and he realised that, for the first time in his professional life, he didn't have a plan or a false name at his fingertips.

"I'm Charlie, Charlie Haywood." Did he detect some alarm in her? Her eyes, which his father would have called Dresden blue, flickered about uncertainly as she spoke.

"Well, welcome, Charlie Haywood. How did you hear about the exhibition? Have you been to the gallery before?"

Afterwards, he did not know what made him say it. Was it that he was nervous? Was it just the first thing that came into his head? Was it that he wanted to make her stay with him? He could not imagine.

"I'm a collector, Evie. And yes, I've been here before. Exhibitions in this gallery are always so well curated, and I like what they have done with your work. This is great. I really like this one in fact."

He turned to the ballerinas, needing to look away from her.

"Oh, thank you. But that one isn't for sale. It belongs to my aunt and uncle. If you were really interested, I could work up a proposal for a new work on a similar basis. I don't know if you are into commissioning work, but if you were, that would be an option."

"Thanks, I may well be."

He cast his eye around the room, and in the heat of the evening and the hubbub of the laughing, drinking crowd, he began to get his native confidence back.

"So, what about this? What's the story here?"

He nodded towards a small canvass with a purple cello in the middle of it, and Evie began to explain that she had spent time with orchestras and that there were a number of pictures in the exhibition in which the instruments were in full cry without their players. The ballerinas, it turned out, were the product of a similar stint with a ballet company in which Evie had been allowed to tag along and sketch during rehearsals. Charlie stared at the canvas and could almost hear the low moan of the instrument in his ear.

"I like it. I really like it. Evie, do you have a studio? Where do you work?"

"I have a studio in Fulham, just off Lots Road. The address is on my card. Do you want it?"

"Yes, I do want it." He stared at her in that way that he had stared down at women many times before. He realised with a start that she didn't welcome it. The skin on her beautiful face grew taut, she looked sideways, and her mouth pursed.

"Sure. I'll just get you one."

When she handed him the card, she did so at arm's length, and she barely even smiled. The Dresden blue of her eyes looked away, but he wasn't deterred. Charlie was not accustomed to giving up, and he wasn't about to do so this time. His experiences had not taught him to doubt his abilities, and he continued.

"Thanks. I am around in Fulham sometimes, and I'd like to look in if that's okay—see what you're working on. I could pop in one afternoon next week if you're free. Maybe we could get dinner after. I could treat you. What is the point in being in the art world if I can't feed a struggling artist from time to time? How about it?"

"Erm...that is very flattering...Charlie..." He winced to think that she had to search around for his name. "But maybe not. I have only just met you, well...and I manage to feed myself most days."

"I didn't mean—"

"I'm sure not. Thank you for coming, and I hope you enjoy the exhibition."

She smiled and was absorbed into the crowd of interested parties. The fabric of her dress shimmied against the curve of her form as she moved away from him. He felt sweat breaking out under his shirt, muttered the most coherent goodbye he could muster at the door, and was gone.

His feet pounded the street on the way back to the Tube station. He could literally have kicked himself. He had completely screwed that up. He had spun her a ridiculous story, one that he would have trouble sustaining if he ever had to see her again. He had annoyed her. He had found out nothing at all about her apart from the fact that she had a studio in Fulham. He felt her card in his trouser pocket and imagined it like a razor blade slicing his fingers. He should have gone around the room studying the prices and working out from the stickers how many she had sold. He should have sniffed around to see if there were any other Darcy relations there. He had done none of it. Worse, he had been brushed off by her. She didn't hesitate. She just said "no." His body was shaking with the aftershock of it.

What was he coming to? This, he decided, was a one off. A girl who took offence at being asked out to dinner was not a girl for him to trouble himself with. So what if she was beautiful. Ethereal. Interesting. He told himself these were characteristics to be found in many places. Evie Pemberton was a chippy one, and she probably didn't even know anything that would be useful anyway. It was obvious that she had money—the fact that she was making a living as an artist with exhibitions in Central London and a studio in Fulham told him that. She probably didn't even need her share of the Darcy Trust. It was stupid and pointless to have spent so much time talking to her. As for asking her out, he was just bored, and that is why he did it. First thing in the morning, he would get on Cressida Carter's case, big time. Crazy Cressida could have the full glittering force of his efforts, no-holds-barred, all guns blazing. There was no reason for him to even see Evie Pemberton again. He passed this thought around in his mind for longer than was necessary.

SOMETIME LATER, AUNTIE BETTY NUDGED A DISTRACTED EVIE WHO STOOD behind the desk in the gallery. The party was almost over, and the guests that remained were still there because they were too drunk to go, not because they were serious customers. There had been a few sales, not that many. Evie watched the students having a good time, and she couldn't begrudge them.

"Who was that chap who stormed off earlier, lovey?"

Evie did not think anyone had observed her in that uncomfortable exchange. She had watched that collector stalk out of the door and down the street, and although she was glad to see the back of him, she recalled how he had fixed her with his eyes, and she couldn't get it out of her head. His hand had brushed hers as she had handed him her card, and the memory of it stung her between the eyes. Even now, when he was long gone, she felt unbalanced by it.

"Erm, I'm not sure, Auntie. I've never met him before."

"Really? I thought you might know him."

"No, never met him before." It was the truth, and yet it felt like a lie. She knew that she was blushing to think of it. "I'm glad he's gone though. He seemed really, *really* arrogant."

"Nice looking though, isn't he? And so tall…"

Chapter 6

April 2, 1820, Pemberley

My sister Lydia has been our guest these three weeks, and already she has made me most uneasy. I remind myself that, although she is foolish, she is also young and widowed, and I love her. I also love my husband, who is not at all foolish but in certain circumstances can be irritable. Balancing the two characters is a task to which, I believe, no woman can be the equal. Only this morning, Fitzwilliam and I were awakened with a shriek through the wall from Lydia's room.

"Well, if that is the best that Lizzy can do, then I shall have to speak with her! She cannot expect me to wear such a dreary thing. She simply cannot. It is not fair. And anyway, in case you had not noticed, I am just as blessed about the chest as my sister, so there is no need for that dreadful, little panel..."

My blood pumped with embarrassment to hear her breathy protests from the next room. Beside me, Fitzwilliam's hand reached for his forehead and his eyes closed in exasperation. I had already regretted installing Lydia in the room next door to my own. It had been in my mind that the view of the lake might soothe her, but alas, it had not. I had considered asking the servants to move her, but it seemed to be both ridiculous and an admission of defeat. It is for Lydia to behave reasonably, even in her grief. It is not for me to place her in isolation in order that we are not disturbed by her histrionics. Her voice whined away from behind the wall, and I could bear it no longer.

"Elizabeth, what are you doing?" asked Fitzwilliam as I leapt out of bed and began pulling on my shawl.

"I will go and speak with her, Fitzwilliam. I know what this is about, and I cannot have her being so rude to the servants or waking us with her dramatics. It is only the next-door room, and she is my sister. She has seen me in my nightclothes before."

I knew that he was about to protest further but did not wait to hear it. His annoyance with me for leaving the chamber undressed and with my hair down was as nothing to the annoyance that he would begin to feel towards Lydia if I could not rein her in. Hair streaming and shawl trailing, I appeared in her room. She looked me squarely in the face and put down her teacup.

"Lizzy. There you are. Now, I cannot wear that *thing* for dinner this evening. What will Lord and Lady Matlock think? It is so dreary, and I am meeting them for the first time. You just cannot—"

"Lydia, keep your voice down. What are you doing awake at this hour? You have roused Fitzwilliam and me with all this nonsense—now be quiet."

To this, she merely smirked.

"Well, I could not sleep, and I am not that loud. You must have particularly fine hearing. Anyway, if your husband still keeps to your bed after all these years, Lizzy…well, you should have nothing to complain of." She laughed and glanced at the maid, Milly, who blushed and looked at her feet.

"Thank you, Milly. That will be all."

I believe the poor girl was more than grateful to be dismissed.

"Well, there was no need for that, Lizzy. Why I am sure that the whole staff knows—"

"Lydia, that is enough! If you wake me again with these morning fits of temper, then I shall move you to the other end of the corridor. And if you are rude to the maids, then you can attend to yourself. My goodness, we have done everything to make you comfortable, but you have to start behaving like a reasonable creature."

"Well, there is nothing reasonable about that dress, Lizzy. It is full black, and look at that thing that she has put in across the chest. I shall look like I am in holy orders!"

"You will not look anything of the sort. You will look like a respectable widow because that is what you are. I wore that dress to Rosings when Lady Catherine died, and it is lovely fabric. It was very costly, and the cut is beautiful. I have said that you can have some lace to make it more suitable for the evening. I want you to feel attractive, Lydia, but I will not have you dressing up in all colours and revealing yourself to Fitzwilliam's relations. It is unseemly—"

"Oh, Lizzy, to hear you go on so, one would think that Wickham had only just died. It has been eight months, and I am sure that he would not like to think of me in that dreadful thing. Look at it. That style went out with the ark—and why should I be covered to the neck? If Wickham were here, he would be fighting for me to at least wear grey, Lizzy."

Her eyes were pleading, and she thrust forward the top half of her body. It was as if we were back at Longbourn and she was a girl of fifteen. I thought in that moment of how young she actually was in mind and in body, and I could not be too harsh with her.

"Very well, I shall offer you a bargain, Lydia. But you have to keep your side, is that understood?"

"Yes, Lizzy."

"Well. You may lower the panel by a couple of inches and have a grey sash so that it is not completely black. I have a single back pearl for your neck to dress it a bit. If you wear it like that, you will feel a little more adorned. But if I allow that, Lydia, please show a little more restraint. *Especially in front of Mr. Darcy.* Try to talk a little less and a little less loudly. When Lord and Lady Matlock come to dinner tonight, try to recall that they are much your elders. Can you do that for me?"

She looked to stifle a smirk but then thought the better of it.

"Yes, Lizzy, I can do that. It is a bargain. I shall not let you down."

"Thank you. And can you try to be quieter in the mornings? You never used to get up this early at home."

I recalled how I was always up for a walk before breakfast at Longbourn while my sisters had to be jostled out of bed. Lydia had never been a girl to be awake at the break of dawn, and I could not account for her.

"Yes, you shall not know I am here. I shall be like a widowed mouse!" She tilted her head and laughed. I gathered my shawl about my shoulders, and as I turned to leave, she bellowed from her dressing table, "But Lizzy! What about shoes?"

At length, and somehow already weary, I returned to my chamber to find an empty space in the bed in place of Fitzwilliam.

It had been, I reflected, an exhausting three weeks. Lydia, since the death of her husband, had spent four months at Longbourn with our parents and three months with Jane and Mr. Bingley at their estate at Bollington. She had, I believe, been somewhat of a trial to all of them, and I did not feel that I could resist having her as a guest any longer. Fitzwilliam had said my sister was welcome. I reasoned that it would be diverting for the girls to have their aunt Lydia present. I had not seen my sister for over two years, and mayhap I had forgotten her talent for drama. When she arrived, she hardly stopped talking for a week. Being trapped in a carriage for three days is quite against Lydia's disposition, and she took out this deprivation on Fitzwilliam and me. She wittered in my sitting room during the day, and our nuncheon and dinner were dominated by her monologues on fashion and acquaintances. Of her late husband, she spoke at length, recalling his past comments about Pemberley and his strong connection to the Darcy family. No servant was allowed to enter the room without being questioned by her on their experiences of the late Mr. Wickham and no feature of the house and garden that he had favoured was allowed to pass unremarked. I had tried not to look at Fitzwilliam's face as he sat at the other end of the table, turning his food over with his fork.

"Hannah, do you know where the master is?" I asked when she arrived to bathe and dress me.

"Yes, madam, he went out riding directly he came downstairs."

"Do you mean that he had no breakfast?"

"I believe not, madam. I understand from his valet that he will be on estate business at nuncheon as well, so it shall be just you and Mrs. Wickham."

I turned away slightly as I said, "I see." I did not want even Hannah to witness the surprise on my face.

As it was, Lydia was a pleasant companion at nuncheon and throughout the afternoon. When we had eaten, we repaired to the day nursery to find Alice and Emma about a game, Frances asleep in her crib, and Nanny repairing the buttons on a smock by the light of the window. My sister and I settled down on the chaise with a girl on each lap, and I read stories that I composed myself until it was time for their afternoon tea. Nanny, Lydia, and I enjoyed tea while Anne and Emma guzzled glasses of milk. We all had cake, and Lydia was quite right when she pronounced wistfully, "What a lovely time this is!"

I did not see Fitzwilliam until shortly before dinner. I was dressed and sat at my vanity. When he came in, Hannah, who had been adjusting the sleeve on my gown, smiled, curtsied, and was gone. He paced around behind me, and the silence was like an ache in my limbs.

"I am sorry that I have been gone all day, Elizabeth. I have had a lot to attend to."

"I understand, Fitzwilliam." I turned on my stool and faced him, hoping he recognised I really did understand. "You will be pleased to know that Lydia has actually been very good today. After this morning, she has been much quieter. She and I played in the nursery with the girls, and she was lovely with them. She has calmed down a little, and she has promised me that she will be on her best behaviour this evening."

I touched his hand and saw his body relax. He smiled.

"Good. Thank you. Shall we ask her to accompany us downstairs?"

"She is already down, Fitzwilliam. She told me she was ready and going down about an hour ago."

When Fitzwilliam and I arrived in the drawing room, we found Lydia plumped down in the corner with a miniature of Wickham in one hand and a small glass of wine in the other. Dim light fell on the jet of her borrowed gown, and she looked up at us only briefly before returning her eyes to his likeness. The picture, which had been commissioned by my husband's father many years previously, had been consigned to a place out of sight until—with Wickham's death and Lydia's visit—I had retrieved it. I had regretted doing so several times although I was gratified that, when Lydia saw us, she quickly put it aside and made her greetings. She did not get up, which seemed a little odd. For all of her complaints, my gown suited her, and Milly had dressed her hair in a new arrangement. Altogether, she looked rather pretty. When James approached me with a small glass of wine upon a silver tray, I wondered whether I imagined the strange look that he gave me. As it was, there was no time to ponder it further when my husband's aunt and uncle were announced.

"Lord and Lady Matlock."

The door opened, and in they swanned, looking every inch the grand, old people they are. Happy greetings were exchanged, and Lord Matlock complained to Fitzwilliam of the road whilst Lady Matlock focused on us ladies.

"Oh, Elizabeth, how slender you are! How do you do it with three babies coming one after the other. It is quite remarkable. And this must be Mrs. Wickham. I am pleased to meet you…"

Lady Matlock smiled and, when Lydia said nothing and did not curtsy, looked about in an embarrassed fashion. Silence fell, and my aunt Matlock blinked slowly. The clock ticked, and the footmen's soles clicked in the hall. I could bear it no longer and gave a slight tug on my sister's arm at which she seemed to remember herself.

"It is an honour to meet you, Lady Matlock. I am Elizabeth's sister, Mrs. Wickham."

"Mrs. Wickham, I hope that you have been enjoying your stay at Pemberley? It is so beautiful at this time of year."

Lydia smiled but said nothing. Just as I thought she was about to speak, she let out a hiccup followed by a giggle, and my mind raced to account for her demeanour.

"It is quite lovely, Lady Matlock, although I am not much of one for rambling about the countryside as my sister is. I would much rather dance. Do you enjoy a dance, Lady Matlock?"

With this, she peered at Fitzwilliam's aunt, who is nearly sixty, but did not wait for a response.

"I do, but being a widow, I declare that I have not had one dance these eight months. I shall be glad to dance again when I am allowed, I can tell you. My husband died a hero, Lady Matlock. A hero. What a thing that is to have a hero for a husband. I cannot imagine anything more splendid—except him being alive, of course. My goodness, did you know that my husband actually grew up at Pemberley? Yes. He had such affection for this place, and can we not all see why? I take great comfort thinking of him running about the gardens as a boy and building camps in the woods…"

Words streamed from her lips, and I thought they would never stop. In fact, not only did they not cease, they grew louder and more insistent. Her hands fluttered around and everything about her was distracting. It was like watching a horseless carriage thunder down a steep hill. Lord Matlock had stopped speaking of the road, and he and Fitzwilliam were turned to us in silence. My husband fixed me with a grave look and, with his gaze, indicated Lydia's wine glass, now left on the small table beside her chair. At the moment I realised her predicament, Lydia seemed to reach the apogee of her confidence.

"I hear, Lady Matlock, that you have an unmarried son who is a colonel of the regiment. Is that not the case? How marvellous. There is nothing like regimentals on a man, is there?"

I knew that I had to stop her.

"Erm, Lydia. Maybe we should allow Lady Matlock to sit and gather herself. She has only just arrived, and it is a long journey from Matlock."

Matlock to Pemberley is only ten miles of good road, but as to that, any port in a storm, thought I.

"Yes, of course, Lizzy. Why, my journey here from Hertfordshire was such a trial. I can well sympathise. It took me a full three days to recover myself! Although, I must say that Mr. Darcy's carriage was vastly comfortable indeed. Mama was so envious to see me disappearing in it, I can tell you…"

"Aunt Mary, is the weather fine at Matlock? We have been kept in by rain here." I scrambled for a topic, and in my panic, the weather was the only one I found.

"It has been reasonably fair…"

"Oh, but it is so cold here, do you not think so, Lizzy? It is far colder here than ever it is in Hertfordshire at this time of year. I wonder that Lizzy manages, for we were never so chilly as girls. She must wear a great deal under her gowns to guard against the wind, for it is bitter!"

"Lydia!" I moved towards her as one might approach a horse who had gone rogue.

"Well, it is true, Lizzy, and I know you think so too, for did you not write to Mama when you were first married that you were cold?"

With this, Fitzwilliam turned to the fire, his body a rage of tension.

"No, I did not say that, Lydia. I have always been more than comfortable in Derbyshire. It is my home, and I love it."

She gave me a dismissing look with which I was well familiar before engaging poor Lady Matlock once more.

"Now, Lady Matlock, it is such a pleasure to meet you at last, for Lizzy is always speaking of you. I am glad that you are come to supper, or I might have thought she had made you up! Now, my sister tells me that your younger son is frightful handsome and extremely agreeable company. Well, I should like to meet him, for I do not see why Lizzy should get all the amiable gentlemen."

Desperate times, I concluded, called for desperate measures.

"Lydia, I need to have a word with Mrs. Reynolds before supper. Would you mind coming with me please?"

"Whatever for?"

I took her arm.

"Well, I shall tell you on the way. Please excuse me, Lady Matlock. I shall be back directly."

Lydia looked confused, but I could tell from her eyes that she was not about to refuse. If I thought, however, that the evening had thus far gone badly, worse was to come. For when we went to move towards the door, my sister's grip upon my arm tightened, her slippered feet stumbled, and she nearly fell.

"Lydia!"

"Oh! My goodness. I am sorry. I am all right, Lizzy."

"I think you may be feeling poorly. I shall see you to your chamber…"

When we were in the hall and beyond the closed door of the drawing room, I am ashamed to say that I almost dragged her upstairs.

"Do not pull on me so, Lizzy! Stop it. I do not feel very well."

"Of course, you do not feel very well. What were you thinking? You are not used to drink, Lydia, nor should you be!" I said when we were safely behind the closed door of her chamber.

She sank down on the edge of her bed and groaned. I turned to Milly, who had joined us at my request.

"Milly, Mrs. Wickham is feeling unwell. She will not be able to join Mr. Darcy and me for dinner. Please, can you assist her to bed and bring her tea and buttered toast in case she becomes hungry in the night? Thank you. Lydia, I suggest that you will be better off in bed. I will visit you in the morning."

I did not wait for her to reply but turned on my heel, clicked the door closed, and departed.

I have enjoyed merrier suppers with my husband and his relations than that which followed. At first, there was a lack of conversation. The room was filled with the sound of silver tinkling on china, glasses being picked up and replaced, and James pacing the room with various dishes, his polished shoes padding around the thick carpet. I knew that I could not allow it to continue, and so, angry and upset though I was, I forced myself to be cheerful. With some effort, I encouraged Lord Matlock to tell us of his recent visit to Town. Lady Matlock, who can be relied upon to discuss her family, was immediately at ease when I asked her how plans for her eldest son's wedding were progressing. Although we are not close, Lady Matlock has always been kind to me. She looked at Fitzwilliam, surly and taciturn, and then trained her eye upon me. I believe that she consciously held out her hand by way of assistance when she resolved to be happy and talkative. Even so, my husband said little. He sat opposite me, slightly in shadow, and when I moved to catch his eye around the side of the candle, I was certain that he looked away.

Our guests did not stay late, for they had some miles to travel home. We bade them farewell at the main door and watched in silence as their carriage clattered away down the moonlit drive and out of sight.

"I am sorry, Fitzwilliam…"

"Elizabeth, I have to write a letter."

"A letter? At this time of night?"

"Yes, there is a problem with the tenant at Rosschapel. I have to write to my steward urgently. I would have done it before dinner but…it is nothing for you to worry over. You should retire."

That was the last he spoke to me before stalking into his study without a glance back. It has now been two hours, and here I am at the desk in my chamber, alone. I am not fooled by the suggestion that a letter was so urgent it had to be written at night nor so long that it would take an age to compose. No. I rather think that there is no letter, but that, after the evening he has had, my husband wishes to be out of my presence. It is sobering to think that I once had to write in stolen moments, while he was preparing for bed, between the soft looks at the dining table and the kisses of the night. Now, it would appear that I have more than enough time in which to account for my movements, and I wish instead that he would come to me. In the stillness, I recall how he gave this book to me, and although he knows that I enjoy writing in it, I have never told him exactly what it is I write. Whatever would he say, I wonder? To write so much, and so deeply of myself and yet not tell my husband, sounds quite wrong; but do we not all need our secrets?

Chapter 7

London, 8 August 2014

From: Charlie Haywood
To: Cressida Carter
Date/time: 08/08/2014 06:26 BST
Subject: Project Darcy

Cressida, can you ask your solicitor in Shropshire who acts
for the Darcy Trust?

From Cressida Carter
To: Charlie Haywood
Date/time: 08/08/2014 06:53 BST
Subject: Project Darcy

You're up early. I hope that you are not emailing me in bed.
I already know. Firm called Galbraiths, Flanders & Waites in
Fleet Street. They do big-ticket private client. Old as the
hills. Any news?

CHARLIE WOULD HAVE SENT HER A FLIRTY REPLY, BUT HIS MIND WAS REELING
with the sheer good fortune of Galbraiths being involved. He had not lost
his touch. His lucky number was up again.

He leaned back in his chair and took a sip of coffee. Outside the office, the London morning was opening, clear bright light filling the sky, taxis putting on their orange lights, early birds arriving at work, and street sweepers swishing down the road. He had thought of her twice that morning and recalled the motion of her foot on the polished floor of the gallery as she spoke to another man. He pushed the thought away.

He surveyed the pile of papers Simon had left for him. A genogram, a few wills from the probate registry, an article about stately homes in Derbyshire—there were all sorts. Simon had worked hard and done a good job. But Charlie was like a bloodhound on a scent. He had read the papers angrily, voraciously. He had a skill for quickly and effectively taking in and assimilating vast amounts of data. It had been said to him that he could have done many other things with that skill than the thing he had done; of course, other people did not understand quite how things had been—how fate had twisted against every plan he had ever had for himself. He decided not to be distracted by that history now. In his mind, the late Fitzwilliam Darcy and his family had emerged from the mist of ignorance and begun to take shape.

Mr. Darcy had been born in Derbyshire in 1785 to a wealthy landowning father and an aristocratic mother. On his mother's side, he was the grandson of the Earl of Matlock. His father was untitled, wealthy gentry. In 1813, he married one Elizabeth Bennet of Hertfordshire. Simon had not learned much about Mrs. Darcy except that her father was a small landowner and she was one of five sisters. Mr. and Mrs. Darcy had lived in an enormous pile called Pemberley in the Peak District and had six children, five girls and a boy. Their marriage ended when Elizabeth died, aged sixty-one in 1853. Her husband followed her to the grave seven years later in 1860. These people had proper money. In addition to Pemberley, there was a house in Grosvenor Square, owned by his descendants until 1947 when they sold it to pay death duties. Mr. Darcy also owned smaller estates in Ireland, Scotland, and the West Country. Cressida had not exaggerated when she called her mother's family "terribly grand."

As for their children, the rich and privileged were always easy to trace. First, there was Anne, born in 1814. Anne had married in 1836, and maybe she wasn't much like her mother as she only had one son. Her son had married, had a family, and so had his kids. The upshot was that there were three women living in Australia by the name of Murphy who were lucky enough to be beneficiaries of the Darcy Trust. Next in line was Emma Darcy. She had married and had children too. A grandson and great grandson of hers had died on the Titanic. They had been in first class, so Charlie reflected as he sipped his coffee that they had been very unlucky to die. The only living descendants of Emma Darcy were Cressida Carter, her mother, and her cousin Jennifer.

The next Darcy sister was Frances, and although she married and had kids, her modern day descendants seemed to have been treated to a torrent of misfortune. Three of her great granddaughters died in the Blitz, two of them in the same raid. At the end of her line in the genogram, there stood only male names, so no worries there. The Darcy's fourth daughter, Beatrice, came into the world in 1820 and only had one child, a daughter who died in childbirth in 1863. Then came the controversial Victoria Darcy, born in 1821 and still causing shock waves in 2014. Victoria's only living female descendants were, as Charlie expected, Clementine and Evangeline Pemberton.

Fitzwilliam Darcy's son, born in 1822, was the last of his children to be born, and his living female descendants comprised an eighty-six-year-old lady named Violet Fortescue, currently living in a care home in Brighton, and her two daughters, both in their fifties and living in what Charlie imagined to be great comfort in the Home Counties. So there it was. Astonishingly, there were only eleven women who benefitted from the Darcy Trust. If Cressida Carter could strike out the Pemberton sisters, then there would be only nine, each of them significantly richer in consequence.

Charlie checked the trust document again. It really did say "all of my female descendants in perpetuity." It was that simple, that bald, that open. What had been in the guy's mind? These Darcy daughters were all married to rich men. Simon had found evidence that Emma was married with a dowry of £20,000. That was an extraordinary sum in 1839. It would be very unusual if she had been married with a greater dowry than her sisters. Why on earth had Fitzwilliam Darcy felt the need to set up this trust? It was completely bizarre. Charlie's coffee was stone cold and his back had started to ache by the time Maureen clattered in, still wearing her outdoor shoes.

"Good morning, Mr. Haywood. Thank goodness, it's you. I thought for a dreadful moment that I hadn't locked up properly on Friday."

"No, Mau, just me. I've been in to get some headspace on this Darcy thing.

It has been good actually. I have got loads done."

The early morning was the best time to work; his dad had said so, and he was right. The memory stopped him in his tracks. Maureen smiled faintly and seemed to consider him over the thick rims of her glasses. She had been his secretary for ten years, and he wondered how much she knew of his life. She arranged his diary and did all of his paperwork. She made sure his tax was paid and his car booked in for its service. She knew the hours he worked and the overwhelming effort that went into appearing nonchalant. They shared the surface intimacy of long-term colleagues, and the truth was that Charlie felt comfortable in her presence.

"Well, I'm glad, Mr. Haywood. There is nothing in your diary until this afternoon when a Mr. Trinder is calling about his business partner. Shall you be working in your office until then?"

"No. I could do with stretching my legs. Anyway, I need to catch up with someone about this Darcy thing. I'm on my mobile, okay?"

She nodded as she stashed her faux leather handbag neatly below her desk. Charlie grabbed his jacket, slung it over his shoulder, and in a flash was out of the door, down the stairs, and onto the bustling street.

Across the road from Galbraiths, Flanders & Waites stood a newspaper shop, a Starbucks, and an independent coffee shop with rickety chairs and a halogen light in the window. It was 9:30 a.m., and Charlie probably had a wait ahead of him, so he bought a copy of the *Times* and *Vanity Fair* and sat in the window of the coffee shop, keeping watch without appearing to do so. It was Monday morning, and he knew that she would never last until lunch without a coffee and a cigarette. Sure enough, at nearly 11:00 a.m., she came. The main door of Galbraiths opened, a big, red bus drove by, and there on the pavement was Isobel Langley-Jones—long legs, sweet smile, looking left and right, and clutching her purse to her chest. Charlie stood, took his jacket from the back of his chair, paid up, and left the magazine and newspaper for the girl behind the till. Isobel did not notice when he joined the queue directly behind her in Starbucks.

"Let me guess, skinny cappuccino with an extra shot?"

"Charlie!" She spun around, grinning from ear to ear. "Wow, what a coincidence. How are you?"

"I'm great, Issy. And you?"

"Yeah, oh, I'm okay, you know." She fiddled with her pretty hair as she spoke, and he tried to recall how long it had been.

"I really am getting you a coffee though. Do you have time to stop, Issy?"

Her eyes darted about and she had that look on her face that told him she was about to say "no" but then changed it to "yes." He ordered their coffees, and they sat at the back on each side of a small, round, not-quite-clean table. They chatted amiably, as well as two people who occasionally slept together but otherwise rarely fraternise can. Isobel amazed him by announcing she had given up smoking. She had passed her legal secretary test and recently decorated her flat. Her cat was well. It was that kind of conversation. He made the error of brushing her hand with his when she reached for a napkin, and she looked suddenly suspicious.

"This isn't really a coincidence, is it, Charlie?"

He felt suddenly guilty for having underestimated her.

"Well, not quite. I had a meeting nearby this morning and hoped that I might see you on your coffee run because...well, I was hoping you might be able to help me. It's going to take a bit of explaining though...it's a long story. Do you want to hear me out?"

She put her head in her hands and let out a strange noise.

"I know that I shouldn't, but I know that I will. Okay. When do you want to talk?"

"Meet me for lunch? Temple Gardens, one o'clock? My treat."

Later that day, they sat on the parched grass, midsummer flowers blooming and the sun blazing.

"Charlie, you remembered that I love raspberries! Lovely and only a little bit creepy." She winked, and he laughed back. Things were okay between them. She was not a girl who took things too seriously.

"'Course I remembered."

She sat back against the slight, grassy incline behind them and passed the red, fleshy fruit around in her mouth. Issy had helped him before, but on that occasion he just wanted a client's telephone number.

"So come on then, Charlie, let's hear it. What do you want this time?"

"I want you to get a file for me."

"You want what? Are you completely mad? I'll get the sack. No. No, no, and no."

"Calm down, Issy. I haven't told you anything about it yet. Don't jump the gun. Eat another raspberry. It's not a current client file that I want. Christ, the file I want might not even be there. This thing is so old that it might have been put through the shredder long ago. This is ancient history, Issy. Nobody is going to care or notice."

"But you do?"

"Yeah, it might be important for a case I'm working on. It might be a dead end. It's just a try, but I kind of need you to help me get started. I didn't know you had got so timid."

He knew that would rile her.

"Okay. So how old is old?"

"Well, the guy I'm interested in died in 1860. Old enough for you? I told you, it's not like I'm asking you to take a current file. This isn't one of your Russian oligarchs or your aristos in rehab. Nobody will notice. Nobody would care if they did notice. Think of it as an antiquarian fetish of mine."

He shot her a glance, and she closed her eyes in acceptance. He moved his arm closer to hers, knowing that she would feel the silent pressure, the knowledge of their history whispering against her skin.

"What is the name?"

"Darcy. Fitzwilliam Darcy."

"Fitzwilliam is a funny first name. We definitely still have Darcys on the books—live ones, I mean. Okay, Charlie, I'll look in the archives, but I'm not guaranteeing anything. It has probably all been chucked out, but I'll have a look."

He kissed the side of her head and said, "Thank you."

"I should bloody think so. You owe me, Charlie Haywood."

She was a nice girl, and he liked her, but she didn't really touch him. When lunch was over, he gave her a hug, and she went back to the office, the sun shining on her bare legs, and the remains of the raspberries in a pot in her handbag to brighten the afternoon. Charlie's mind was buzzing with the Darcys, but he knew that, for all his efforts, Issy might find nothing. The archives of Galbraiths, Flanders & Waites were long and deep, but whether they contained documents from 1860 was a different question. It was a long shot, and only time would tell. So, he headed back to the office. He worked on another case and answered some emails. He talked to a Mr. Trinder about a new instruction. He listened to Simon's account of having trailed the Lebanese trophy wife through every naughty knicker shop in West London.

By six o'clock, he didn't have much left to give the day, and so he left. He sat in the leather driver's seat of his Porsche, started the engine, and was gone. Imaginary faces of historical Darcys danced around before his eyes, and he played the matter around in his head. Without knowing how or why, his mind returned to her honey-blonde head and her moving hands. He cursed himself again that he had made such a hash of meeting her and thought of all the things he did not know about Evie Pemberton. He probably never would know those things, and it didn't really matter. But it nagged him, nibbled at his consciousness, intruded on his peace. Who the hell was she, and why did he care?

He could not have explained to anybody why he did it. The heat was gone from the day, the pavements full of people in suits walking home from the Tube. There was a guy giving away copies of the *Evening Standard* when Charlie stopped at the traffic lights, and his voice seemed too loud to be real. Charlie grew up in London and knew the way to anywhere on instinct. He had looked at Evie's card more times than he would care to admit. All of the signs seemed to point and all of the roads seemed to lead to her. Before he knew where he was, he was headed away from home, straight into the heart of Fulham. He knew the street, and the studio was easy to find. Suddenly realising how bad it would look if she saw him, Charlie parked opposite, turned the radio down, and simply looked. The studio was pretty obvious. There was a massive canvass obscuring part of the window from the inside and the broken clay model of a lute in the front garden. Tired, late summer flowers blew against the low, red brick wall, and a black cat lay across the pebbly path. It was a single-story building on the end of a terrace house. There was no reason to think that the house had anything to do with her, of course. It was a strange looking place, and Charlie noticed that, instead of steps, there was an ugly, concrete slope leading to the front door and a series of unsightly, metal bars attached to the wall. The contrast with the other houses—all polished, pastel coloured front doors and gracious bay windows—was striking. He wondered for a moment who lived there. The whimsy of his state of mind and the appalling fact that he had gone to her studio for no good reason woke him with a jolt. It was a mindless, ridiculous act. If she saw him, it would be even worse. Holding that thought, he turned the key, indicated left, and with one, strong hand on the steering wheel, got himself out of there.

Later, in his flat, fatigue was catching up with him when his iPhone buzzed the arrival of an email.

```
From: fluffyissy@hotmail.com
To: Charlie Haywood
Date/time: 08/08/2014 22:55
Subject: Result

Attachment: doc.pdf

I can't believe I am doing this. See attached. There
wasn't much in there--just some letters. Not the original
handwritten ones. For some reason, somebody had typed them
up in the 1940s. So it is not even a struggle to read. You
have the luck of the devil, and you don't deserve it. If I
lose my job, I am moving in with you.

Issyxxx
```

By midnight, still sleepless, he had read the lot several times. There was *something* there. It was almost beyond comprehension, but it was true. Dots linked up with lines in the darkness and dazzled him. He felt the familiar rush of success, the drunkenness of it swelling him. His head was singing with it. After ten years of searching for people's secrets, the avenues of discovery still amazed him. There was a secret in this Darcy marriage—a real secret—and these letters proved it. Who would have thought that it could come back to haunt the descendants of Elizabeth Darcy two centuries later? Involuntarily, he recalled the sight of Evie Pemberton, dwarfed by her own canvas. He dismissed that vision. It didn't matter. This was his brief, and as usual, he was on it. He deleted Issy's email details and message before he forwarded the file to Cressida Carter. The subject read, "We are on to something."

Chapter 8

June 1, 1860
Pemberley

Galbraith,

 I write further to my last letter and very much regret the need to do so. Since writing, I have become aware of a piece of servant's gossip that, it appears, has been commonly known at Pemberley for some time. I shall not bore you with the circuitous manner in which it reached me, but, inevitably, a number of people here are aware of it.

 You may or may not recall Hannah Tavener. There is no reason you should, but she was Elizabeth's maid throughout our marriage and travelled with Elizabeth everywhere. She was always with us when we went to Town, and you may have seen her at Darcy House when you called. In any event, she was a loyal and trusted servant to Elizabeth, and I am not romantic when I say she was also her friend. Hannah nursed Elizabeth during the fever that killed her, caught the fever herself, and was dead within three days of her mistress. I attended her funeral and, you may recall, made a significant gift to her family for whom her wages were a source of financial security. However, coming as it did so hard upon the unexpected loss of my wife, Hannah's death seemed simply one of a barrage of sorrows.

 I now learn that, in her last hours, she made a declaration that Elizabeth had asked her to dispose of something and that she had failed to do so. I have no idea what it was that Elizabeth may have wished to destroy or her reason for asking Hannah to do it. I have had each of the servants—whom I know to have gossiped about this—in my study, and I regret that none of them knows anything more. I have interrogated the rector who gave her the last rites. He concurs with the story and recalls that Hannah, who was delirious at the time, pleaded with him to assist in "getting rid of it for Mrs. Darcy."

Thus, my enquiries have foundered. I do not need to spell out to you, Galbraith, what my fears are with respect to the Rosschapel business. If there is something abroad that Elizabeth knew of and that may reveal truths known only to us, then I want it to be found. If you have any wisdom as to how I should proceed, then I would be glad to hear it.

Yours,
Darcy

Chapter 9

U nusually, it is early morning, and I write while Fitzwilliam sleeps. These past mornings, I have woken feeling most poorly and have not been able to stay abed. I have benefited greatly from a cup of tea and a walk around our sitting room. I hear birds outside and the soft tread of maids in the corridor. My husband's breath and the scrape of my pen are the only sounds within this room, and I find it calming. How little time in life is as peaceful as this? At some point, and soon, he shall roll over, his hand seeking me. The cold sheets against his skin will wake him, and then I shall have to stop. He will want to know how I am feeling and whether I have had enough sleep. He leaves me in no doubt of his concern for me. He could not be more attentive. Even so, he never speaks of whether this, our fourth child, is to be a daughter or a son. When I have been with child previously, he has made a show of assuring me that he did not mind. Now, he says nothing, and I wonder whether he was ever in earnest. I shall not raise this matter with him. I shall not be the one to say it. When he wakes, I shall return his kisses and laugh my best laugh. For it does not do to be downcast, and if I can think this child a boy with happy thoughts, then I shall.

As it is, there is much to be jolly about. Along the corridor, Jane and Mr. Bingley sleep in their chamber, for they are to stay for two whole weeks on their journey north to see Mr. Bingley's relations. They bring with them Miss Bingley, still unmarried, but I cannot mind that because the presence of my sister Jane is a tonic, and I shall bear any number of Miss Bingleys to be with her.

It was mid-morning when their carriage clattered into the courtyard at Pemberley. Fitzwilliam and I watched as it teetered under the weight of so many trunks and cases loaded on the back and as Jane and Mr. Bingley, smiling, and Miss Bingley, chattering, seemed to fall out. Jane rushed towards me, skirts billowing, face beaming, and I almost burst. What with her confinements and mine—and the distance from their estate in Leicestershire—it had been nearly a year. There were cries of "Oh, Lizzy" and "Oh, Jane." To hear us exclaiming at each other reminded me of Lydia, and I wondered whether Mr. Darcy was annoyed. It was strange that, when I glanced at him to check, he was looking at me hard, and he was fixed with an almost imperceptible smile playing across his lips.

"Lizzy, it is no good. You shall have to stop having all of these children. Those of us who live to the South cannot cope without your visits any longer. The sense-deficit in Hertfordshire in particular is now grown so great that it shall soon be considered a country-wide emergency."

"Oh, Jane, now I will not have you blaming me thus. You could ask Mr. Bingley to move here. Or, you could stop having babies yourself and visit me more often."

We laughed, and Miss Bingley, who was not a lady to be left out, interjected.

"Mrs. Darcy, how wonderful to see you." We bobbed curtsies to each other. "I say that you should both stop producing infants, which must be so trying, and end your exile from Town, which must be the most diverting place that any of us have available to us. Do you not agree? I simply cannot imagine missing the season."

"Oh, Miss Bingley, I can, and I rather think that Mr. Darcy can as well. He was thrilled the first year that we missed it due to Georgiana's being married and my being confined. He could hardly suppress his joy."

She looked away from me, and her eyes fell upon Fitzwilliam who was well out of earshot and speaking with Mr. Bingley. Caroline, who must be all of thirty years, looked suddenly sad, and I regretted referring to my husband in that way. It had become apparent to me in the earliest days of my marriage that, despite her rudeness, she was much more to be pitied than feared. Her admiration of my husband, who hardly even looked at her in all the years of their acquaintance, was so powerful that, even now, she could not properly hide it. Within a year of becoming Mrs. Darcy, I had resolved to be as kind as possible to her. I reminded myself of that resolution now.

"But your challenge is taken Miss Bingley. I shall have to make sure that you are as diverted as we can manage on this visit. I will do my best. I hope that we shall hear you play? We may even have to have dancing one evening, although you may have to excuse me. I am currently a punishment to stand up with, I believe!"

Both Jane and Caroline looked at my belly and laughed.

Cloaks and bonnets were removed, trunks carried above stairs and unpacked. Servants scurried from room to room. The horses were taken to the stables to be rested and refreshed. As Jane and Mr. Bingley were shown to their room, Caroline close behind, I stood at the bottom of the staircase, feeling rather small. Fitzwilliam's hand came to the small of my back.

"Elizabeth, shall we visit the day nursery while our guests are settling in?"

He was right that we had not been today. I had been so busy with Mrs. Reynolds and anticipating Jane and her family that our usual routines had been thrown asunder. It surprised me that he thought of this as I had come to think that maybe it was I who most particularly wished to visit the day nursery each morning. I was surprised, but I was glad.

"Yes, Fitzwilliam. Let us go up together."

He offered his arm, which I took. When we turned the corner and with nobody watching, I quickly kissed his cheek.

Later, I sought out my sister. Mr. Bingley was out riding with Fitzwilliam, and Caroline was still in her chamber, no doubt considering her various outfits. I knocked gently on Jane's door.

"Come."

"Only me." I peeked into the room where I found her sitting on the bed, her maid unpacking gowns and frockcoats. "Can I tempt you with a walk, Mrs. Bingley? It is not too cold, and you will find my pace most unchallenging!"

She smiled broadly, donned her bonnet and shawl, and we were gone. Arm in arm, we limited ourselves to the closest path to the house. Jane spoke of their recent visit to Longbourn. Being now resident in Leicestershire, it was rather easier for the Bingleys to visit Meryton than it was for us, and inevitably, they did so more often.

"Shall your husband be decorated with medals, Jane, for consenting to live within tolerable distance of our family?"

"Sometimes I think that he should be, Lizzy, although I must say that he never says so. He is such an amiable man, so generous hearted. He speaks not a word of reproach. Not even about Lydia…"

"Now that is a feat indeed. To have Lydia in his house for three months and not complain. I cannot manage that, and she is my sister!"

"Well, I could not have coped, Lizzy, if I had not had you to write to. I can manage her, but I need to express myself sometimes, or it is quite unbearable. I was so sure that time would be a healer—that things would improve. But, do you know, I think she has got worse? She sleeps hardly at all. Lydia, who had to be winched out of bed before she was married is always last to retire and first at the breakfast table. Not that she eats a great deal, of course. That is another problem, and Mama frets on it enough for the whole country."

"Yes, she was like that when she was here. She kept the most extraordinary hours and had the servants attending her at all hours of the morning. She even managed to wake Fitzwilliam, and he always starts his day before me."

"Well, she is just the same. And one would think that she would be tired, but she does not appear to be anything of the sort. She remains…well…odd in company. She either is so quiet and withdrawn that one wonders if it is really her, or she is agitated by the most amazing, nervous energy. It was such a godsend when Maria asked her to stay in Margate. Papa had been dealing with the situation by hiding in his library, and Mama…well, she was at the end of her tether. Everyone agreed that a change of scene would be just the thing."

I pondered this for a moment, for I did not want to say wrong. Our dear friend Maria Lucas had been married the previous year to a gentleman of Margate, and she had kept up correspondence with both Lydia and Kitty. She had no doubt also heard of Lydia's misfortunes from her mama, Lady Lucas, with whom our mama visits weekly. In any event, Maria is well settled and a great evangelist for the benefits of seaside living. She kindly invited Lydia to stay for a few months, and she could hardly have had a more enthusiastic response from either Lydia herself or her family. It is now oft repeated that getting away from home is just what Lydia needs and that the sea air and a change of scene will set her up. But is that really true? Are we not all saying that because we want it to be real? I detected an oddity in Jane's tone. There was a reservation that had not been there before, and

I had a sudden sense that she was holding back.

"Well, let us hope, Jane. Have you heard anything from Margate?"

"I have had one letter from Lydia, and I believe that Kitty has heard from Maria."

"What did they say?"

"Well, Lydia's letter was like every letter she has ever written to me. She wrote of what a splendid time she is having and how she has made a number of new acquaintances. She is pleased to be wearing grey and some mauve, and she has attended some small dinners and assemblies with Maria and her husband. Everyone is charming, and all is perfect. You know how she is. All of her geese are swans."

A sudden rush of wind rustled the shrubs to the side of us, and Jane looked down at her pale blue slippers pattering across the gravel.

"What is it you do not say, Sister?"

"Oh, Lizzy, it is probably not anything new to worry on..."

"Jane! I told you about the evening with Lord and Lady Matlock, and that was a confidence indeed. Now you have to tell me what is troubling you."

"Well. I have heard from Kitty, and she has had a letter from Maria. It was not a complaint exactly. Maria writes to Kitty regularly, and this was just one of her letters. But...well, she did say that they were finding Lydia rather difficult to control. She was pushing herself forward in company and being very raucous. They attended a local assembly where Lydia, apparently, took herself around the room without an escort, introducing herself to all of the gentlemen and initiating gossip with the ladies."

"Is she drinking?"

"The letter did not relate that, but I do not believe Maria would say even if she were. Poor Maria. She has been so generous, but I am at a loss as to what to do. What worries me is that Maria really knows Lydia. They grew up together, and Maria knows how difficult she can be. She knew about the elopement with Wickham; everyone in Meryton did. Maria is no stranger to the facts. And she is reserved. She would never intimate to Kitty that anything was wrong unless it was serious. Lizzy, I am most worried about what she is *not* saying."

The sight of Lydia staggering about my parlour came back to me in a flash, and I felt an ache in my ribs as the baby pushed up against them.

"I agree. I think we should write to Aunt Gardiner and see what she thinks."

"That is a good idea, Lizzy. Let us do that."

She squeezed my arm and touched her gentle hand to my belly, and we turned back to the house.

Later, I was sitting up in bed sipping my tea when Fitzwilliam joined me. He paused slightly in the doorway as he approached, and his eyes were caught by the flame from the fire. His valet had undressed him, and in the dim light, I could see the lines of his body beneath his lawn shirt. I believe that he caught me looking at the lower part of his neck. He smiled lazily as he lay on the bed beside me.

"You look very pleased with yourself, sir."

"I am, for I believe that I have a happy wife. Am I right?"

In fact, I had been worrying over Maria's letter about Lydia and wracking my mind for solutions to our dilemma. I could not trouble him with it, and so I kissed his forehead.

"Yes, you are right. It is lovely to have her here, Fitzwilliam. It has been too long. Do you think that Charles may ever be persuaded to move into Derbyshire?"

"Well, maybe. But Leicestershire is convenient for him as it is nearer to London. He has a lot of business interests there."

"Well, you have interests in Scotland and the West Country—and there is Rosschapel in Ireland—but we do not have to live in any of those places."

"No, but I employ men to represent me where necessary, and in fact, when it comes to Rosschapel, there are still problems with the tenant. I rather fear that I may need to visit at some stage."

"Oh." I looked at my mountainous belly and then at him. He had told me of an arduous visit to Rosschapel with his father many years previously, and I knew that, if he were to go there, he would certainly be absent from Pemberley for a month if not more. "Not soon, I hope?"

His hand reached out for mine.

"No, Elizabeth, not soon. You must not worry yourself about it. It is for me to deal with, and it is not urgent. If I do need to go there, I will go for the shortest time I can, and you will have plenty of warning. But as for Bingley, he needs to be close to London for business. In any case, if he ever tries to take Caroline any further distance from the attractions of Town, he will have a fight on his hands, I'll wager."

"It is not for Caroline to decide, surely! It is a kindness that Jane is willing to have her on a permanent basis. For myself, I cannot understand why she does not spend more time with the Hursts. Before we were married, Jane and I fancied Caroline and Louisa were as close as we were, but now it seems that they are not, and poor Jane has to put up with Caroline day in and day out!"

"Well, that is as may be. I do not know, Elizabeth. But of course, if the Bingleys moved to Derbyshire, they would be even further from Longbourn, and I believe your parents would miss their frequent visits greatly."

I ran my fingers through his dark, curled hair and murmured my agreement. The scent of him and the feel of him came over me. He had netted me, and he was pulling me in—through the water and past the rushes to a place I knew well. I would not yield to it immediately.

"Speaking of Miss Bingley, I hope that you noticed the vividness of her skirts and the volume of bosom on display this evening, Mr. Darcy. I believe it was for your benefit."

He looked at my nightgown-clad bosom, much increased by my condition, and smiled a pale smile.

"Indeed? I am afraid it quite escaped my notice, Elizabeth. Mayhap she should focus her attentions on men who are not married to beautiful women."

With that, he pulled back the bedclothes and began to kiss my neck. Our limbs moved against each other in the half-light. The orange of the fire flickered, and the world outside the bedposts was quite forgotten.

Later, on the verge of slumber, Fitzwilliam pulled me into his warm embrace.

"Has Jane heard anything from Lydia in Margate?"

"No," I answered. "Nothing at all."

Chapter 10

T he ring of the phone in the studio was like an alarm. She set it loud so that she would hear it in the back garden or if she had music turned up loud. On this occasion, however, it was early morning, and she was scrambling to get the key into the lock. She just made it.

"Hello. Evie Pemberton speaking."

"Hi. Hello, Miss Pemberton. This is Charlie Haywood. We met at Cork Street last week. I hope this is not a bad time?"

There was a beat of silence, as though he were considering whether he needed to say more. She recalled him immediately. His name had lodged in her brain, and the memory came back in an instant. It wasn't completely welcome.

"Erm, no this is a fine time. What can I do for you?"

"Well, first of all, I wanted to say 'sorry.' I hope I didn't give you the wrong impression at the gallery. I'm sure you don't need charity dinners, and I'm sorry if it sounded wrong. You will have to forgive me for bad chat. I didn't mean it."

Evie did not know what to say to this. A candid apology did not match her notion of the kind of man Charlie Haywood was. She recalled his tall figure before her and the fit of his crisp, white shirt over his broad shoulders in the summer heat. His voice did not seem to match her notion of his arrogance. She was momentarily silenced by it.

"And secondly—in fact, I suppose, the main reason that I am ringing—is

64

that I really did like your work. It was an impressive corpus, and I'd like to see more if you'd let me. I am sorry to ring so early, but I have a meeting on the King's Road this morning, so if you were in your studio, I could come over after?"

She wasn't entirely against it, but she wasn't enthusiastic either. In her mind, she was conflicted. She thought of the swagger of his smile when he looked at her in the gallery and the sheer chutzpah of the man to ring up like this when she had brushed him off! Maybe she had misinterpreted him at the exhibition. Men were a foreign country to her now, and she acknowledged that she might have misread the signs. Then, she remembered the pathetic number of sales she had made, and the word "collector" danced around her brain. It wasn't in her character to push him away when he was being so polite.

"Sure, that's no problem. I am in the studio all day today. Come over whenever you like."

"How about eleven?"

"That's fine. I'll see you then."

Charlie replaced the receiver in his Notting Hill flat and gazed out of the sash window over the streets below. It would be good to find out more about her and her sister. She might actually know some useful information herself. The rumour was obviously out there in the family because that is how Cressida Carter found out about it, so maybe Evie knew the truth or an element of the truth. Cressida Carter. Just her name turned his stomach. Since receiving Mr. Darcy's letters, she had bombarded him with emails and calls, suggesting all manner of avenues for his enquiries. She was obviously thinking of nothing else. For Charlie's money, she had no idea how to ferret out a secret.

Simon had done a good job of amassing a few documents, and to kill time between now and his visit to Fulham, he sat down to read them. Right at the top of the pile was a PhD thesis from 1975 on the privately commissioned work of leading portraitist of the mid-nineteenth century, Alfred Clerkenman. Charlie was about to start tutting at Simon's lack of focus when he spotted a "Darcy" in the index. He turned to the page and read. It spoke of a momentous group portrait—a fine and detailed conversation piece. It was said to be a monumental work, the kind of art that melts its observer into a space on the floor. The painting was called *Mrs. Darcy and Her Daughters* and was commissioned in 1826 by Fitzwilliam Darcy. It featured his wife and their five daughters, ranging in age from five to eleven. The girls were seated around their mother in her private sitting room, variously holding books, toys, and musical instruments. It was judged to be an exquisite example of Clerkenman's work, perfectly showcasing his eye for detail and human sympathy. The few who had been admitted to its presence had been astonished. And it was "the few" because for some reason Fitzwilliam Darcy had adamantly refused to allow it to be exhibited publicly. He had been approached by a number of galleries, but the answer was always "no." After his death, his son followed the same line, and after that, Clerkenman went out of fashion, and the galleries stopped asking. The thesis author had seen it but only by private arrangement with the owners in their home.

In 1975, this painting was still behind closed doors. Where was it now? Charlie chewed it over in his mind. There was no illustration, only the description, and his imagination burned with it. It sounded beautiful, but would it be? It felt like it must be meaningful, but why and how? How could he square this painting with the cuckolded Mr. Darcy? He had been mulling for a long time, and his coffee had gone cold when he realised that it was time to set out for Fulham.

When he knocked, she opened the studio door so fast that he wondered whether she had been watching through the peephole. She said "hi" and "welcome" and swept her honey-blonde hair back from her face. She was slightly flushed and wearing a loose-fitting shirt with the sleeves rolled up over tatty Levis. There was a fleck of blue paint on her Converse trainers. Somehow, he knew she was more herself in this outfit than she had been in the dress at the gallery. The curves of her body under the camouflage of her costume didn't escape him. She had Buddy Holly jangling quietly in the background, and the unexpected familiarity of it struck him. A memory came to him of watching his parents jiving around the church hall to "Peggy Sue," his mother shrieking with laughter, flinging her arms out with joy. He felt a sense of comfort that was almost alarming. Evie made them tea in the tiny galley kitchen at the back of the studio, and they talked about the weather and his journey. Charlie's mind dwelled involuntarily on the light shampoo fragrance from her hair as she handed him his cup, and he battled to set his wayward thoughts aside. He congratulated her on the show, and she explained that it was her first and she was still buzzing from it.

"So you should be."

"Thank you." She smiled, and it warmed him. "It never would have happened without my old tutor from Camberwell. He has contacts at the gallery and has been pushing for it for ages. I don't deserve him. I do have some stuff here that was not exhibited if you're interested. There wasn't room for it, and it doesn't all 'fit' if you know what I mean. But if you like, I can shunt stuff around so that you can see it."

"That would be great. Yes, please."

She immediately stood and started shifting dusty canvasses about and pulling sheets from their faces to display them. The air was suddenly full of paint dust, so she opened the French doors to the back garden.

"Sorry! I should have done this first. I forget how dusty they get."

The sunlight crowded into the room, and the green of the grass reflected on her porcelain face.

"Don't worry about it," said Charlie, suppressing a cough.

He looked at the previously obscured images and saw that she was right. They would not have "fit" with the work exhibited at Cork Street. But they were really good. They were vibrant, interesting, and challenging in an unlikely way. He liked them. He *really* liked them. He was struck by guilt that he had lied to her in order to see these pieces, and he was wretched to think that she would have hopes that he was a real, long-term scale buyer. He could buy a couple, of course, and would. One thing he was not lacking was cash, and the thought of having an object made by her hands in his home reassured him greatly.

"These are great, Evie. More ballerinas as well. They would have exhibited well alongside the big piece."

"Thanks. I know, but there was so little space, and these were the early ballerina paintings. I was worried that they were rather immature, so I left them out."

"You're too harsh on yourself. I love them."

"Wow. Strong words. Thank you."

Was she teasing him? He couldn't tell. He hadn't been teasing her.

"Seriously. I am surprised that you haven't sold these. I hope that you made some sales from the exhibition."

"Yeah, well a few. I had a really good review in the *Art Monthly*, which was amazing, but it hasn't led to all that much. I am always surprised when people are actually interested though. I can't get past the idea that nobody but me and my sister and my uncle and aunt would actually like this stuff."

"No way, Evie. That's ridiculous. You must have other family members who would like it too."

They laughed, and she did not want to spoil the moment by saying she did not.

"My old tutor might be good for one or two. He taught me at Camberwell, and as I said, he's been a bit of a hero helping me to launch myself. I must admit that I love doing the work…but I'm not so great at selling it."

He found it hard to credit that she did not make a good living from painting, but that was what she seemed to be suggesting.

"Well, isn't that better than the other way around? Some artists can sell coal to Newcastle, but if the work isn't worth the time they spend tweeting about it, then what's the point?"

They drank more tea and talked with an ease that surprised them both. Evie dragged a few ill-fated attempts at working with clay out of the shed at the back. As she did so, she thought it was crazy to show a potential collector any examples of her work that had gone wrong, but she somehow knew instinctively that it didn't matter. They laughed at them together, and quite against her expectations, everything felt fine. Evie had lost track of time, but Charlie knew that it was at least two hours since he arrived. It was a trick of the trade that he was astoundingly good at estimating time. It was part of the watchfulness and awareness that came with the territory, and out of habit, he was always measuring out time like so many spoons of sugar. He had asked Maureen to clear his diary for the morning, but his iPhone had begun buzzing away in his pocket. He hadn't looked at it. He didn't want to leave. When the studio phone rang, he didn't think he had ever heard a louder ring.

"Hi, Evie Pemberton. … Hi, Milena. … Oh my God, is that the time? Okay. Give me five."

She clunked the phone down, and he had a sinking feeling that he was about to be politely turned out.

"Sorry. That was home. I live next door, so I usually go home for lunch. It's just sandwiches, but my sister's there, and it's kind of nice."

He was about to say that he'd give her a ring when she astonished him.

"If you'd like to join, you'd be welcome. It's nothing special, but it's food, and it's only next door. If you don't have anything else planned, that is…"

"Erm, thanks, that would be great. I don't have to be anywhere."

"Okay, well, let's go."

She put their tea-stained mugs in the sink, and he watched her tussle with the Banham lock on the front door, yellow sunlight pouring down on her head. Eventually, she locked it, and they walked the few steps to the next door and went in.

"'S'me," called Evie as she gestured for him to follow her. "Clem? Milena?"

A lilting eastern European accent came back from some unseen place. "We're in here, Evie."

Charlie followed her diminutive figure through the hall, along a slightly faded Chinese runner, and past stacks of unframed prints and canvasses. There was a suitcase open on the floor and seemingly full of medical kit. A grandfather clock with the mechanism taken out stood in the corner.

"I've got someone with me," called Evie as they walked through a set of double doors into an airy dining room. The patio doors were open at the other end of the room, and outside a light breeze played fallen petals across the grass. You could hear the low moan of traffic on the King's Road, and a carriage clock ticked on the mantelpiece littered with postcards and keys and the general detritus of a busy life. His eyes rested on her, and he cursed himself for not having guessed. Even in the wheelchair, you could see that she was Evie's sister. Her hair was held back by a red Alice band, and a napkin had been tucked into the collar of her top. It fell over her chest like a flag on a still day. And that was how her body was generally; it was still. It had no movement in it, you could tell. The chair sat around her like armour, rising high behind her head, the footrest catching the soles of her feet below.

"This is Charlie Haywood. He came to the studio to look at my work. Charlie, this is my sister, Clemmie."

She turned to him, and he knew from the gleam in her eye and the tilt of her head that it was a challenge. She hadn't warned him because she wanted to see his reaction. Did she expect him to fail? At that moment another woman, plump and black-haired came in, holding a glass of orange juice with a straw in it.

"And this is Milena, my sister's nurse, who lives with us. Lena, this is Charlie."

They all smiled and said "hi." Milena reported that she and Clemmie had spent the morning listening to Radio 3. Milena had checked through Clemmie's meds and fixed some buttons that had broken off her cardigan when she fell from her chair the previous week. Clemmie had napped sitting up, and while she was asleep, Milena had made her bed. Auntie Betty had rung to say that she would pop in tomorrow. That is how the morning had been: quiet, domestic, unhurried. When Milena brought the sandwiches in, Charlie made a point of sitting next to Clemmie.

"When I came over to look at your sister's work, I didn't expect to get fed, so thank you for having me."

"You're very welcome. Did you go to her exhibition? I wish so much that I could have gone myself, but the gallery doesn't have disabled access, so I would have been camped outside on the pavement, which might have cramped her style." Her eyes twinkled as she laughed.

"I bet you wouldn't have done, but you have plenty of her paintings here unless I am mistaken?" He looked around the room.

"Yes, they don't get any choice," interjected Evie, biting into a sandwich.

"We like the pictures, don't we, Clemmie?" asked Milena who was feeding Clemmie hers in tiny pieces. "They brighten the place up."

"They do," said Clemmie between mouthfuls, "but one day my sister will hit the big time, and we'll sell the lot and move to Mayfair."

Thus, they laughed and ate their lunch as the mid-afternoon unfolded. Milena entertained them with tales of her Bulgarian relations who had just discovered Skype and wanted to video-call her every time the cooker was playing up. Clemmie and Charlie talked happily about the best walks through the Royal Parks. He was not a man for the Tube or the bus. If he wasn't driving, he liked to walk around London. It took him a moment to realize that he shouldn't have mentioned it. He was uncharacteristically abashed.

"You don't need to be embarrassed. I used to be able to walk. I haven't always been in this thing. And anyway, now that I am, Lena pushes me, so I still get to feed the ducks in Green Park. I just scare them a bit into the bargain." She smiled brightly, and he was reassured.

"Have you always lived in London, Charlie?"

"Yes, I have. I live in Notting Hill now but grew up in Hackney. I can't imagine living in the countryside. I think the silence might kill me. And the darkness—how do people sleep in the darkness of the country? I couldn't do it. How about you? Fulham born and bred, or are you girls city immigrants?"

Clemmie laughed, and he got the feeling that, if she could, she would have thrown her head back in merriment.

"Fulham, born and bred—and this house, born and bred. We were both born in this house, and we have lived here all our lives. Our mother was an early adherent of the giving-birth-at-home craze. Said there was no call for hospital unless one was ill, and childbirth was not illness. Of course, now we are far more familiar than any of us would like to be with the inside of the local hospital. But anyway, that's an aside. Evie and I are SW6 natives."

"There can't be many people in London who live in the house they were born in," he said. He wasn't sure whether it was fortunate or not. Evie's face tightened slightly, and it occurred to him that she was considering the same question.

"Your mum sounds like quite a lady. Did she have a romantic name as well?"

"Romantic?" Evie's eyes flicked up as she said the word.

"Well, Clementine and Evangeline, they are romantic, unusual names, aren't they? I just wondered if it was a family tradition."

Evie sat up straighter and seemed suddenly troubled. He tried to recall whether she had ever actually said that Clemmie was short for Clementine. He feared that she had not, so he should not have said it. Her brow furrowed slightly, and he decided not to worry about it. Clemmie herself put an end to this train of thought by answering the question.

"I'm afraid not. Her name was Nora."

It was Evie who ended it all by standing up, stretching, and saying that she had to get back to the studio. Charlie was immediately brought back to reality. He should not linger anymore. It was three o'clock, and he had work to do. He realised as he got into the car and started the engine that he hadn't thought about the Darcy Trust at all. It was obvious now, of course, why Simon had not been able to find anything about Clemmie. She didn't work or really do anything because she was disabled. Her life was within those four walls. It was listening to the radio and watching the breeze in the garden. It was eating sandwiches with her sister in the house that she had been born in. She had been looking tired towards the end of lunch, and as he left, he noticed Milena advancing towards her with a blanket.

What did it cost to have a live-in nurse he wondered? He thought of the bottles of meds and the tubes and of Milena's fingers popping bits of broken up sandwich into Clemmie's mouth. The idea that Evie needed the money from the Darcy Trust to pay for her sister's care crashed over him like a cold shower. He had thought that she wanted for nothing, but maybe not. She didn't dress like a rich woman, but she was not the sort of girl who would. She had said that she didn't sell much at the exhibition, and that household was obviously being supported from somewhere. His mind flickered to Cressida Carter and her grasping expression when she sat in his office. He took off the handbrake, steered angrily out of his parking space, and sped towards the office.

BACK IN THE STUDIO, EVIE FELT DISCOMBOBULATED. SHE OPENED THE French doors to let the air in and put the canvasses back into their stacks. She could not recall the last time she had felt relaxed. She let the sensation wash over her. It brought back memories of childhood and a world before her parents died when her sister didn't need twenty-four-hour care and the house didn't have ramps and bars all over it—memories of when a guy being interested in her was just a guy being interested in her and not a series of "what-ifs" so complex and convoluted that it made her head ache. She would not let herself fall into the trap of self-pity; it wasn't her.

As she washed up his cup, she realised how much he had surprised her. It was hard to believe that he was the same man who had come strutting into the Cork Street gallery. Without a crowd, he was much kinder, and he hadn't turned a hair when he saw Clemmie clamped inside her wheelchair. There was none of the toe-curling embarrassment and the bizarre, whispered, patronising pleasantries they had all become accustomed to. He had talked to Clemmie as if she was a normal girl, and the smile on her lips had lit up the room. Evie felt warm from it, but she could not allow herself to think of him as a man or even a friend. She focused her mind hard on him as a potential collector. He had said he wanted to buy two of her ballerina studies, and she took them aside, thinking she would give them a clean. One wasn't framed, and she contemplated making him a frame that could be treated as part of the work as a whole. She could tell what he liked from the pictures he had honed in on.

It was coming up for six o'clock, and she was just about to lock up and go home when the phone rang its ear-splitting ring again.

"Hello, Evie Pemberton."

"Hi, Evie. It's Charlie. I...erm...I just wanted to say 'thanks' again, and

I wondered what you were doing on Saturday evening?"

There was a silence, and a vision of his confident face appeared before Evie. Her thoughts began to race.

"It's just that my cousin has just started seeing a ballerina. She is with the English National Ballet. They have four tickets to see *Onegin* at Covent Garden, and I thought you might like it. They were going to take my aunt and uncle, but my aunt hasn't been well, and her doctor says she needs rest. It would be the four of us if you're up for it?"

He was obviously at pains to emphasise that it wasn't a date, and for a confused moment, she did not know how to react to this. It did not take long to resolve her emotions. Evie loved the ballet and loved Covent Garden, and her feet almost left the floor in anticipation.

"I'd love to. Thank you."

Chapter 11

I could not have picked up my pen at this time yesterday. Today is a different story. I have managed to get up and move around my chamber a little. I am tired, and my back aches like the low moan of an orchestra tuning up. I would like to reach down to check my ankles, but it is uncomfortable to do so. This morning, Hannah said that they were still rather swollen, and they do not feel right even now. Should I walk to the window or attempt turns of the ankle as Mama suggested? I reprimand myself for being so vain, but I do not want Fitzwilliam to see them. The feeling that I have not pleased him sickens me. I am unsteady with the nausea of it. I can recall the touch of his hand upon my body, and I want to scream.

Mama has taken Beatrice and is presently cradling her in my sitting room. I can hear the pitter-patter of her slippers upon the carpet and the soft lilt of her chatter through the door. Occasionally, she makes some remark to Nanny or Hannah, and if I did not feel so wretched, I would laugh at the imperious tone she adopts with them. Although I have made merry at her expense all my life, I am now contrite, for I have never understood my mama better than I understand her now. It was Georgiana's suggestion that we name our fourth daughter Beatrice. I wanted him to name her and waited, waited for him to make his preference known. If he had named her, as he named Anne, Emma, and Frances then it would have made it better, more bearable. It would have been as though he were saying, "She is mine, and I do not mind that she is another girl." But he did not. He smiled a pale smile at me as I lay in bed. He peered at her, his hands clasped behind his back. The skin of his face seemed to tighten against his bones, and the blood seemed to drain from my head correspondingly. When she cried a hungry wail, he turned away. I tried to recall whether or not he had turned away thus from our other daughters and could not.

I cannot rid my mind of that awful day in Lambton. At the time, I did not record it here. I fancied that, if I did not write it down, then it would be as if the mortifying business had not occurred. But that was silly of me, was it not? For we cannot wish the past away. We cannot undo it by way of silence. Did I not say when this book was begun that it was to be a faithful record of my days? It was wrong of me to rebel against my own rule. It was also futile, for it has assisted me not at all. The recollection of the event haunts me now just as it did when it happened—more so even, for it has come to seem prophetic as well as embarrassing.

I had been large with the babe but still fit to be seen and to move about. Jane and Mr. Bingley were nearing the end of their stay with us. Jane and I had chattered, wandered, and laughed; it was as though we had not been separated for nearly a year. In the mornings, we sat beside each other and wrote our letters, and in the afternoons, I dozed in my sitting room while she worked her embroidery. Mr. Bingley and my husband kept to themselves, riding after breakfast and sitting up after dinner with glasses of whiskey. One morning towards the end of their stay, Jane expressed a wish to go into Lambton. She had some baby clothes to deliver to a Mrs. Waugh who is an old acquaintance of our aunt Gardiner. Aunt Gardiner had grown up in Lambton, and I was dimly aware that her family had been friendly with the Waughs, who lived in the village opposite the rectory. Jane thought to go alone, but I would hear nothing of that. I was feeling marvellous, and Hannah needed to go into Lambton for ribbon in any event. It was decided that we should all three travel together with Hannah attending to her errands while Jane and I visited the Waugh household.

The parcel of tiny caps and smocks was well received, and we had a lovely tea with the young family, whom I had met on a few occasions. Mrs. Waugh's mother had grown up with our aunt, and we were told they had played together like sisters. I came bearing a basket, but Mrs. Waugh had made a lovely sweet loaf, which we enjoyed. The children of the house scampered happily about us and stared in wonder at our carriage parked outside on the road. I had begun to feel rather fatigued, and a slight twinge had begun in my side. Confident that Hannah would be finished with her tasks and waiting by the carriage, Jane and I stood, bid our farewells, and made for the door. As soon as it opened, Hannah ceased her discussion with the driver and moved towards me, her beige cape billowing slightly in the breeze.

"Are you ready to depart, Mrs. Darcy?"

"Yes, Hannah, we are—"

The woman seemed to come from nowhere. I saw her low, wide person amble towards me, a misshapen stick and a sprig of flowers gripped like weapons in her red, raw hand. Quite unexpectedly, she alarmed me, and I must have drawn back. She let out a laugh that splintered the air, and I felt Jane's hand rest lightly on my back.

"Mrs. Darcy, ha!" She extended her gnarled forefinger towards my belly, and I shrank back.

"You will need to keep on with these until you give your master what he needs, Mrs. Hoity-Toity. There have *always* been Darcys at Pemberley, and they won't be stoppin' for you!"

Hannah's lean arm came from nowhere to push her away. The driver leapt down from his seat, his face ablaze with righteous indignation. I believe that he must have heard the words, for he looked too mortified to speak himself. Hannah suffered no such disability.

"Get away! Shoo!" she said as she put her body between the old lady and me.

The door to the carriage was open and—shaking, befuddled, hardly knowing what to think—I climbed in. Jane and Hannah followed, and we were away. The words of the strange old woman rang in my head like a bell that would not stop. "There have always been Darcys at Pemberley." My husband is a Darcy as was his father before him, but where is my son? And what shall I do if he never comes? The unanswered question sits on my belly like a boulder. It hounds me night and day. Now, I realise in horror that it is even worse than I thought. It is not merely a private trial for me to be battled and borne. It is not merely the question of making the boy-child and keeping love alive between Fitzwilliam and me. It is a matter of public business to be gossiped about and speculated on by strangers. It is a thing commonly spoken of by those around us like the price of meat in the market and the weather in the fields at harvest. I tried to speak with greater calmness than I felt.

"Hannah, who was that woman?"

"She is just a mad old crone, madam, well known in the village. She makes a business of spouting nonsense and…" She looked at Jane and then trained her eyes back on me. "Well, nobody heeds her words, madam."

This was no comfort to me when I knew that, on this occasion, she was right: there have *always* been Darcys at Pemberley.

"I see. In that case, we shall say nothing more about it. But I do not wish Mr. Darcy to know of this. Hannah? Jane?"

I looked at them both hard, and they knew not to argue with me. If Fitzwilliam knew that I had been accosted by a stranger in the open street about my failure to provide him with an heir, he would be angry, but his anger would avail me nothing, and his pity I could not bear.

So it was that, some weeks hence, the event had not been spoken of. My poor body had swollen to a great size, and I was upon my bed. The village midwife stood over me, winked at Hannah, and said, "It shall be like shelling a pea, Mrs. Darcy." She had also said that it "would not be yet a'while." As she said these things, she had raised her eyebrows and tilted her pink round face to one side. These predictions, it turned out were quite wrong. That very afternoon, I began to feel the familiar stirrings and tightenings about my person, the odd discomforts, the overwhelming sense of what was about to happen. We were in the small dining room, and Mama, who had been with us for two weeks, was asking about the number of bedrooms at Broughton Park. My mind narrowed and focussed on the matter at hand. I schooled my body to show no signs until nuncheon finished and Fitzwilliam had gone to his study. His tall frame walked out of the room and away like a flame dying down in the grate. Did he look weary, or did I imagine it? A strange spasm came in the lower part of me, and I pressed my fingers to the edge of the mahogany table.

"Mama—"

"I would not have you think that the credit of a house is all in the number of bedrooms of course, Lizzy! Indeed, it is not. After all, Bollington, elegant though it is, is actually quite ill served for chambers above stairs. But on the other hand, there is a standard below which a really great house cannot fall and—"

"Mama, I think I shall lie down. I am not feeling well."

A look of anguish for more than the business itself crossed her face.

"Of course, child. Come, stand."

She gestured to me, and at length, I rose. Her hand came to the silk of my sleeve and brushed off some imagined fluff. For a moment, she was silent, and her eyes met mine, but when I looked away in pain, she began to chatter in her usual manner. The lace of her cap bobbed about, and she wanted assurance that I had eaten enough, and did I want my shawl, and how many hours had I slept the previous night, and so on. As soon as we were in the privacy of my chamber, she closed the door behind me. I crouched on the edge of the bed, dug my fingers into the fabric of the bedspread, and turned to her.

"Mama, please call for Hannah."

She came, and the midwife came too. The afternoon stretched into the eve, stretched into the night until I was sick with pain and sweat and fatigue. About my person I felt hands unfastening my clothes, Mama's soft fingers unbuttoning my sleeves, Hannah stripping me down to my shift without seeming to look at the swollen, straining, purple-lined indignity of my body. There were sounds in the room of trickling water and closing doors and linen being shaken out. There was the solid rumble of words exchanged between Mama and Hannah and the maids and the midwife. Were those footsteps outside the door? More than anything there was the ceaseless scream of pitiless agony within me. It raged, and I cried out. Before my eyes, the canopy over the bed shifted shape, and its colours became sharp and angry. Voices around me grew inaudibly quiet and deafeningly loud. The sheets were taken from under me, a great wet wad like a snake beneath my legs.

From somewhere my voice came forth.

"Mama, Mama, it is very bad…"

"Hush, child."

"But it is very bad, Mama. It is worse. It is worse than before. It is worse than the girls."

"I know, Lizzy…hush, child."

She ran a warm, dry cloth across my brow and looked at Hannah who was busying herself with some task on the other side of the bed.

"But it is much worse than the girls…what do you think…?"

"Madam," said Hannah, stopping her work and fixing me with the steady, green stare of her eyes. "I beg you not try to talk, madam. I fear it shall profit you naught."

A fresh wave of bone-shaking, frame-splitting pain took me, and I said no more.

When the matter was finally concluded, I fancied that I had been there for a hundred years. Mama held my hand and mopped my brow, and Hannah and the midwife saw the blood-spattered, flesh-squeezed, first moments of my child's life. The pain was almost beyond me, and in my mind, I clung to the side of a great incline, desperate to survive. The cry went up.

"It's out. The baby's out. Well done, Mrs. Darcy. Linen, Milly!"

My head flew back on the soft cushion of my pillow, and my breath came hard, fast, and loud. The cry of my babe soared like a flare on a battlefield. My arms reached up, withered by exhaustion. In the corner of my eye, Hannah was folding blankets around the child, tucking and securing them. When she looked up and advanced towards me with the warm bundle in her arms, I knew what her words would be.

"Congratulations, madam. You have a daughter."

Chapter 12

Evie considered herself in the mirror and wondered whether she had been right to let Milena take charge of her appearance for the evening. She was wearing a pale blue shift dress, which had cost more than she could afford, and unfamiliar make-up coloured her face. Momentarily, she worried that she had put too much on or that it was too garish, but the simple fact was that she was so used to seeing her bare face staring back at her that it was a shock to see it made up. She stuffed her phone, bank card, and keys into a clutch bag and recalled her mum saying that nothing ruins an outfit like a great, clunking handbag slung over the shoulder. She looked okay, but was she getting her hopes up? Was she being ridiculous? Milena had tried to force her into heels, but at that, she drew the line. On went her flat, gold ballet pumps, and that was *dressed up enough* as far as she was concerned. He had texted that morning to say that he'd get a cab and pick her up at five thirty so that they had time for a drink before the performance. She thought of how expensive a cab from Notting Hill to Covent Garden by way of Fulham would be and shoved some cash into her clutch bag. He had made it clear that this wasn't a date, and she should not behave as if it were. The stairs creaked as she walked down and joined the girls in the dining room.

"Lena, who is this beautiful woman? I didn't hear the doorbell." With this, Clemmie smiled broadly, and Evie was ashamed to think of how she had longed to get out of the house on so many nights.

"You look lovely, Evie. You'll knock 'em dead, as people say."

"Milena!"

"I know, I know. It's not a date. Even if it looks like a date, and he thinks it's a date, and you look like you are going on a date, it's not a date, I know…"

At that moment, the doorbell really did ring. Evie headed towards the door, unlatched it, and there he was.

"Hi."

"Hi."

It occurred to her that, if this evening was to be enjoyable, they would have to break through the "hi" thing. Evie had never had a problem making conversation, and she wasn't going to be beaten by Charlie Haywood. She looked at him squarely and decided to act as if she went out to the ballet with a devastatingly gorgeous man every night of her life. Spying the waiting black cab behind him, she grabbed her clutch and left the house, light with excitement.

All her life, Evie had loved being in black cabs. The back seat was like a bench and encouraged a sense of proximity to other passengers that was absent from ordinary cars. The cavernous inside suggested unlikely objects and journeys, and the sight of the city racing past the windows set off a song in her. The late afternoon rush was on, and buses jostled with taxis and bikes as people jay-walked and crossed the roads in flocks. The heat of the sun warmed Evie's neck, and the breeze through the open window rustled her hair slightly. When they arrived, the cobbled square of Covent Garden was littered with street performers, late shoppers, and people heading home from matinee performances and shopping expeditions. The warm buzz of an evening just beginning and of souls who had been cooped up all day letting loose was all around. Evie realised how unfamiliar it was to her.

Charlie collected the tickets from the box office, and they headed together up the frosted-glass staircase. The bar at the top was half-full with early arrivals, and the sun crashed through the white iron and glass of the vaulted roof. Drinks were ordered, and they settled at a table with a view of the city. The buildings of a dozen ages and the irregular roofs of countless shops, offices, flats, theatres, and secret spaces stretched out below them.

"What an amazing sight," said Evie. "Our grandparents used to bring us here when we were children, but they were strict opera buffs. We never came up to the bar. I think they would have thought it was a waste of time when we could be downstairs studying the programme!"

He laughed. "You'll be telling me you brought your own sandwiches next."

"We did! We really did! They were serious high culture vultures, and I didn't know that it was so amazing up here. You can see everything. It is like being on Parliament Hill but warm and glamorous and not windy. Are you a regular?"

"Not as regular as I'd like to be. I like it here," he said leaning back in his chair. His long, fit body stretched out before her, casually. Evie took another sip of her wine. "And I like the opera and the ballet, although I don't think anyone would call me a buff. I just enjoy it, you know? I don't really understand it."

"I know just what you mean. But…well, I don't go often, but when I do, I don't really try to understand it. I love the way you can really sit and think while you are watching."

"Sure, of course. Don't worry, I won't be asking you questions about it later. This isn't a late night talk show on Radio 3."

They laughed, and she felt something deep inside her relax and unravel like a ribbon from a gift. She took another sip from her cold, white wine and felt it coursing around inside her, loosening her up.

"So, did you say that it is your cousin and his girlfriend we are meeting?"

"Yes—Peter—and the girlfriend is Tatiana. She is Ukrainian, and between you and me, she is a bit out of Peter's league. He and I are about the same age, and he grew up in London as well, so we have been hanging around together all our lives. He is great really. He's kind, and he's loyal and funny in a bumbling kind of way. He is almost comically English."

"Well, it must be nice to have family you can go out with. I have an uncle and aunt who live in Putney, but apart from them, it is just me and Clemmie."

"Really?" His conscience twitched slightly to think of Simon's genogram back at the office, stretching out in all directions with uncles and aunts and cousins multiple times removed. It appalled him to think he knew more about her family than she did. "You must have other family. You just don't know them, right? Don't they say that we are all sixth cousins or similar?"

"Well, I guess so, but I don't know who they are. They might be living next door. How funny would that be?"

He wanted to ask her about her parents, but he guessed that it wasn't a happy story, and he couldn't bear to break the joy of her mood. Her beautiful smile took over her face, and her small body was electrified with the anticipation of the evening. He didn't dare imagine that he might be the cause of her excitement. He thought of the endless drawings and paintings of ballerinas and knew why she was so glad to be there. He was about to ask about her interest in ballet when she spoke again.

"Actually, I guess, I know that I do have other relations because…well, there is this weird trust thing that I know about. I get…well, I know that there must be other family out there, but I don't know anything about them. We get…well, we hear from this trust every year. Clemmie and I, and so did my mum before she died. So I guess that there must be family out there. I've never really thought about it. My mum didn't really talk about her family."

Charlie couldn't help but look away slightly. Not for the first time since meeting her, he wondered at himself and what he had become. The old Charlie would have been questioning and subtly pumping her for information. He would be leading her in a charming dance in which she would reveal everything she knew. She wouldn't even have known, but by the end of the conversation, he would have all the information he needed. As it was, the thought of the Darcy Trust sent a shudder through him, and he did not want to waste time with her talking about it.

"You can't stop my mum talking about family. She is a non-stop, self-taught genealogist, and we get to hear about it the whole time."

"Does she live in London?"

"Berkshire. It's where she is from. She lives in a nursing home. She has a problem with her legs, and my dad died a few years ago. She isn't in great shape bodywise, but her mind is fine, and unfortunately for the staff, she has an iPad and access to the internet. That is how the whole family history thing started. Speaking of family…"

EVIE LOOKED UP AND SAW A MAN IN BRIGHT RED TROUSERS AMBLING TO-wards them with a huge grin on his face. On his arm was a tiny woman who was waving frantically. You could see that he was related to Charlie; he had the same wavy brown hair, and there was a similarity about his nose and the way his eyes wrinkled as he smiled. But that was where it stopped.

Peter was a kindly looking, presentable guy. Charlie...there was a magnetic force about him, and she didn't know whether to be frightened or just to relax and trust her luck.

Introductions were exchanged, and it was immediately obvious that spending an evening with Peter and Tatiana would be no hardship. Everyone was excited about the performance. Tatiana was the only one of them who had seen *Onegin* before, but that was in Kiev. While Charlie and Evie had been talking, the place had filled up. The floors of the bar and foyer swarmed with feet clicking about in strappy sandals, and silk scarves of all colours had been slung over chair backs. Women touched up their lipstick in the loo, and men leaned over the bar, giving their orders to the staff who strained to hear over the din. Before long, it was announced that the performance was about to begin, and the crowd started herding towards the auditorium. People around them ran to the cloakroom to deposit bags and fumble around in their purses for tickets. Charlie handed Evie her ticket, and she tried not to think of the eye-watering price on the front of it. She noticed that the name on the tickets was "C. Haywood" and wondered at his story that his cousin had bought these tickets and then given them away because his parents couldn't use them.

"Ready?" He smiled at her.

"Let's go." She smiled back and wondered whether she was imagining the suggestion of a hand near the small of her back as she walked slightly ahead of him through the crowd to their places. The four of them plumped down in the red flap-down seats, and Evie leant back, luxuriating in the sight of the vast curtained stage before her.

When the curtain rose, light, colour, movement, and verve screamed into the space in front of them. Lithe, powerful bodies bolted about, and the sound of their feet on the floor was like a dozen heartbeats. Evie felt lifted up by the energy. She could just make out the head of the conductor bobbing away beneath the stage, and the swell of the music seemed to sweep her up. Her mind went back to the paintings that Charlie had said he would buy, and she continued planning the frame that she would make for one of them. Unconsciously, she was almost drawing a picture on her knee with the end of her finger when she realised that Charlie was looking at her. She smiled palely in the murky light of the auditorium, and he looked away. His leg was by her leg, and his arm was by her arm. His proximity to her was real.

It made her face burn. It made her feel *things*, and she wondered what she was supposed to do about it.

As the lights went up at the end of the first act, Evie felt the usual rush of exhilaration. They stood, and Charlie suggested they head out and up to the bar. The crowd had already begun surging down the aisles and staircases.

"Do you think we will get served? There are so many people here," said Evie.

"I have already ordered the drinks," replied Charlie reaching into his pocket for his iPhone that, unbeknownst to her, had been vibrating away for the last ten minutes of the performance. When he got into the corridor, he looked at it and saw that he had a missed call from his mother's nursing home, and knowing that he had to call back, told the others that he'd catch up as he walked towards the main entrance to get some signal.

Peter held his arms out to Tatiana and Evie. "Well, look at that. A beautiful woman on each arm. Come on ladies, let's go and find our drinks."

The three of them ambled up to the bar, talking about the performance, Tatiana's commentary by far the most informed. Soon they were installed at their table, sipping drinks and smiling at the old ladies who came in ball gowns and the teenagers who preferred skinny jeans and Doc Martens.

"But then you get all outfits here, don't you?" said Peter. "Now, my mum, she wouldn't be seen here without a long dress, but that is just her generation, isn't it?"

"I suppose so," answered Evie. "How is your mum, Peter?"

A look of confusion crossed his face. "Erm, she's fine thanks."

"I hope she's not too sorry about missing the performance."

"Erm…" Peter wracked his mind to recall what element of Charlie's strict instructions he had obviously forgotten. He wasn't sure. "No, not *too* sorry." He hedged his bets. Wanting desperately to change the subject, he went for an obvious question. "So how did you come to meet my reprobate cousin?"

"He came to an exhibition that I…well, that I was at as well, and we met there."

"Oh, that sounds very civilised. I didn't know that he was an art exhibition kind of chap. Mind you, come to that, we did take my parents to a show at the Royal Academy, but that was a few years ago. I didn't know that he was really into it."

Something started off in Evie's mind like an alarm sounding in the distance. She strained to hear it.

"He collects art, doesn't he?"

"Collects it? I…well…I don't know. He has a couple of nice pictures up in the flat but one of those I know for a fact belonged to his dad. Maybe he has started collecting things. He hasn't told me. I'll have to ask him about it. That's the thing with Charlie: he can turn his hand to anything. He's got such a mind—photographic memory you know. With his brains, he could have done anything, but in some ways he's a funny chap. Likes to plough his own furrow. He's so intelligent, but my parents have always said that he wastes his talents with this snooping business of his."

"Snooping?"

"Well, that's what they call it, but that's because they disapprove. Doesn't bother me. I say. 'To each his own,' and nobody could deny that he has made a success of it. You know, he's a self-made man, and he's got it all. The swanky flat, the shiny car, women throwing themselves at him—"

Peter stopped, coloured, and reached for his drink. He wasn't an intuitive man, but he knew that was the wrong thing to say. He searched around for a fresh direction.

"Actually, I always fancied getting involved myself, but you can't ask your cousin for a job, can you? Anyway, I would worry that I am not discrete enough for it."

Thoughts and questions started unfolding in Evie's head. She recalled that he had practically run away from her when she brushed him off at the gallery and never really said exactly what kind of art he collected or how he started out. He had known that Clemmie was short for Clementine, but she hadn't told him. He had paid for the ticket and pretended not to have done. He obviously had money, but she had no idea where from. Now Peter was talking, and it was like the babble of a foreign language. Snooping? Disapproving? Discretion? What did it all mean? She felt a tremble in her fingers and tightened her grip on her wine glass to stop it.

"Must be fun though, don't you think? All that secret cloak and dagger stuff. I must admit that, before he started it up, I didn't think that private detectives really existed."

"Private detectives?"

"Yes, you know. Trilby hats, big mackintoshes, oversized magnifying glasses."

He squinted with one eye and peered at her. She felt momentarily as though she were in a cartoon.

"I thought they were the sort of thing that you got in novels and films but not in real life. In fact, it turns out there's a whole world of the buggers. And he gets sent on all sorts of assignments, you know. A lot of it is matrimonial. Marital problems of the super-rich. You know, husbands checking up on their wives and that sort of caper. Although there is other work as well."

She wanted to take a sip of her wine for strength, but she could not move. She knew in her bones that there was a grave error here, an untruth, laughing at her. It was more than the fact that he had not told her what he did for a living. People must do that all the time, and maybe he was embarrassed. But there was cruelty in his saying he was a collector when he wasn't. It was malicious. The unkindness of it crept over her, and she wanted to get out.

"In fact, he was telling me only the other night that he's got the strangest case he's ever had land on his desk. A really odd business. It seems that there is this trust set up by some fella from the dim and distant that pays out to all of his *female* descendants. Now this has been going on since forever, but Charlie has been approached by one of the women who is convinced that two of her relations, two sisters living in Fulham, I think he said, are receiving the money when they shouldn't be. Story about someone or other being illegitimate or some such. So there is Charlie, raking about in the history of this family, trying to prove that these two women aren't really supposed to get anything. Apparently, it is going to be a tricky one to prove, but if anyone can do it, Charlie can. He's that sort of chap. Personally, I wouldn't know where to start—"

He looked up, and she feared that her face betrayed her. Her mind darted, and she felt her pulse quicken. Her palms dampened with sweat, and she pressed them to her dress. She told herself to be calm, but how could she be? It was shaming to think that she had sat here gaily telling him about the trust only an hour ago. It couldn't be a coincidence. It was mind-bendingly confusing, but it wasn't a coincidence. She remembered how he had deftly led her to the subject of family history, how he had subtly asked her about her finances, and how he had turned up at the gallery and then at the studio and jumped at the chance of lunch with her and her sister. The thought of him sitting at their dining table, while all the time he was working against them, made her shudder. Her head throbbed. She reached for her clutch and stood.

"I'm sorry, Peter, Tatiana. It was nice to meet you, but I have to go." She didn't wait for their replies, turned, and was gone.

Her gold ballet pumps pounded the floor down the stairs, through the foyer, and out onto the street. It was still light, but a duskiness hung in the air like a scent. A street acrobat somersaulted a few feet in front of her, and his audience clapped. A woman eating outside in a nearby restaurant cackled at a joke and dropped her fork on the ground. Evie felt sick, angry, and lonely. She recalled the cash that she had stuffed in her bag, ran across the cobbled square to the strand, and held her hand out for a cab. The memory of how he had made her feel turned to shreds. She thought of the make-up and the too expensive dress. She wanted to rip it off and throw it in the Thames.

"Lots Road, please."

"'Course, love."

She sat in the cab and tried not to cry. She saw the driver glance at her in the mirror and could tell from his expression that he knew she had had a bad evening. He could not have guessed how bad. The city whipped past. Lights were on and revellers were about, but it looked grey and joyless to her. She could not even process what Peter had said. It was crazy. Nobody could know about that trust except the people who got money from it and the lawyers who dealt with it. A memory crept back to her, like sunrise through drawn curtains, of her mum sitting her down on her eighteenth birthday and explaining that she would be getting this income for life—and Clemmie too. Mum called it their *Darcy money* and said it was like pennies from heaven, like gold dust, and it had saved their bacon a million times. Spend it on important things, she had said. Don't waste it; use it to make your life better; use it to make things happen that otherwise wouldn't. Her own mother had said to her, however many decades previously, that she was not to spend it all on stockings and chocolate, which, Evie concluded, amounted to much the same advice.

The Darcy money had been Evie's blessing in a sea of misfortune. It paid for Clemmie's care and treatment in specialist centres. It paid for physical therapy and speech therapy and the endless slopes and bars and lifts and gadgets that had been required for them to remain in their home—to say nothing of the fact that it was the Darcy money that enabled Evie to work as an artist and follow her dream instead of the requirements of her circumstances. It was the thing that saved her from being Clemmie's full-time, life-long caregiver. How could it be that they were to be disinherited, disentitled? What kind of ill wind had blown this man into her life: a stranger who lied to her about who he was, followed her about, and spied on her to trick her out of money she needed? The spirit-crushing dishonesty of it blindsided her.

Her phone started to buzz in her clutch, and when she looked, it said "Charlie Haywood calling." She rejected the call, and moments later, a text arrived.

It's not what you think. Please can I call you?

The cab turned into the King's Road and sailed into Fulham, the pastel-coloured doors of home streets unfolding all about her. When the house came into view with its ramps and bars glistening in the orange sodium stream of the streetlight, she felt tears prick her eyes. Clemmie would be in bed, but she could see the lamp on in the sitting room and the shape of Milena moving about within. She couldn't go in crying. She moved the flap back on the driver's cab.

"I'm sorry. Do you mind if we just wait here for a second?"

"'Course. No problem, lovey." He smiled a kind smile and handed her a pack of tissues he took out of the glove compartment. She wondered how many times they had come in handy like this. He stopped the meter but didn't hurry her as she dried her eyes and tried to look normal.

When she stepped into the house, Milena was on her in a second.

"Well? How did it go? I thought you would be much later than this. I hope he complimented the dress. As soon as I saw it, I knew it was the one, and it really brings out the colour of your eyes."

Evie tried not to look at her as she slipped off her shoes.

"It was fine, Lena. It was a short performance; that's why I'm back so early. All fine here?"

"Yes, we just had a quiet evening—you know, like normal. Clemmie had a bit of trouble with her soup, but after a cough, she was fine."

"Okay. Good."

She slipped her ballet pumps into the cupboard in the hall, and Milena, who had a nurse's instinct for crisis, hovered behind her.

"Evie, would you like a cup of tea?"

"No, thanks. I think I'll just go to bed. I've got a bit of a head."

With that, she raced up the stairs, closed her bedroom door, and flung herself on the unmade bed. The buzz of her phone started again. It was him. She rejected the call and turned the damned thing off.

Chapter 13

September 12, 1820, Pemberley

The better and more contented part of my day has been spent lying on my bed, playing with my daughter. Beatrice is eight weeks old, and though she is small yet, she is mighty. Her tiny hands grip my fingers with a great ferocity, and her eyes, which are still bright blue, flick about at every turn. Her lovely, toothless mouth has smiled at me, although Mama has denied it and said it was not a "proper" smile. I do not hold with such cynicism. She has a chin just like Papa's and such power to her kick as I can hardly credit. As I look at her now, I feel a sense of joy that I cannot name.

The door moans open, and my sister Kitty appears, clutching a book and tilting her head towards her niece.

"I thought you were napping, little one?"

"She was, but what is the purpose in sleep when there is kicking and giggling to be done?" I answered on her behalf.

We laughed and lay either side of Beatrice, tickling her tummy and marvelling at her person. Kitty discovered the game of dangling one of her curls on Beatrice's nose and was most pleased at this.

"Kitty, where is Mama?"

I had not seen her for some hours. It occurred to me that she may be somewhere in the house, irritating Fitzwilliam. The Mrs. Darcy of years gone by would have removed her from him by some process of coaxing and persuasion. I would have had her in my sitting room chattering for hours beyond number or rooting through my dresses by way of diversion. Now, if she is in his presence and causing him annoyance, I find I do not care. Is this how love dies? Does it falter on the road of complacency and acquiescence? If I do not tend to him as once I did, is it not he who has made me feel thus? A feeling of darkness and loneliness is welling up inside me, and I know not how to push it down. Kitty's voice breaks through from somewhere.

"She is lying down in her room, Lizzy."

"Ah, of course."

"Yes, you know Mama. It is just…you know."

"Her nerves?"

"Yes, those old friends of ours."

I lay flat on my back, exhaled, and stared at the canopy above the bed. I felt, rather than saw, Kitty's eyes upon me. She opened her mouth to speak but said nothing, and then she began shifting about on the bed and straightening out Beatrice's smock. I turned onto my side and focussed on her pretty face. She was my sister, and I did not need to dissemble with her.

"Kitty, have you seen Mr. Darcy this morning?"

"No, Lizzy. He was not at breakfast when Mr. Braithwaite and I were." She paused and looked at the view of the lake through my window. "Do you not know where he is?"

I had no idea where my husband was. He had continued to sleep in my bed these past weeks, but I fancied this was more out of habit than desire. I feigned sleep, and he did not try to wake me. In the darkness, I turned to my side away from him and listened to his breathing, wondering whether he would ever touch me again. My mind returned to Kitty who looked at me enquiringly.

"I do not." I stretched and closed my eyes. "He is displeased with me, Kitty. That is why he stays away."

There was a moment of silence before she spoke again.

"I am sure everything will be well, Lizzy. It always is with you and Mr. Darcy."

I touched her hand with mine and smiled, for she was a young wife, and it did not do to worry her. She had already confided to me that she had missed her courses and prayed every night that she may be with child. We inspected her tummy before bed some nights ago, laughing like girls at its unpromising flatness. I would not have her fearful that her marriage may sour like old milk as mine has, and so I resolve to concern her no further.

"Thank you, Kitty. I hope you are right."

Yesterday was Beatrice's christening day. It had been decided that, like all Darcys, she should be christened in the chapel at Pemberley, and the rector of the church at Lambton joined us for the day for the purpose. Georgiana, whom we had asked to act as godmother together with Kitty, had arrived with her family in tow. Hannah dressed me in my favourite day dress of the season, and Beatrice lay upon my bed in the Darcy christening gown when a light tap came upon the door.

"Come," I called without looking.

"Elizabeth." I was astonished to hear Fitzwilliam's voice and spun around to see him advancing towards the bed, dressed for the service.

"You do not usually knock," I said, possibly more harshly than I meant. I thought of the things that had passed between us in this room, on this bed, and flushed.

He looked past me to Beatrice—in the gown in which he himself was christened—but said nothing. *Shall you not even ask after your daughter, Mr. Darcy? Is her sex so offensive to you that you shall turn your back on her thus?* Having glanced at his daughter, he trained his eye on me.

"That is a handsome dress, Elizabeth."

"You have seen it before; it is not new."

"That does not stop it being handsome, does it?"

He smiled faintly, and I knew not where to look. I looked away and said nothing.

"It is pleasing to see you looking a little better, a little more yourself. I know that the birth of the babe was difficult, but—"

"Beatrice. Her name is Beatrice. You have not forgotten, surely?"

The skin on his face tightened, and he flinched. Quietly, he replied, "Of course not," and ran his fingers through his hair.

"Are you ready, Elizabeth? I thought we might go down together. Everyone is waiting in the drawing room."

I shuddered at the implicit criticism—at the knowledge that I was failing him as a hostess as well as a wife.

"Yes, of course," said I, slipping my hands under Beatrice and gently lifting her to my arms.

"Would you like me to…?"

Fitzwilliam gestured towards her tiny form, but I looked away and held her firmly to my chest.

"No. You need not trouble yourself," and I walked a step ahead of him out of the room.

The service was short but touched me as I had not expected to be touched. I looked down at the crinkled face of my fourth daughter and considered how small she was against the world and how cruel it may be if I did not protect her. Our party clustered like ducks on a riverbank around the small font and said our prayers. Georgiana and Kitty made their vows as godmothers, and when it seemed to grow even chillier than before, Hannah produced an extra blanket for the baby. When it was time to depart, Fitzwilliam shook the rector's hand, thanked him, and ushered me out.

I felt his presence near me throughout the day, but we did not speak. I was busy chattering with Georgiana and Lord Avery and with Kitty and Mr. Braithwaite. Mama, as we know, can talk for the county, and so she kept me engaged as well. Cook had laid on a special nuncheon with several of my favourite things, although I did not recall having requested them. I ate, I believe, more than I needed and talked more than I ought. My eyes strayed to him across the room where he was speaking to Lord Avery and sipping from a glass of wine. Little Archibald played around them and, having tired himself, sat down on the floor near his father's feet.

In that moment, across the crowded drawing room, the possibility of it struck me like gunfire. If I did not produce a male child, would Fitzwilliam leave Pemberley to Archibald? He was his nephew, and he was the grandson of Fitzwilliam's father—as much a Darcy as any future sons of our daughters and more so than any future husbands of our daughters. I had heard of it happening in other families—of despairing gentlemen passing over their daughters in favour of brothers, uncles, nephews, cousins. Indeed, upon Papa's death, it shall happen to Longbourn although that will not be of his choosing. Georgiana's husband was aristocratic, but his prestige outstripped his wealth. If the Avery and Darcy estates were merged, they would be great indeed in land and status. I saw how Fitzwilliam offered Archibald a hand to help him up from his place on the floor and felt I may boil over.

A great conflict raged within me. I knew Fitzwilliam had overlooked many disadvantages to his union with me. He had suffered expense and mortification at the hands of my family. He had submitted himself to the silliest of talk and allowed himself to become an object of curiosity amongst my kin. For all of this, I had failed him. I had not given him the one thing that he needed, and I was wretched to think on it. At the same time, I see his stiff expression, and I cannot sympathise with it. For the children of my body are the children of *his* body, are they not? How could it be right that they be passed over in favour of a nephew? Why is it that the production of boys is a compliment to the father whilst the birth of girls is in some way a poor reflection on the mother? I cannot hold with that analysis, and I cannot be content with my situation.

Chapter 14

After Charlie's first two calls, they had started going straight to voicemail without ringing, so he knew there was no point. He sent her another text and looked out of the window onto the street below. It was 6:00 a.m., and a smattering of unlikely people milled about haphazardly. There were a couple of early morning runners, workmen cleaning the streets, girls hobbling home from the night before. He looked at them and wished his life was simple. He wished that it didn't involve a constantly expanding and deepening tissue of lies he couldn't control. The irony of her refusing to listen, now that he was willing to tell the truth, did not escape him.

The crazy thing was that it must have happened in a few minutes. He had not been on the phone to the nursing home for long. They had called to say that Mum had taken a minor fall and was fine but was asking to see him. He said he'd visit in the next few days and had been mentally rearranging his diary as he wandered up to the bar to find an astonished looking Peter and Tatiana and no Evie.

"Has Evie gone to the ladies?"

"I don't know…I don't think so." Peter's face betrayed both creeping guilt and overwhelming ignorance, and he forced a smile. "She just got up, said goodbye, and scarpered, didn't she, Tatty?" Tatiana nodded, and Charlie's stomach tightened.

"She just left? Why? What did you say to her?"

"Nothing, old chap. We were just sitting here, talking about your work—"

"*My work*? Peter, I told you not to mention that!" He raked his hand through his hair and started looking about for some glimpse of her.

"Sorry, I forgot. I don't see why she should run off just because you run a private snooping outfit. We were having a good chat actually. I was telling her about that trust thing you were telling me about the other day, and she went all white, didn't she, Tatty?"

They were nodding to each other, and Tatiana was speaking, but Charlie couldn't hear her. His head was spinning. He bolted through the crowd, down the stairs, through the foyer, and out on to the street. Assuming that she would have gone for a cab, he ran across the square to the headlight-blinking, pedestrian-swarming hullabaloo of the Strand. He looked left and right for a glimpse of sky blue and honey-blonde, but there was none. There was no sign of her. She was gone.

He paused on the curb like a diver about to slice the water, thinking about how happy she had seemed, how he had wanted to touch her smiling face but didn't dare. How the thing could have unravelled in such Technicolor, he hardly knew. He needed to think, to regroup. Pulling out his phone, he texted Peter to say he wasn't coming back and began the long, lonely walk back to his flat. His feet worked the warm pavements of the West End and the edge of Hyde Park. The streets were full of couples looking for restaurants and ladies teetering around on unfamiliar heels and shivering slightly when their bare arms met the chill of the late evening. It was five miles to Notting Hill, and by the time he put his key in the lock of the flat, it was dark. He had come to a few conclusions.

Firstly, he would contact Cressida Carter and tell her that he couldn't work for her anymore. He was tempted to just cut her dead—say he was too busy. But in the end, sense and his need to protect Evie, even if she wanted nothing to do with him, won out. It would be much better to tell Cressida that he was not going to carry on with it because it was going nowhere; it was a *no-hoper*, and she was wasting her money. There was always the possibility that she might give up and Evie would be left in peace. Then he thought about that treasure trove of Darcy's letters he had sent to her, and he knew that she would be stupid to just let it drop. Somehow, he knew that, to protect Evie, he would have to beat Cressida to it, find whatever they were looking for, and get rid of it. He couldn't leave Evie to face this thing on her own. And that was just the thing. He would help her even if she wouldn't speak to him, even if she never knew. He got her into this, and he would get her out of it.

His mind turned to what she may be thinking and feeling—to the somersaults her mind must be making. She had not answered his calls or texts and had turned her phone off, but maybe he would have more luck when she had calmed down. He wasn't going to give up.

The sound of more people in the street found its way through the windows, and Charlie took a shower and made himself a strong coffee. He read through the most recent barrage of emails from Cressida and sighed. She was full of ideas for finding the "lost" whatever it was that was going to prove Victoria Darcy was illegitimate. He chewed it over in his mind, and by 9:00 a.m., he was ready to call her.

"Hi, Charlie, you're an early bird. It's a Sunday!"

"Hello, Cressida. Well, I have always been an early to work kind of guy, and what is a weekend anyway?"

She laughed down the line.

"I've been going through everything we've got actually and having a bit of a think, so I thought I'd better give you a call. It's not easy for me to say this, Cressida, because I've got my pride, but I think we are going to have to draw a blank on this one."

There was silence on the other end—big, empty silence.

"I've had my guys looking at it from every angle, and we are on a hiding to nothing here. We can't prove that Victoria Darcy was illegitimate. The thing is that, historical recordwise, there's nothing there. Even if it is true, we can't prove it. It's a waste of your money to carry on, Cressida."

"You can't be serious." Her voice shook slightly. "If it is about money, you don't have to worry. I can afford to pay you—"

"It's not about money, Cressida. I know that you're good for my fees. It is about not carrying on when it wouldn't be fair to you. I told you right at the start that this was a tall order."

"But you haven't even tried to find this lost document that Darcy talks about in his letters. You haven't even tried." He could hear the shock in her voice being replaced by anger.

"What document though, Cressida? We don't even know what it is, or was. I'm a private detective not a miracle worker. How can you or I find something when we don't know what we are looking for, or where it is, or if it even exists?"

"Well, we could go to Pemberley and look for it, or we could go to this place in Ireland and look for it there. You haven't even tried. You have taken my money and you have given up the ghost before we have even started!"

"Look, I'm sorry about it, Cressida. I'm not going to get into an argument about it. It is just the way it is. I'm afraid that I am going to have to terminate. I'm sorry. I won't be sending you a bill for the last week or so, so there is nothing more to pay, and I guess it is a case of 'thanks for coming to me; sorry I couldn't help.'"

There was a brief silence in which he could almost feel her hackles rising.

"Well, some private detective you are. Fortunately, I've got a bit more gumption, and if you think I'm letting it go, you've got another think coming. I won't be recommending you to any of my friends; I hope you know that. You are completely overrated and a total bastard."

The echo of silence was all he heard as the line went dead.

Later, he drove over to Fulham. He had called four times, and Evie hadn't answered. So he put on some clothes and went over there. He pulled into a parking space a little away from the house and ran through in his mind what he would say. At just the moment he knew he had been sitting there too long, the door of the house opened, and Milena wheeled out Clemmie. Evie followed behind them, locking up and then buzzing open their car, which was parked right outside. It was a big people mover, obviously adapted with a ramp at the back to take a wheelchair, and Evie and Milena worked as a team to open it out and line up Clemmie. Evie looked beautiful but slightly deflated. She had no make-up on, and she was wearing a green cotton dress with canvas pumps. As Milena pushed the wheelchair up the ramp and began to secure it, Charlie saw his chance and got out of the car.

"Evie."

She turned and squinted into the sun. Seeing him, she looked like she had been kicked in the gut. He tried not to think of the memory of her grinning face the night before.

"Evie, can we talk?" he said as he drew closer.

She didn't even say "no." She just turned away, got into the car, and drove off. He could not recall a time when a woman had walked away from him like that, but he knew deep down that she was well within her rights to do so.

IN THE CAR, THE GIRLS SAT IN SILENCE FOR A WHILE. THEY WERE DRIVING over to Putney for Sunday lunch with Auntie Betty and Uncle John. Evie had been hoping that it might take her mind off things. She had never imagined that he would come over like that—be standing there in the road, staring at her without blinking. After a period of silence, Milena ventured a question.

"Was that Charlie?"

"Yes."

"And…"

"Lena, I don't want to talk about it. I'm sorry."

"Okay, darling. In that case, we won't."

She squeezed Evie's knee, and nothing more was said. They soon discovered that there was a huge charity cycle ride taking place, and they had to drive a different way than normal. Evie sighed as they sat there in lines of traffic, moving like cold syrup, the heat of the city afternoon pressing against the windows. She knew that Milena could have pushed her on what had happened and was grateful that she did not.

In fact, lunch wasn't too bad. The food was delicious, and Clemmie was her usual ebullient self, laughing enough for two even though she had the least cause of any of them. By the time they got back to the house, she was even more exhausted than usual and troubled by a slight cough, so Milena started her bedtime routine. Evie went next door to the studio. She had hoped that it would take her mind off things, but everything there reminded her of him. She recalled them laughing over cups of tea and her hauling canvasses about on the floor. She took the two pieces that he had said he wanted and turned them to the wall. She switched on the lights, took out a blank canvas and her oils, and started painting, angrily, viciously, throwing colour and shape into the empty space. It was dusky outside when the ear-splitting ring of the studio phone started up. For a moment, she thought it might be him again and considered ripping the socket out of the wall and hurling it across the room. Letting it ring longer than usual, she decided against this and picked up. It was Milena.

"Evie, come quickly. Clemmie has a temperature and is struggling to breathe."

"Coming." She slammed down the phone, ran out of the front door without locking it, and vaulted over the low wall, scrambling for her keys to the house door. When she got to Clemmie's bedroom, Milena was staggering under the weight of her sister's limp body.

"Evie, bring the chair closer. She fell when I tried to move her forward."

Clemmie's short breaths were firing out of her in loud, angry gasps. Evie recalled how Milena had said that Clemmie had choked on her soup last night and then how she had been coughing in the car on the way home from lunch. She knew immediately how it had occurred—how a problem swallowing had led to a problem breathing and to a fever. How that had led to a fall. How the whole scenario had resulted in her poor, contorted, terrorised body fighting for oxygen. It was like a play that they had all seen before. There was an awful inevitability to it. Evie immediately jumped to Milena's side, and they managed to prop her up against the side of the bed. The wheelchair was just out of reach, taunting them.

"Hold this. I've called an ambulance. They didn't know how long. Her temperature is dangerously high. I told them that."

Milena deftly managed Clemmie's tubes whilst holding her up and speaking softly between her strangled breathing. Evie ran to the stair lift and moved the straps into the right places, her hands shaking. She came back to the bedroom and, stroking her sister's face, spoke to her. Clemmie just moaned in response, and heat radiated from her like a stove. Together, sister and nurse manoeuvred her into her chair.

"Where is that ambulance? I'm calling again." Evie took out her phone and dialed 999.

"Hello. … Hello. My sister has a raging temperature and can't breathe, and she has taken a fall. She is a quadriplegic, and we have been waiting for an ambulance for ten minutes. Where is it? … Yes, that's the address."

Behind her, Milena spoke coaxingly to Clemmie and eased an inhaler into her desperate mouth.

"What? … Forty minutes? We don't have forty minutes!"

She ended the call and looked down at Milena, furious.

"They can't come for forty minutes because of this bloody bike ride. People, able-bodied people, have fallen off their bikes, and all the ambulances are busy!" Tears came to her eyes. "Forty minutes is too long, Milena. We will have to take her. I'll go and open the car."

With that, she flung herself down the stairs and out the door. She practically ripped the back doors of the car open, and her hands were shaking as she unclipped the ramp to release it. She was hot with anxiety, cold with fear, and her face was wet with tears. The ramp was slightly caught, and she pulled it hard to release it, making a tiny cut on her thumb.

"Evie, what's wrong?"

She spun around to see him standing there in the road and almost couldn't compute his presence.

"Leave me alone."

"No. I saw you run out of the studio. What's happening?"

He moved her aside and secured the ramp for her.

"Tell me what to do."

She didn't even answer. She just ran back into the house, head thumping and body shaking.

THE DOOR WAS OPEN, AND HE STOOD IN IT, PEERING UP THE STAIRS. He could hear the sound of Evie and Milena talking and an awful gasping and crashing. It didn't sound good, and however much she might hate him, he could not leave. He knew it was wrong to stand about without announcing himself, so he shouted up the stairs.

"Evie, I'm down here; if I can help you, I will."

There was a great crash, and he was sure she let out a cry. After what felt like an age, Milena appeared at the top of the stairs.

"Charlie, come up. We need another pair of hands."

He took the stairs two at a time as she explained.

"Clemmie choked on some food yesterday evening, and she now has a very high temperature and can't breathe well. It is very common with quadriplegics, but she must go to hospital as her breathing hasn't improved, and her temperature is climbing. The wait for an ambulance is so long that we are going to have to take her to the Chelsea and Westminster ourselves. They have care there that I can't give her here. Evie can hold her tubes in while you and I get her into the chair. Then we can take her down the stairs on the lift and into the car. Got it?"

"Yes." He had got it, and that is what they did.

As it was, Charlie picked Clemmie up himself and placed her in the chair while Milena strapped her in. To a symphony of tortured gasping and encouraging remarks, they brought her down the stairs, outside, and into her place in the car. Evie ran to the door and slammed it shut. Milena, who was standing over the patient, called out to him.

"Charlie, would you mind coming just to the hospital with us? When she is in this state, she is a two-person job, and Evie will have to drive."

He looked at her poised as if in flight in her summer dress and pumps, her hair all out of its hair band. There was no emotion except fear on her face.

"Sure, but I'll drive so Evie can sit in the back."

Her eyes flashed at him, and it was agreed. When they arrived at A&E, the girls went in with Clemmie in her chair while Charlie parked the people mover in the hospital car park. Walking back through the dingy underworld of badly parked cars and abandoned wheelchairs, he fingered the ticket and wondered how long he should hang about. Inside the hospital, he found a Costa coffee on the ground floor. He sat down and texted her.

How's it going? Has she been seen? I'm in Costa with your car keys and parking ticket. I can stay or go home, whatever you want.

It was about an hour later that she appeared. Her pale face peeked out from under messy hair, and she had that look about her that everybody gets when they are in a hospital. That look of not having slept or eaten or worn the right clothes. Of having been taken unawares; of not having read the right books or seen the right films; of being lost and lonely and confused. She approached his table and sat on the edge of the chair opposite him.

"Thanks for waiting." She seemed to want to speak more, but nothing came out.

"It's no problem. How is she?"

"Okay. They are going to keep her for a few days. She will be fine. It has happened before."

"Good. Well, I'm glad that she has been seen."

She looked at his face and placed her hands flat on the Formica table. A whisper of a question played across her face before she closed her eyes for a beat. She looked exhausted.

"Evie, do you want me to drive you and Milena home? You look done in."

"Thanks." She looked up, and he wondered whether that was the shadow of a smile. "I'll drive. But you come too. You left your car on our street right?"

They drove through the night in silence. Milena insisted on sitting in the back so that Charlie and Evie could talk if they wanted, but somehow it didn't happen. She changed gears, steered, and indicated like an automaton, and it was only as they parked outside the house that he spoke.

"Thanks. Is it okay if I call tomorrow?"

"I suppose so."

Chapter 15

April 2, 1821, Pemberley

An almost imperceptible joke played across Colonel Fitzwilliam's face, and he smiled into his teacup before drinking. His much-anticipated arrival took place an hour ago, and now he is in the drawing room, with all of us hanging on his every word. The girls, I thought, may combust with excitement in the hours before he alighted from his horse and sauntered into the hall. Ann and Emma have not seen him for two years, and this is the first time that he has met either Frances or Beatrice. Frances potters about on the floor, and Beatrice lies in Georgiana's arms next to me on the chaise. Questions have been fired at our guest from all directions, and he has fielded them creditably. Has he ever seen a cannon ball? Has he brought his uniform to Pemberley, and shall he wear it to church? Does he wish to sit on a rocking horse in the day nursery? Their little faces opened up towards him like flowers.

Cousin Richard himself is quite unchanged from the easy mannered, kind, and agreeable man whom I met at Rosings when I was a girl of not one and twenty. He jumped off his horse after a long and perilous absence and smiled as if he had been to Lambton to post a letter.

"Darcy, Lizzy, where are all these young ladies then? I cannot have people being born into the family and not exposed to my company!"

He kissed my cheek and gave me a brotherly embrace after shaking hands with Fitzwilliam.

"I thought you would have seen enough of battle and may wish for some rest before they are unleashed on you."

"No, Lizzy. There is never too much battle for me—you should know that. You are looking very well. Darcy is obviously looking after you, as well he should."

My husband threw a withering look at his cousin who was well used to such banter. "You will have to forgive us, Fitzwilliam, for greeting you without the children. We were not sure whether you could stand their exuberance, and I would not want to tire you out when you have only arrived."

"You have not lost your humour, Cousin. I'm glad to see that. After spending a week at Rosings with Anne, I shall relish it! I am in need of song, laughter, and conversation—and lots of it. Now, where are those girls? I wish to see my relations. Are they all as beautiful as Lizzy?"

He winked at my husband who only flinched slightly at his manner of referring to me.

"They are," he replied and led his cousin into the drawing room without further ado. Since that time, Georgiana, Lord Avery, and Archibald have joined us, and altogether we have been a merry party. I notice that my husband favours Archibald with conversation and enquires after his progress at riding. My fingernails dig crescents into the flesh of my palms. I see him smiling upon his nephew when he plays with Anne and Emma on the terrace outside. When Fitzwilliam and Lord Avery stand by the fire and talk, I wonder whether they are speaking of it even as I look upon them. Their heads incline towards each other, and I hear the low mumble of their male voices. I do not know their words. Shall they ever be confided to me? Has my husband suggested to our brother that his living son may take the place of my non-existent one, or shall he leave that proposal for later? Wild ideas flame up in my mind, but I fight against them, determined not to be consumed. Archibald comes in from the terrace and presents himself to me with mud on his hands.

"Aunt Elizabeth, may Anne and I run to the folly?"

"You may, Archibald, but you must also take Emma, for I think she would like to go, would you not?"

I look at my second daughter who frantically gasps her assent. It is agreed, and they are off, storming into the distance, their little bodies twitching up the hill, pastel-coloured shapes against the green relief of the lawn. I stand at the door that gives onto the terrace and watch them go, the sun on my face, a light breeze rustling my skirts. Archibald's little breeches pound away, and he is easily outstripping the girls in their cotton frocks. I feel the beginnings of resentment and hurt growing inside me. Fitzwilliam appears at my back and says nothing. I bristle at his nearness, but ultimately, I have not his appetite for silence.

"Archibald is a good runner, is he not?"

I feel the faintest touch of his finger against my forearm.

"Not as good as you, Elizabeth."

My mind flipped to us running together in the woods when we were first married, and my confessing to him that I had, as a girl, run from Longbourn to Meryton for devilment, and none of my family knew. I considered for a moment how we had once been with each other and how things were now, and I wanted to cry out. If he thought he could flirt his way back into my good graces, then he was wrong.

"You flatter me, sir. I would not be up to that now at my age and after bearing four children. I would do myself an injury. No, I think I shall leave the athletics of the household to young Archibald."

"Nonsense…"

He was about to speak further when a cry went up in praise of Frances's having taken three consecutive steps, and we were all distracted.

Later, our exhausted children were put to bed, and Archibald climbed wearily into his father's carriage and, with his nanny for company, went home. It had been decided that the grown-ups would dine at Pemberley and then, as it was a full moon, make a late night progress to Broughton Park where Richard was to stay with Georgiana and Lord Avery. So it was that we found ourselves, as the evening was settling into night, in the small dining room—Fitzwilliam and I at either end of the table, and Georgiana and Richard on one side facing Lord Avery, who seemed to turn his food around on his plate in a melancholy manner. Servants came in and out of the room with platters and dishes and sparkling decanters, and candle light flickered across our faces like quicksilver. Richard's jokes were so diverting and so numerous that, by the time our puddings were placed before us, I had an ache in my belly and in my cheeks. I caught Fitzwilliam looking at me from his place and wondered whether he was troubled by my easiness with his cousin. He had never become accustomed to our addressing one another as "Richard" and "Lizzy" but I could not overly regret this. For, if it was a discomfort to him to think of my enjoying a friendship with his cousin, then it was equally a discomfort to me to know that our nephew was to be promoted above all of our own children as his heir, simply because he was a boy.

When the meal was at its end, Georgiana and I retired to the drawing room and left the men to their dimly lit port and serious conversation. Her hand slipped over my arm, and she snuggled to my body as we walked down the corridor to our tea.

"Oh, Lizzy, it is just like old times, is it not? I am glad we are alone for I want to play a new piece of music, but it is not yet perfected enough to be presented to the men."

I smiled at her as we approached the drawing room.

"Well, in that case, I shall look forward to hearing it. But you should not be shy in front of the men for they are none of them great musicians. Certainly, not Fitzwilliam. He sang for me once after a great deal of cajoling on my part, and I must say that I do not plan to push the point again."

The memory made me smile in spite of my mood.

"Oh, Lizzy, where did you learn to be so diverting?"

"Your brother could make jesters of us all, Georgiana. It is one of his talents."

She sat down at the piano bench and began to rifle through the music sheets she had fetched with her from Broughton Park. Her fine head, still as blonde as sunshine, tilted towards her lap full of papers. She continued to chatter, and I was glad that she did not look at my face as she spoke.

"…not the only one though. Fitzwilliam is quite the *best* of brothers. I could not hope for a better one. For he has been such a wonderful uncle to Archibald recently. We are so fortunate."

"Indeed? I mean has he been more than usually attentive?"

I felt a sting in my eye and straightened my body.

"Why yes. Archibald is being quite spoilt. Fitzwilliam has been coming to Broughton Park so frequently. He has some business with Henry. I do not understand, but it requires lots of hours closeted in the study, and heaven knows what they find to talk about. But when he has visited in the last few weeks, he has been so agreeable with Archibald. He has taken him out riding and asked him about his books. And little Archie is becoming most comfortable in his company, for which I am glad. For he is so shy around Henry's brother, who I must say is rather fearsome with him, but Fitzwilliam has been quite the opposite."

"Well…I'm glad to hear it…"

"Only this week Fitzwilliam was in Henry's study for the whole afternoon, and he still found time to discuss the harvest with Archibald, *the harvest, Lizzy!* There are many men who would simply not make the time for a little boy."

"No indeed…"

"And it is so good for a boy to have attention from an uncle as well as a father—do you not think? I am sure that your sisters are attentive aunts to the girls, more than I. I try to do my best, but I fear that, having grown up with so many sisters, Mrs. Bingley, Mrs. Lander, and Mrs. Braithwaite must be the experts when it comes to being aunts to young ladies. And Mrs. Wickham as well, of course."

"Well, they are loving aunts, to be sure. But I shall not have you feeling underused, Georgiana. If you are ready, there are all manner of duties to be performed, from walking guide to doll's house chatelaine."

I smiled and tried to relax myself. Georgiana, I observed, settled herself down in her usual place next to my own. Marriage and motherhood had hardly aged her, and her tall figure, beautifully dressed, seemed to fold down like a length of starched linen, and she looked about in the anxious manner she always had. She fingered the edge of the chaise arm and beamed at me as I poured the tea with a shaky hand. Nobody could be sweeter, and I know that she says nothing that she does not say in earnest. Even so, knowing that my husband's frequent recent absences from Pemberley were due to extended visits to Broughton Park—and that he had been favouring his nephew with his attention—was a bitter taste indeed.

"I shall try, Lizzy. Perhaps I should visit more often, and I can be cajoled into whatever nursery game I am required for! Speaking of games, Lizzy, I cannot help but think that my husband and your husband are about some mystery or other."

"Whatever do you mean?"

"Well, Fitzwilliam has been visiting every week! He never used to come so often. Now he seems to be within Henry's study whenever I look. I say 'Where is Lord Avery?' and the answer then comes, 'He is in his study with Mr. Darcy.' Regular as clockwork. Whatever can they be about?"

"I cannot say."

"Oh, Lizzy, if you do not know, then I give up, for you know everything about Fitzwilliam. He is like a drawing for which you already have the outline."

"I am not sure that he would like to hear himself so described, my dear. And in any case, I do not think that I do know everything about him, for how can anyone know everything about another? It is quite impossible."

I felt in that moment that I scarcely knew him at all.

We heard the rumble of Colonel Fitzwilliam's jolly laugh before the door opened, and the men joined us. Wishing to avoid my husband's conversation, I moved to take my place at the pianoforte, but he followed and moved the bench for me to sit on. The others laughed and chattered and would have been quite unaware of Fitzwilliam's touch behind me and whisper of my name as I sat at the instrument. I could not bear to look at him and so did not do so. I shuffled forward slightly, freeing the small of my back from the heat of his hand and kept my face from turning to him. I felt rather than saw him stiffen behind me as I began to play. Georgiana, I knew, was a more accomplished performer, but she was enjoying her tea, surrounded by all of her favourite gentlemen, and for myself, I was glad of the solitude. My fingers worked the keys of their own motion, and the sound smashed around me like a portcullis. On the other side, my companions chattered and laughed, but I could not focus on them. Later, Georgiana played while I sang, I hope, merrily. By the time our guests made to leave, the black sky was palely lit by the moon. The great front door was opened, and the chill of the night pecked at our faces as we said goodbye. The Averys and Richard clattered into the waiting carriage, and through the window, I could see the pale sheen of Georgiana's gown being pulled and straightened for comfort. Fitzwilliam and I stood at the top of the stairs, waving but not touching. As the carriage pulled away and the horses' hooves beat their path across the gravel, Mr. Darcy surprised me by taking my hand in his. He spoke not but led me back into the house, across the vast echoing floor of the hall, up the stairs, and into my chamber. As he closed the door behind us, he dropped my hand and ran his fingers through his hair.

He turned to face me.

"Elizabeth," said he, and I knew I could pretend no longer.

Chapter 16

London, 3 September 2014

After weeks of dry heat, it had rained in the night. The ground was damp and the colours all slightly brighter than before. A back-to-school–September feeling hung in the air. In Bishop's Park, Evie sat on the bench facing the river and waited. She had asked him to meet her there, and she didn't give an explanation. For his part, Charlie had been bemused by the suggestion of Bishop's Park. It is an unprepossessing and oddly shaped patch of grass on the edge of Fulham with an unimpressive bit of the Thames snaking past. There were overflowing litterbins, bedraggled runners, and not much else. It wasn't an obvious place to meet, but it had been what she wanted. He saw her some time before she heard him coming and thought how tiny she looked sitting in the middle of the ageing park bench. He sat down beside her, looking straight ahead, and there was a moment of silence before she spoke.

"What do you want from me?"

It was a simple and reasonable question but blunt, and he hadn't rehearsed an answer.

"I want you to listen and try to believe me."

She closed her eyes and tilted her head back slightly, her fine features luminous on a dull day.

"I don't see any reason why I should believe anything you say. I don't think you have ever said a true word to me, have you?"

"I have, but I've told you a lot of lies as well."

"Well then," she said as if it ended the matter. He didn't move. "If I do hear you out, it's not because I trust you. It's only because I want you out of my life. Once you have said what you've got to say, you can go."

He had not expected her to be welcoming, but the hardness in her voice chilled him. He had to force himself to withstand it—to speak in spite of her frostiness. There was nothing for it but to say it straight.

"I am a private detective, and I find out people's secrets for money. I'm very good at it, and I have my own business, which has a lot of clients and a lot of work. I'm sorry I didn't tell you what I did for a living, but I'm telling you now."

He glanced towards her, but she was motionless.

"There was a reason I didn't tell you the truth. Until recently, one of my clients was a woman called Cressida Carter. You don't know her, but she is your sixth cousin. She is one of the other beneficiaries of the Darcy Trust. There are eleven of you: you and Clemmie, Cressida, Cressida's mother, a teacher called Jennifer Craig, three women in Australia, an old lady called Violet Fortescue, and her two daughters. You all get money from the trust every year because you are the surviving female descendants of a guy called Fitzwilliam Darcy who, before he died in 1860, set up the trust. The reason that Cressida came to me is that she got wind of a skeleton in the Darcy family cupboard—a very old skeleton. The rumour is that one of Fitzwilliam Darcy's daughters wasn't really his daughter. She was the illegitimate love child of his wife, Elizabeth Darcy and somebody else, nobody knows who. Her name was Victoria Darcy. She was born in 1821 and you are her fifth great granddaughter."

Evie let out a nervous laugh. He had prepared himself for the fact that she may be angry or resentful, but what if she didn't even believe him? Agitation and irritation were written on her face.

"Can you just stop? Who even are you? I don't know any of these people. I've never heard of them."

"I know, Evie, but it's important you know this."

"How dare you tell me what I need to know?"

The scent of her hair too close to him and the sight of her chest rising and falling as she breathed, not quite calmly, threatened to engulf him, but he fought it. He had to focus his mind if he were to help her.

"Because knowledge is power. Because if you don't know a fact and somebody else does, it can be used against you. Because if you walk away not knowing this, it will be my fault. Not everyone is like you, Evie. Some people are cold and hard and greedy."

"And some people are liars. For all I know you are making this up as well… Anyway what does it matter who my fifth great grandmother was or that I'm related to some woman called Cressida who I've never heard of? It's all crazy. You are crazy."

"This is why it matters. What Cressida Carter is on to is the fact that if all this is true then you and Clemmie are not really descendants of Fitz-william Darcy. And if that is true, then she can stop you continuing to get money from the trust."

"She can't just stop it. That's ridiculous. I've been getting money from the Darcy Trust since I was eighteen and so has Clemmie. We are entitled to it. If we weren't, the lawyers would have stopped it."

"If Cressida Carter can prove that Victoria Darcy was not the daughter of Fitzwilliam Darcy, then she can approach the lawyers, and they will have no choice but to stop it."

She glared at him disbelievingly, eyes sparking.

"They can't! They just can't. Do you know how much I need that money? Do you know how much it costs to care for Clemmie? Between Milena and other caregivers I have to get in and her holidays in specialists centres? I had to borrow to adapt the house and buy the car, and the repayments are massive. I could never pay them if the Darcy Trust wasn't there. I just couldn't."

"I kind of guessed that."

She looked at him for the first time since he arrived, and there was disdain in her eyes.

"You guessed it, and you still did this to me? You don't even know me, and you have come into my life and started this…this thing. You sit there going on about all these people that you know about, but it's a load of shit."

"Evie…"

"You know everything and nothing. You know all these names and dates, but you don't know anything about me or the things I live with day after day. You don't know that Clemmie used to be a normal girl before her poor body was mangled in the car crash that killed our parents—both of them in the same minute, the same moment."

AN UNFAMILIAR BELL RANG IN EVIE'S MIND, AND SHE REALISED THAT SHE had never spoken the words out loud in all of the five long years that had elapsed; she had never actually said it. Quickly, mind racing, she recovered herself.

"You don't know what things are like for us."

"I know enough; that's why I'm sitting here with you."

"I wanted to tell Milena just so I'd have someone to talk to, but I can't because she would be so anxious about her job. I want to tell my aunt and uncle, but they'd be worried sick because they could never afford to help me if I lost the Darcy money. My sister, as you know, is currently wired up to the nines in the Chelwest. You have brought this on me, and now you think I should sit here and listen to you. I don't know how you sleep at night."

"Evie, I'm not your enemy. I know it feels like it, but I'm not."

"If you're not my enemy, then who are you? You said that you were working for this woman."

"*Was.* I *was* working for her. I told her I couldn't do it anymore."

"Why the change of heart? Wasn't she paying you enough? Did you find a job that was even less noble to take up your time? Did you get bored trying to rob a disabled woman of the only income she has? Did you find out that you could get even more money by ruining somebody else's life?"

"No. I..." There was a moment of brittle silence as he searched around the darkness in his mind. "I realised that you really needed it and...well...I don't want to work against you. I want to help you."

She looked away, and her stomach tightened.

"I am not hiring you."

"I didn't mean that. Look, I haven't told you the worst thing yet, but you need to know it. I said I was telling you the truth, and here it is. When I was working for Cressida, I did find something—something important. It was a batch of letters that Fitzwilliam Darcy wrote to his solicitor. The letters suggest very strongly that there was a secret surrounding Victoria. They also talk about some sort of mystery document that Elizabeth Darcy tried and failed to destroy before she died. Putting those two things together, the missing document might reveal the truth about Victoria. Basically, although the letters don't prove anything, they lend a lot of credence to what Cressida Carter suspects."

"So..."

"Well, she has those letters, Evie. I sent them to her. So she knows she's on the right track. When I rang her to say that I wasn't going to do it anymore, she…well, she didn't give me any comfort. She said that she wasn't going to give up. She was going to carry on the search."

"The search for what?"

"For Elizabeth Darcy's lost document, whatever it is. The smoking gun. The elusive proof that what she says is true."

"And if she finds it, I'm screwed, right?"

"She won't find it. I'm going to find it. I've got an idea where to look, and I'm good at finding things. If you don't trust me to do it on my own, then come with me."

The suggestion sat in the air between them. Would it take flight or drop to the ground like a stone? For the moment, it hovered, and Evie considered it.

"If you'll let me, I'll email you the letters. Read them. See what you think. Then we can talk again. How about that?"

Evie's mind bombed about like an out of control rollercoaster. Worries fought with fears in the pit of her stomach. She kept seeing Clemmie's face in the harsh hospital light. If they lost the Darcy money and Evie had passed up the opportunity to save it, she would never forgive herself.

"Okay. Send me the letters. I'm not promising anything. But send them to me."

"Thanks. I will."

"Charlie?"

"Hmm?"

"Why did you tell me that you were a collector? How could you?"

"I don't know. I'm sorry. You made me nervous, and I said a stupid thing. I'll still buy those two paintings though. I do want them."

"If they're for sale…"

"But they are, right? Please let me buy them. Name your price and I'll pay it."

"I'll think about it," she said, standing up.

He took the hint and rose from the bench. Both in their trainers, he towered above her. She stared at the two buttons opened to his chest before looking down at the damp ground.

"Can I give you a lift home?"

"No, thank you. I'd like to walk."

With that, they said goodbye and parted. He turned on his heel and walked out of the park the way he had come in, Evie watching his long, lean figure shrink into the distance. Once he was out of sight, she stretched and began to run. Strange names and long ago dates swam around in her mind. They meant nothing to her. She was not a history girl. She had never been interested in the past. It was dry and boring and colourless, and it wasn't her bag. She told herself that *he* was not her bag either. She recalled how she had felt standing so close to him and rejected the thought. Her feet pounded the damp paving slabs, and cool air swept over her sweaty face as she moved through the familiar streets. She wanted to push her body as hard as it would go and increased her speed until her breath hurt in her chest and her muscles screamed out in pain. She wanted to run it out of her, to work herself so much that it would all go away.

When she got home, she took a shower and changed into clean clothes. Their household computer was fitted with voice recognition technology and set on a high desk so that Clemmie could use it from her wheelchair. Evie switched it on and blew on her coffee to cool it. She was not surprised to see that he had emailed her already, attaching a PDF of Mr. Darcy's letters. She opened it and began to read, mystified afresh by how this had come into her life. Strange, old-fashioned phrases, written centuries earlier by people she knew nothing of, cantered around the page. It seemed too ridiculous to credit that her whole life was about to come crashing down because of this.

Sometime later, Evie and Milena piled into the car and headed to the hospital for visiting hours. Milena could see the anxiety on Evie's face although she could not possibly have guessed what had caused it.

"Try not to worry, my lovely. They just want to see her stabilised, then she'll be back home, and we'll all be as before. It is part of Clemmie's condition that these things will happen sometimes, but it is manageable."

"It is manageable as long as we can get her to hospital."

"I know, but we did in the end, didn't we? With the help of…well, we managed it. Try not to worry about what might have been. It is a waste of your energy. Come on Evie, onwards and upwards?" She smiled a kind smile and caught Evie's eye.

"Okay, Mummy Milena. Onwards and upwards. Have you enjoyed the morning?"

"Yes. Well, I would have enjoyed it more if Clemmie were not in hospital, but yes. I met a friend of mine for coffee at Parson's Green. Did you know that there is a new respite centre opening up near Brighton? My friend is a nurse, and a client of hers is going there for a holiday. Apparently, it's all mod cons, and there is swimming and all sorts. You know how Clemmie loves the seaside. It might be worth a look. Shall I see if they have a website?"

Evie immediately thought of the cost, and her moment of calm was shattered. She heard his voice in her head: *knowledge is power.* She saw his face, and her hands began to sweat slightly against the steering wheel.

"Yes. Why not? Sounds like it would be right up her street."

Milena's confidence had not been misplaced. Clemmie looked well under the circumstances, and the doctors were happy with her progress overnight. They said what they always did: that these kinds of incidents were inevitable, and it was a case of learning to deal with them. It would never be possible for Clemmie to be free of these horrors. They were a part of her life and Evie's. It was agreed after much discussion that Clemmie would be discharged the next morning provided that she continued to improve. With that happy knowledge, Evie and Milena had kissed her goodbye and headed home to make sure her room was nice and her favourite food was in for dinner.

Evie's head spun like a wheel on fire and she could not stop it. When she got home, she printed out the letters of Mr. Darcy and looked at them again. They were short, curt, and elliptical, but they said a lot. They spoke of a man who she just knew in her gut was good even though he lived so long ago, so far away. "There are men who, if they knew the full truth, would say I have been a fool." He had written it. But what did it mean? She didn't understand, but something about the whole thing touched her like a hand in the darkness. It touched her that a rich and powerful man long ago had thought to protect the interests of his unborn granddaughters and great granddaughters. It touched her that, in his last days, he had been wracked with worry for the recovery of this mystery document his wife had tried and seemingly failed to destroy. It touched her that love could be so strong, that it could cut through pride and money and faithlessness and misfortune.

Later that evening, she helped Milena make Clemmie's bed. It was a large bed, higher than standard and with a great harness fixed to the ceiling above. It was a monster in many ways, but the sight of it reminded her of her sister sleeping peacefully. A feeling inside Evie reached its zenith and galvanised. Issues that had previously confused her into inaction crystallised, and she was less afraid. She knew that she would not—could not—let her sister down. After Milena had gone downstairs, Evie stood alone for a few moments before she drew the curtains and switched off the lights. In the dark, she took out her phone and texted him.

OK I'm in. Call me and tell me what we are doing.

Chapter 17

April 2, 1821, Pemberley

Elizabeth, I shall not have this."

"You shall not have what, sir?"

He paced the room, his slim figure throwing a shadow on the deep pile of the carpet. In moments such as these, I was tempted to call him "Mr. Darcy," for it never suited him as well as when he was angry.

"This—this *distance* between us. Your manner with me. I will not have you moving away from me."

I looked away from him and turned the ribbon from my sleeve about my finger.

"Nobody observed me."

"*I* observed you."

My eyes closed, and I felt the sting of early tears building. Anger jostled with despair inside me. If he knew that I was thus undone, then he did not show it but continued to turn about the room in a distracted fashion.

"You avoid conversing with me. You walk out on your own or with the girls. Since Beatrice was born, I have barely seen you."

"You have seen me in bed every night, sir. I have denied you nothing."

"What on earth are you suggesting?"

With this, he looked straight at me, and his face blanched. It was a challenge but not one that I was afraid of. My courage rose, and I resolved to speak the truth and live with the consequences. I moved towards him, and he stood stock still, a query playing about his face.

"You know very well what I am suggesting. I have been a good wife to you, Fitzwilliam. You cannot deny that. I have loved you and your family. I have borne you four children. I have been mistress of this house. You have wanted for nothing…save for—well…"

"Save for what?"

"You know. How can you force me to say it when you know?"

"I do not know. I do not have the pleasure of understanding you. Speak plainly, Elizabeth."

The cruelty of it choked me, but I forced the words out like bile.

"You have wanted for nothing save a son."

With that, he opened his mouth slightly and turned away, apparently silenced.

"And now, this business with Archibald is all around me, and you expect me to continue with you as if nothing has changed. You expect me to smile and laugh and play your favourite music on the pianoforte when you have betrayed me thus."

He turned back to me, but as I spoke, his expression changed somewhat.

"Betrayed you? *Now*, I am utterly lost, Elizabeth."

"I have never shown Archibald any unkindness, and I shall not. He is only a child, and it is not his fault that I have failed you and you have given up hope. But you cannot expect me to rejoice in it, Fitzwilliam."

"Rejoice in what? What 'business with Archibald'?"

"Is this a night for forcing me to speak painful truths when you already know them, sir?"

"No, it is not. Elizabeth, if I knew what you were talking about, I would not be asking."

"I am talking of your plan for Archibald."

"*What* plan?"

He jerked his arms out questioningly, demandingly. I could not stop.

"Your plan, sir, to make him your heir. You think I do not know, but I see it. I see that you must have a son, and I have not given you one. I know that there have always been Darcys at Pemberley, and so do you. Archibald is your father's grandson, and he is a better candidate for your estate than our daughters are. I can guess your reasoning, and I hope that, in time, I can accept it. I grew up in a household in which daughters were the regret of their parents, and I can do so again, but you cannot expect me not to be hurt, Fitzwilliam. It is quite impossible."

I considered, in the aching silence that followed, the magnitude of my words and strained not to blink as he stared at me, fixedly. His voice, when it came, was rather quieter than mine had been.

"*You* are impossible." He paced about before me. "Is this what has been in your mind? Is this the reason for your manner with me of late? No wonder you have been out of sorts. It is nonsense, Elizabeth. It is fiction. It is the creature of your imaginings, nothing more. I have never had a plan to make Archibald my heir, and I never will. You are my wife. The girls are my children. How could you suggest that I would dismiss their claims in favour of Archibald? It is ridiculous."

"It is not ridiculous. It has been done by other men."

"I am not other men."

He looked at me hard, and I could not look away.

"I never thought to hear anything so risible from your lips. Archibald is no more a Darcy than any of our other nephews. And he is not my child."

Anxiety raced with relief inside me, and I could keep neither from bubbling up by way of tears.

"Then why have you been so odd with me of late? Why did you not name Beatrice? I thought you were ashamed of her."

"Ashamed? Certainly not. I thought you wanted to name her. I did not comprehend that I *was* being odd with you. I have been attempting to care for you. I know that the birthing was…difficult."

"How do you know that?"

"Mrs. Bennet told me. She thought that you may be unwell in yourself as a consequence and that I should know of it."

I wanted to speak, but my mind reeled to think of such a conversation as must have taken place. The thought of Mama discussing such a subject with my husband, whom she found most intimidating, was one that my mind could hardly manage.

"I suspect that she exaggerated."

"I do not know whether she exaggerated. I am minded to think not. I never thought to see your mother embarrassed in discussion, but I believe she was. She came to my study the day after Beatrice was born. She was acting in your best interests, Elizabeth, and so was I. I have been worrying about you night and day. If I have seemed 'odd,' then that is the reason."

He blinked and straightened slightly, and I could not but smile. How could we have misunderstood one another in this manner after so many years? The occasion called for some straightforward questions.

"Well, why have you been visiting so much at Broughton Park? Georgiana tells me that you are there every week and closeted with Lord Avery for hours at a time and taking Archibald riding when you are not so engaged. What is it that keeps you there?"

"I have been helping him with some estate business. My God, if you had asked me, I would have told you, but I thought you would find it dull. If I had imagined that you would invent this sort of torture for yourself out of my absences, then I never would leave the house."

He looked at me, and his face softened slightly.

"But, maybe I have been in error not to confide in you more. I confess that there are some areas of life that I have seen as my domain—my responsibility to resolve without embroiling you and making you anxious. Perhaps I have done wrong?"

His eyes were questioning, and he began his customary pacing about the room before me. After a short silence, he began to explain himself.

"Avery, you know, is not as wealthy as he looks. His estate has been poorly managed by previous generations of his family. They have made bad investments, and they have been reckless husbands of their land. Avery is paying the price. There are all manner of problems arising from old decisions that he has inherited from his father and grandfather—great problems—problems so great that he was faced with the possibility that the whole estate may have to be sold."

"Sold?"

"In its entirety."

"Poor Georgiana."

"Well, I hope that now it will not come to that. I have made a small loan to him that has allowed him the opportunity to make some changes. I have been helping the man to take charge of his own property, Elizabeth, in order that he and his family, including our sister, can stay there."

"You should have told me before."

"I did not want to worry you when you have had so much with which to concern yourself. In any case, I have never wanted my time with you to be shared with my business affairs. When I am with you, I want to be only with you. The sparkle of your company is too good for talk of money and land and tenants and shares."

"But it concerned Georgiana. What if she had lost her home while I did not even know they were in crisis?"

"I suppose when you put it like that, you are right. Have I been high-handed again, Mrs. Darcy?"

He looked at me sideways, and I saw his body relax with the acknowledgement.

"Maybe a little, Mr. Darcy. But I have been worse, and I am sorry for it."

"Do not be." He moved towards me, and his strong hands came about my waist. "But understand this: I love you every moment as ardently as I did when I married you. More. Nothing can dull it, still less extinguish it. And as for our children, I by no means believe that their number is complete, do you not agree?"

I smiled, and as he went to kiss my neck, the thing I least expected to occur took place. A light tap came upon the door, and after an unusually long pause, Hannah entered, bobbed a rather flustered curtsy, and said, "I am sorry for the intrusion at this late hour, sir, madam, but Mrs. Wickham is in the drawing room."

Chapter 18

On the road to Pemberley, 17 September 2014

The engine of Charlie's car gave a low, expensive rumble, and the M1 stretched out ahead like a gleaming carpet of jet with green fields on each side, sun shining above like a firework. They had set out at 6:00 a.m. and had been going for three hours, cutting up the country at speed, putting London behind them in favour of an unknown, unpredictable landscape. There had been a little chatter at the beginning, but for some time now, she had been asleep, curled slightly in the capacious leather seat beside him. He glanced at her and saw that she was stirring. She juddered into wakefulness and sat forward, rubbing her eyes.

"Oh God, sorry. How long was I asleep?"

"Only a couple of hours."

She smiled at this. "How embarrassing. I hope I didn't snore or dribble or loll my head around in a way that made it look like it might fall off or anything like that."

"No—no snoring, no dribbling, and no lolling—just sleeping, and you must have needed it. Go back to sleep if you want, Evie. The Sat Nav says it is still over an hour to Pemberley, and you will need to be on form when we get there."

He could tell from looking at her that she would not go back to sleep now. She straightened herself jerkily and had that wired look of the recently rested, caged animal. He could feel the worry seeping off her. The sun through the windscreen caught the gold in her hair as she turned to speak.

"I've never pretended to be anyone I'm not before. I hope I'm up to it."

"Of course, you're up to it. Try not to sweat it too much. It sounds wrong, but in a way, you can be yourself. You are not pretending to be a different personality; you are just pretending to have a different life. For the next couple of days, you are Evie Jones, studying for your PhD on the work of Alfred Clerkenman. You are studying through the Open University, and I am your supervisor. Simple. Don't let it become a big thing in your head. Evie Jones has the same personality as Evie Pemberton, she just does different things. It's like…you are just being a different version of yourself for a while."

"A different version of myself? Feels like a barefaced lie to me. This is normal for you, isn't it?"

He smiled and glanced at her. She was right, of course, that when it came to using cover stories and false identities, he was a veteran. He had claimed more names to more people than he could number, and it had never been a problem. As for the rest of this situation, there was nothing "normal" about it. Charlie could not remember an occasion when he had taken three days off work for the sake of a possibly fruitless and certainly unpaid expedition to Derbyshire with a beautiful woman who hated him and was only tagging along out of self-interest. Even Maureen had not been able to hide her surprise when he mentioned it the previous week.

"Holiday is it, Mr. Haywood?"

He had never taken a holiday except over Christmas in all the years she had been his secretary. Until recently, he had never cancelled a meeting, failed to meet a deadline, or sacked a client. He considered telling Maureen the truth, but it was too complex to contemplate.

"Yes, Mau. I guess it is."

It didn't feel like a holiday. The worry of the ways in which it could go wrong gnawed away at him. They might be found out. They might find that Cressida was already there. They might find nothing and go away empty handed, then she would be in the same position as before, and Charlie would have failed her. He had thought carefully about how best to get into Pemberley, and it had been a challenge to come up with a plausible story that would get them both in for an overnight stay, together. He knew that Evie could not pretend to be anything wildly different from what she was. She was too honest, and he hated the thought of compromising her with more lies. Eventually, he recalled the elusive painting of *Mrs. Darcy and Her Daughters* and hatched the idea of posing as art historians.

He had quickly discovered that Pemberley was still in the private hands of the Darcy family. It had not been gifted to the National Trust or opened up to the public as so many great houses had. The Darcys simply didn't need the money. So there could be no casual visiting, no taking of tea in the vintage style café or hanging about in the gardens, no posing as an engaged couple looking for a wedding venue. It was a sealed box. If he wanted to get in, Charlie would have to engineer an invitation. When he wrote to the current Mr. Darcy, he claimed that they were both at the Open University, knowing that it was difficult to check, and he was amazed at his luck when he had a call only days later.

"Hello? Is that Mr. Haywood? This is James Darcy. You wrote to me." He sounded old and somewhat distracted.

"Hello, Mr. Darcy. Yes, I did. Thank you for getting back to me so quickly."

"Yes, well, don't like to keep people hanging on. Not fair, you know? Anyhow, thank you for your interest in the Clerkenman painting. It's a bloody great thing, hanging up in our drawing room. My wife tells me that we also have some of the sketches that the fellow made when he was painting it, but you might have to hunt about for them."

"Thank you, Mr. Darcy. I would love to see those. That sounds very interesting and valuable for my work."

"Yes, well...you are welcome to come up and bring this...this Evie Jones with you. It is a long way from London, and my wife is still looking for the sketches, so why don't you stay a couple of nights? We've enough bedrooms to billet an army here, and it is just Mrs. Darcy and me."

"That is most generous of you, and we would like that very much."

They arranged it there and then, and Charlie could hardly believe his luck. Now, here he was, driving to Pemberley with Evie in the passenger seat, their overnight bags slung in the boot. Following the Sat Nav, he came off the motorway, and the landscape around them changed. Villages with dry, stone walls and low cottages with hanging baskets sprung up around every corner. The roads narrowed and wound like coils between patchwork fields, and cows watched lazily from the sides. When, forty minutes later, they reached the village of Lambton, Charlie pulled into a parking space in front of the pub.

"We are nearly there. Pemberley is five miles away but I thought you could do with a coffee?"

"I could." She smiled at him for the first time that morning. "Thank you."

It was a dark, cosy kind of place with a dog curled up by the bar and a mishmash of unconvincing, *olde-worlde* odds and ends hung on the walls. Evie sipped her coffee and shivered slightly to be out of the sun.

"I'm feeling so nervous."

"Try not to worry. I'll do as much of the talking as I can. It will be fine. Just remember: you're an academic. If you are a bit standoffish, then that will be no more than they expect. They are two old people. They probably won't be paying that much attention anyway. Just look at the paintings, get out your notebook, and try to relax. You will charm them, Evie."

"Hmm. I'm not so sure. What if they rumble us?"

"They won't. Why would they?"

"What if we don't find anything? We don't even know what we're looking for after all."

That, he knew, was a far more likely outcome, and he paused before answering her.

"Well, we'll cross that bridge if and when we come to it. But let's be optimistic. If there was anything that could have revealed the truth about Victoria Darcy, then it must have been a document of some sort. Looking at it from first principles, it has to have been either a letter or a series of letters, or a confession of some sort. I guess that it could have been longer—a diary maybe. Whatever it was, Hannah Tavener hid it, and as far as we know, nobody has ever disturbed it. So, we have to get into her head. Try to think like Hannah, and ask yourself: Where would she have hidden her mistress's dirty secret in an emergency?"

He noticed how she bristled at his words.

"And how are we supposed to do that?"

"We are about to go to the place where she lived and died. Think about it. You will sleep in rooms where she worked and look at the views she saw every day. We're going to eat at a table she served at, see the face of her mistress. Whatever it was, she knew she had to get rid of it. Her mistress, whom she had served for many years, was dead, and Hannah may already have been sickening with the fever that killed her. She was desperate. But judging from the letters, she was levelheaded and trustworthy. Try to think yourself into her life. What would she have done?"

"You know, you are actually quite creative. Have you ever thought about acting?"

"No way. I don't have the ego for it."

She smiled quietly and drank the last of her coffee, placing the cup back on the saucer before looking straight at him.

"I don't believe you."

"It's true."

"Okay. Well you can't have grown up wanting to be a private detective. You must have thought about doing other jobs?"

"Not really. I sort of fell into it when I was quite young. I didn't go to university because…well, I didn't go, and I got a job and did well. Before long, I was too busy to think about other things. It just happened and carried on happening."

Across the room, the barmaid leaned on the bar and caught his eye. He looked away just in time to observe what many might have missed. Evie's eyes flashed between him and the unknown woman before she began to blow unnecessarily on her coffee. Charlie inwardly cursed. Now was not the time to start telling Evie about his life or allowing her to see things for herself. He dreaded to think what Peter may have said to her, knowing perfectly well that his family disapproved of his business. They didn't know the half of it.

"What did your parents do?"

There was a moment of silence as he looked at the table, blindsided.

"My mum was a primary school teacher."

"And your dad?"

"Vicar."

"You're kidding!"

Having said it, he recovered some of his composure.

"No, I'm completely serious. He was a vicar in an inner city parish in London."

"Wow."

His eyebrows twitched up as he looked her, wanting to laugh from relief. "Why 'wow'?"

"Why 'wow'? Because I'm wondering by what kind of crazy path the son of a vicar and a primary school teacher winds up not going to university when he obviously could and running a high-class snooping agency. It is just so…"

"Just so what?"

"Unlikely. You are a very unlikely man."

"If you say so." He shrugged. "But who wants to be a likely man? Come on, Evie. Let's go and find your fifth great grandmother's document."

The road that led to Pemberley was narrow and undulating. The Sat Nav had got confused, and Evie had the map out on her lap and had been calling out contradictory instructions as the greens and yellows of the fields whipped past the windows. It was obvious that she was not one of life's navigators, but Charlie couldn't be annoyed with her. The road began to skirt a wood, and he wondered how long to let her continue before he took the map and actually found the house. Just then, the sunshine that had been shaded by the trees broke through in a clearing, and right before them in the green of the valley stood the gleaming, grey stone of Pemberley. He had seen pictures, but they had not done the place justice. The light seemed to shine on it and through it like a piece of porcelain. Almost involuntarily, he stopped the car.

"My word," said Evie. "Is that it?"

"Sure is."

"Did my ancestors really live here? Something must have gone wrong in our branch of the family."

They laughed and continued on the winding road past woods and thickets and along streams to the massive turning circle in the front of the house. As they had turned into the great drive, he had seen a tiny figure appear at the top of the swooping stone staircase in front of the main door. By the time they got close, they could see that there were two people waiting for them.

James and Honoria Darcy came down the steps to greet them as they got out of the car. James walked with the aid of a stick and squinted through spectacles that slid down the bridge of his nose. Honoria's tweed skirt moved stiffly in the breeze, and although she was the wrong side of seventy, she was very pretty. She held out her hand.

"Mr. Haywood, Miss Jones. I am Honoria Darcy, and this is my husband, James. Welcome to Pemberley."

True to his promise, Charlie did the talking.

"Thank you, Mrs. Darcy. It is a pleasure to be here. My colleague and I are excited to see the work you have. And it is such a lovely day; we were hoping for a walk through your grounds as well."

"Yes, of course. You can't leave without having a potter about the gardens.

I love them. My husband isn't so good on his pins, as you see"—James Darcy smiled weakly and looked at his stick—"but I would love to show you around. First of all, let's get your things in and get you settled. You are with us for two nights, I believe?"

"Yes, that is what I arranged when I spoke to Mr. Darcy. It is very generous of you to put us up."

"Oh, don't be silly! You can see that we don't want for space." She gestured to the vast Palladian mansion behind her, and Evie stifled a laugh.

"Now," continued Mrs. Darcy, "let us get you inside. We have put you both on the guest corridor, which is very comfortable. Miss Jones, we have given you our best guest bedroom."

"Oh, thank you, Mrs. Darcy," said Evie.

"You are welcome. It has a wonderful aspect, and I hope that you enjoy staying in it."

THE FOUR OF THEM TROOPED THROUGH THE GREAT HOUSE LIKE A BAND OF ants, Charlie and Evie carrying their bags, their feet tapping on tiled floors and their eyes flying up to colossal oils and tapestries upon the walls. The staircase was laid with a carpet so thick that Evie could feel its luxury through the thin sole of her ballet pumps. On all sides, faces in antiquated costumes stared out at them. Men, young and old, were pictured holding books or sitting atop horses or standing in fields and brandishing guns. Amongst the women, there were wigs, beauty spots, bustles, ruffs, and skirts so wide they looked like sails. There were ringlets, buns, and creamy shoulders rising above shiny bodices of all colours. Where is Fitzwilliam? Evie found herself wondering. Where is Elizabeth?

She had been in her room for about ten minutes when there came a knock on the door. She jumped up.

"Come in."

The door creaked open, and Charlie's face appeared. His eyes widened as he looked around the room.

"Wow, you lucked out here. This is twice the size of my room…more than."

"I know, it's huge, isn't it?" She glanced up to the great, silk paper-clad walls and the vast curtains. "And as for the bed…" Pausing, she looked at the enormous, mahogany four-poster and wondered that it didn't have a stepladder to help her into it. Charlie's eyes rested on the massive pillows and layers of blanket and counterpane. They each stared for a second too long before turning to each other and then, blinking, turned away. Evie's face felt hot as she watched him walk towards the long windows and gaze out. Before him was a perfect view of the back of the estate: a lake glistening in the sunshine, rippled by ducks, a folly, wood bordering green.

"And this is quite a view as well."

"I know. The colours here are amazing. Makes me want to do some painting." She moved to the window and stood beside him. "Do you think we should go down and start pretending to be interested in this painting?"

"We *are* interested in this painting," he replied.

They smiled at one another and were gone.

THE MAIN DRAWING ROOM AT PEMBERLEY WAS LIGHT AND AIRY. THE WALLS were hung with a fine, green silk paper and an enormous, pale Chinese carpet covered the floor beneath their feet. Honoria Darcy was pouring out tea from a delicate teapot and offering sugar lumps and milk. She was laughing quietly and chattering away, but Evie could hardly hear her. She had been staring at *Mrs. Darcy and Her Daughters* ever since she entered the room, and she was in danger of looking peculiar if she did not turn away. Charlie seemed to understand that she was stunned by it and had been busy deflecting attention, turning on the charm for the Darcys and asking them about their sons and grandsons and the history of the house and garden. It wasn't enough to blind Honoria Darcy to Evie's admiration.

"It's a lovely painting, isn't it, Miss Jones? I've always thought it rather striking."

"Yes, Mrs. Darcy. It's beautiful. It's so characterful. All of them look like real personalities, and the detail is amazing."

Honoria Darcy clutched her pearls and nodded her agreement. "Yes, well, I think that we had better leave you young people to it. I hope that you have everything you need. Come along, James." She helped her husband to stand, and they left.

Evie looked back at the painting. It was a vast board of colour and character. At its centre stood Elizabeth Darcy: "My late beloved Elizabeth." She was slim and good looking with curly, chestnut brown hair around her face and wearing a dress of dove grey and white. Her eyes jumped out of the picture, and Evie tried to fix the expression that danced in them. Those were eyes that a person could know and laugh with. Around her slender waist was a band of teal so silky in appearance that one wanted to reach out and touch it. She held a small folded-up fan in her hand. It occurred to Evie that, whoever her fifth great grandfather may be, Elizabeth was her fifth great grandmother. She felt an unexpected loyalty welling up inside her.

Around the mother, sat the daughters, and it was obvious that they must have individually sat for the artist as each looked quite different. Evie checked the note Charlie had given her. They were in age order in a semicircle around Elizabeth. Anne was tall and dark and wore a serious expression. Emma was round-faced and played a harpsichord. Frances was fair and, unlike the rest of the family, had blue eyes. Beatrice was curly haired and sat beside a small, black dog. Finally, there sat Victoria in the far right of the picture, holding a finely dressed doll in her small, plump hands. Of all the girls, she looked the most like her mother. Her pale skin was luminous, and her thick, wavy hair hung over one shoulder. She cannot have been older than five when the likeness was painted, and although she was dressed in a child's clothes, there was an air of knowingness about her. Her shoulders were fine and straight, her limbs quite long and slim, her eyes laughing, confident, and almost challenging. Evie couldn't place the room they were in. It was not the drawing room, but it was a large and richly furnished space, and the windows looked to give out onto the garden at the back of the house towards the lake. Charlie advanced behind her and stared up at the canvas.

"You like it?"

"I love it. It's beautiful. I never expected it to be like this—to be so distinctive. I thought it would be like those dry, old group portraits. You know: the ones in the National Gallery that nobody ever looks at where all the faces are the same and the eyes look like marbles. This is completely different. It is so alive. You can feel them. It's like they are about to get down from the wall and pour themselves tea. Do you know what I mean?"

She looked at him, and he nodded.

"I agree that it's lovely…she's lovely," he said looking at Elizabeth Darcy's face and letting her eyes lock with his. "Right. So let's start looking around in here. There are a lot of books with blank spines. We need to check what is inside them—and behind as well because stuff could be easily hidden at the back of the shelves. You can discount anything that is typed; what we are looking for is handwritten."

Evie stared at him for a moment, uncomprehending. She had almost forgotten why they were there. She soon recovered her memory, and fuelled with tiny cups of tea, they began the search, each at one end of the room. Great clouds of dust brushed their faces as they upset books that may never have been moved. Drawers were pulled out and rummaged through and cabinets opened, and Evie found herself crouched on the grate, feeling around the tiles. Every corner was breathlessly investigated, and Evie's heart was in her mouth. Would they be discovered? Would they strike lucky? What were they even looking for? In the end, it was all for nothing. If Elizabeth Darcy's lost document was in the house, it was not in that room.

Later, supper passed contentedly. They sat at one end of the vast dining table, the four of them dwarfed by their surroundings and the great table like an ocean between them. It was obvious that James and Honoria enjoyed having guests to entertain, and as the light slipped from the sky, they ate salmon, drank wine, and talked about the house and its history. They had, it turned out, been married for fifty years and had two sons and grandchildren who visited in fine weather.

"Fifty years? That is quite some achievement, Mrs. Darcy," said Charlie.

"Yes, fifty years indeed. We were married in Lambton Church. You probably passed it on your way in. Lovely spire. And the children and grandchildren were christened there as well. Of course, in the past, they would have been done in the chapel, but it was decommissioned during the war, and my husband's father didn't apply to renew the licence after that. Even before then, it had fallen into almost complete disuse. It's a bit of a shell now."

Charlie became visibly more alert.

"There's a chapel?"

"Yes, of course. All of the Darcy girls you see in your painting would have been christened and probably married in there. It was still in use then for special occasions. It's a bit of a shame, but really, there are no private chapels left in England. They are quite a thing of the past, even in grand houses. There is simply no call for them."

"So what happens in the Pemberley chapel now?"

"Nothing, Mr. Haywood. I'm afraid it's rather mothballed. I know"—she stood, slapping her napkin down on the table, and it occurred to Charlie that she may have had too much to drink—"I'll give you the guided tour now. You will be all right in here, won't you, James darling?" She stroked her husband's shoulder, and he nodded.

In no time at all, they were bombing down draughty corridors, straining to keep up with the old lady. Honoria had promised Evie that they didn't dress for dinner, but she had changed into a fresh blouse, and Evie noticed now that her flats had been replaced by an elegant pair of blue courts that presently clipped along the floor ahead of them. Not quite knowing the form and not wishing to do the wrong thing, Evie had put on the linen dress she wore to her exhibition. The chilly air of the windowless corridors deep in the heart of Pemberley cooled her bare legs as she scampered to keep up. When they arrived at the mahogany double doors, Evie assumed they were about to give on to another corridor, but no. Honoria flung them open, reached inside for a switch, and there before them was illuminated the dried out, unvisited former glories of the Pemberley chapel.

"I'll get all the lights on for you—just a minute," muttered Honoria, her heels dragging on the floor and her arms searching behind a great velvet curtain for switches. "There..." she said as the yellow light fell on them, illuminating it in sections like the stage of a theatre.

It smelt like a place that nobody went, and the air inside was cold, damp, and thick with unknowns. Wooden pews sat expectantly and looked empty and sad. The altar had no cloth, and the candlesticks had no candles, albeit that they were spattered with wax, the telltale signs of former life. Up the walls climbed great marble reliefs, figures sporting with animals entangled with plants like an allegory of creation. The roof was domed and beamed with colourful lettering and images of Christ and the apostles. The sound of their feet moving around echoed in the great, empty space.

"Mrs. Darcy, this is amazing," said Charlie, eyes turned to the ceiling in wonder.

"Isn't it? Nobody comes in here now, which is awfully sad. James and I go for our Sunday service in the village, and the children aren't interested really. So there you are."

When all the lights were on and the dust had settled around them, Honoria begun cantering around, pointing out plaques and effigies and polishing the lectern with the edge of her silk scarf.

"The rood screen, you know, is pre-Reformation! How about that?"

Evie wondered what a rood screen was and, not for the first time, was grateful for Charlie.

"It's remarkable, Mrs. Darcy. There can't be many of those left in England. And it is in very good condition too. Thank you for letting us see it. It's a real privilege."

"Oh, you're welcome, Mr. Haywood. Whatever is the point in having such a dreadful, old mausoleum if we don't occasionally let in the light?"

Chapter 19

April 3, 1821, Pemberley

I t is that part of the morning that feels like night, and I am at my desk in my outside cloak. My hand shakes slightly as a write, and I can hardly credit that events have turned out as they have. Beyond the wall, I hear Fitzwilliam's voice rumbling away indistinctly to his valet, no doubt with some last-minute instructions, some explanation of sorts. Will it be believed, I wonder? What shall be said of us in our absence, and how shall the speed of our departure be accounted for? Some hours ago while I paced the room, Fitzwilliam sat in this seat and wrote to Galbraith with the basic facts of the matter and a promise of more detail later.

"We must have somebody in our confidence, Elizabeth."

"But can we trust him?"

"Of course. I would not tell him if I did not know that he could be trusted."

I knew this to be true and slowly exhaled. I had a notion that we should tell Georgiana, but my husband would not hear of it. He had reasoned that, although she would never mean to betray us, she would have to tell Lord Avery, and her sweetness was so great that one day she, inadvertently, may let down her guard. Thus, it was decided that between us, Lydia, Galbraith, and Hannah there would be fixed a ring of silence, never to be broken. That was some hours ago in the pitch of a night in which neither of us slept.

Presently, Hannah, who has also gone without sleep, has entered the room and is collecting underskirts into a trunk. She has packed, with her usual foresight and good sense, only plain, warm, and serviceable clothes.

This is not a time for finery; this is not a time for show. In a moment, I shall have to give her this book. It shall be placed in the trunk and unpacked I know not where.

"Hannah, are you going to be warm enough in that cloak?"

"I'm sure I shall, madam. Thank you."

I considered it for a moment and tried to focus on her slim figure in the half-light.

"No, we have no idea of the conditions, and I fear that we may be treated to storms and I know not what. You shall take my old, green cloak. You know—the one I had made the first winter I was married?"

"That is very generous, madam, and unnecessary, I'm sure."

"Nonsense, Hannah, take it. It is thicker than yours, and the lining is very warm. I cannot have you catching a chill."

She smiled, bobbed a curtsy, and left me to myself. The sounds of the house creaking to life began to moan around me. I heard a door opening down the corridor and the sound of clanging pales in the hall beneath. It does not escape me that I would usually be sleeping in great comfort while a world of people work around me. At some point, and soon, I must put down my pen and seek out my sister. What sort of condition shall she be in this morning, I wonder? I cannot credit that she has stolen more than a wink of sleep, and although it cannot be good for her to undertake the journey before us, there is nothing else for it.

The connecting door opens, and Fitzwilliam stands before me without his jacket. Shadows fall across his handsome face, and he smiles slightly, maybe not as much as I would like.

"Are you ready, Elizabeth?"

I nodded, and together we walked out of my chamber down the carpeted corridor towards the night nursery. The door eased open without a sound, and Nanny, who sleeps on a small bed against the wall, startled awake and sat up. In the darkness, I felt my way towards her and touched my hand to her bed-warm shoulder as I spoke in a whisper.

"Shh. Do not trouble yourself, Nanny. There is no need to get up. I am sorry to disturb you thus, but Mr. Darcy and I have to go away. I am afraid I do not know how long we shall be gone, but it may be some months hence. I shall write often, and we shall return as soon as we can. Everything you need here shall be provided in our absence."

The poor lady was plainly astonished, and I squeezed her arm in what I hope was a friendly and confiding manner. My soul screamed out for this dreadful matter to be concluded, but I know that it cannot be hurried. It will move at its own pace like the seasons of the year, and neither raucous noise nor quiet prayer shall speed it.

"Mr. Darcy and I just wanted to see the children before we left. We shall not wake them, and if you do not mind my husband's presence for a moment, there is no need for you to get up."

She nodded, blinked, and looked utterly bewildered. With that, I beckoned Fitzwilliam into the room, and together we looked at Beatrice and Frances in their cots, everything grey in the half dark. To see their tiny blanket-clad bodies shook the inside of me, and I began to feel unsteady. At that moment, his warm hand came around my waist, and I leaned forward. Holding my stray hair away, I touched an almost imperceptible kiss to each of their plump cheeks, and we left to visit Emma and Anne in their respective, adjoining bedrooms. Emma had thrown off a part of her blanket, and I tucked it about her narrow shoulders, stroking her hair—chestnut brown. In the next room, Anne stirred when I bent down to kiss her, and I froze in fear that she may wake and be distressed by our unaccustomed presence at such an hour. Her profile against the white of her pillow was so like Fitzwilliam that, in that moment, I wanted to weep. I gripped the side of the bed and told myself it was for the best and not for long.

When I stood, my husband's arms were waiting for me. In the darkness of our daughter's chamber, he embraced me and planted a kiss on the top of my head and then on the insides of my wrists. Quietly, he spoke. "Let us be away." And we were.

Chapter 20

Pemberley, 18 September 2014

J ames Darcy sat at the head of the breakfast table, surveying his unopened post, removing the supplements from that day's edition of the *Times* and tutting quietly as Charlie, Evie, and his wife contemplated the day.

"I have left all the sketches in the drawing room for you, Mr. Haywood. I hope that you and Miss Jones are comfortable in there?"

"Yes, thank you. Very comfortable. The light is great. I'm sure we will enjoy examining the sketches next to the painting itself."

Mrs. Darcy smiled a broad smile and poured tea for them all. "Super! James and I have to go out this afternoon, but we'll be back for dinner. It is your last night tonight, so I'll ask Cook to really spoil us. Don't forget that, before you leave, you must make sure you have a walk around the grounds. They are lovely at this time of year if I say so myself." She glanced at Evie's ballet pumps. "If you need footwear, Miss Jones, you are welcome to borrow from the boot room."

"Oh, thank you, Mrs. Darcy," said Evie, regretting that a stable full of wellies, saddles, and wax jackets was an unlikely hiding place for the document they were attempting to find.

And so, pleasantries were exchanged, toast buttered, and tea milked, and they began to eat. Evie, worried that she was being too silent, was just about to ask about the history of the garden when James looked up from his letters.

"Good grief…Honoria, do we have cousins called Carter?"

Charlie, who was drinking his tea at the time didn't flinch or turn a hair at the mention of the name.

"Carter? Not sure, darling. Don't think so. There are the Carter-Arnolds in Buckingham but they aren't cousins; they are Aunt Mabel's in-laws."

He shook his head and refocused on the handwritten letter in front of him.

"No, this letter is from a Miss Carter. Come to think of it, the name rings a bell, but I'm not sure why. Reckons she's some sort of cousin. Lives in Shropshire. Finds herself up here from time to time. Wants to come and meet us when she's in the area. Oh well. Why not I suppose..."

"Let me see that, darling." Honoria's hand shot out to take the letter. "It could be from any old Tom, Dick, or Harry."

Mrs. Darcy's pretty eyes scanned the letter, and Evie's heart was in her mouth.

"Well, she writes nicely, and what attractive writing paper." She put the letter down beside her and picked up her toast. "It can't do any harm I suppose, darling, although I must say, I've never heard of her. Just goes to show, one doesn't know where one's relations are these days. I should make it a project of mine to do the family tree so that we don't get taken unawares by these things." She laughed and looked at Charlie who smiled back.

HE FELT, RATHER THAN SAW, EVIE STIFFENING BESIDE HIM AND FOUGHT the impulse to reach his hand out and touch her. Worry was cascading off her like steam. He wanted to reassure her that, if Cressida was writing to the Darcys, at least they knew that she wasn't going to turn up while they were there. If she was invited to come for tea one day, it was hugely unlikely that she would be in the house long enough to be able to do the kind of searching they were doing. Even so, the knowledge that she was true to her word, that she had not given up, and that she was on his tail, bit at him. The clock was ticking, and they could not go away empty handed. Honoria Darcy's kindly face came back into focus.

"I'm sure you'd find plenty of information, Mrs. Darcy, especially with the internet being what it is. You might enjoy it as well; I know my mother did when she researched our family."

Before long, they were speaking of Charlie's mother, the weather, the marmalade, and the traffic around Matlock on a Saturday. If it had not been for the fact that he saw him pick it up as they went to leave, Charlie would have thought James Darcy had completely forgotten Cressida's letter. As it was, he tucked it into his breast pocket as he and Honoria left Charlie and Evie to get on with their day's work. Absent the Darcys, they walked to the drawing room in an uneasy silence. As soon as they were safe in the room, Evie spun around to face him. Without thinking, he reached out his hand and held her shoulder still.

"Try not to worry about it. Focus on the positives. At least we know that she won't just turn up out of the blue while we're still here."

THE FEELING OF HIS HAND AGAINST HER STIRRED HER, AND ALTHOUGH part of her wanted to move it away, she didn't. She looked away instead.

"You're so calm. But then I suppose, it's not you who is about to lose everything!"

"You're not about to lose everything either. We just have to think really logically."

"Oh, Charlie, this is crazy! We are going to need more than logic to recover this thing. It has been lost for two hundred years, and we have no idea what *it* is!"

"I've been thinking about that. Elizabeth Darcy died in March, and at that time of the year, the house would have been full of fires. So, if it were just a letter or a couple of pages, Hannah would have simply thrown it in the fire. It makes no sense that she would have failed to get rid of it. No, I think that, whatever it is, it was quite large, and that is why she didn't just burn it. For my money, it must have been some kind of diary or lengthy confession."

Evie sat down on the pale chaise and looked up at Elizabeth's glittering eyes in the painting.

"We have to try to get inside Hannah's head. She is given this thing to destroy, and she knows that she has to do it. But it's too big to burn. Elizabeth is dying or has just died. The place is likely to have been chaos, and Hannah was probably upset herself. She might have been starting to feel ill as well, who knows. She thinks…let's hide it somewhere then return later and destroy it when there is more time. She didn't know that she was about to die too. Question is: Where would she have put it?"

"Surely, she would have just hidden the thing in her bedroom."

"No. Not enough privacy. Servants usually shared rooms, so there would have been at least another girl in with her—maybe more. And anyway, a woman in Hannah's position would have had very few belongings: a couple of dresses, an outdoor cloak, her shoes. She would not have had any way of concealing it in her room. No, I think she would have chosen somewhere inside the house—not in the servants' quarters—somewhere she thought would not be disturbed."

"Okay, if you say so. But where? This place is huge. We can't search it all; we only have today, and then we're leaving. There just isn't enough time."

"I've got an idea where we can look."

"Where?"

"Well, you might not like it, but—"

"Where?"

"Honoria's bedroom."

"We can't do that, Charlie. That's awful—"

"Hear me out. If you don't want to do it, I'll do it. You can wait outside."

"But she's an old lady, and she's kind. We can't go through her things. It's just wrong."

"I'm not going to go through her things, Evie. If this document were sitting in a drawer somewhere, it would have been found. I would just check behind paintings and around the fireplace for secret compartments. I'd check the floor for loose sections and look under the bed. The thing is, in these grand houses, the mistress's chambers are handed down from generation to generation. The old widow goes to the dower house, and the new lady of the manor goes into her bedroom. So chances are that Honoria sleeps in the room that Elizabeth slept in. It's an obvious place. We can't go away without looking, especially with Cressida sniffing around."

Evie imagined Cressida Carter arriving in that very room for tea and cakes and went cold at the thought. Her face whitened, and she shivered.

CHARLIE KNEW THAT HE HAD FORCED HER TOO FAR, THAT THE SUM TOTAL of dishonesty and trickery was about to push her over. He sat beside her on the chaise and looked straight ahead at *Mrs. Darcy and Her Daughters*.

"Look, I know you don't want to do it, so I'll do it. All you need to do is keep watch in the corridor. I'll be in and out in no time, and nobody will know. I won't disturb her things. I like her too. I know that you don't believe me, but ransacking old ladies' bedrooms isn't my bag either."

"Really?"

"Of course not."

"But you do this sort of thing for a living. Doesn't it ever bother you? Don't you ever feel sorry for the people you prey on? Don't you ever worry that maybe you shouldn't be doing it?"

He paused and looked down at his hands. The truth was that until he had met Evie, he had never been troubled by it for more than a moment. His work was his work. He did it. He was good at it. There was nothing else to say and nothing else to think about. It had made him rich. It had saved him and Mum when the chips were down. It gave him some way of filling time between spending money and sleeping with women he didn't love. Occasionally, he had thought of the heart-melting, soul-elevating goodness of his father and felt ashamed, but that was a fleeting thing. It was there in his mind, and then it was gone and worrying him no longer. Now, this woman had come into his life, uninvited, and turned the whole thing on its head.

"Of course, I do."

His words appeared to startle her. She looked straight at him, and Charlie sensed that a question whispering around both of them for a long time was growing loud and starting to scream for an answer.

"Charlie?"

"Hmm?"

"Why are you doing this?"

A moment of quiet crackled between them.

"Can't you guess?"

"I don't want to guess. I might guess wrong. Tell me."

"Well"—he looked down at his feet and laughed uncomfortably—"I'm doing this because I like you. I like you, and I want to be with you. I want you to be safe and happy, and I don't want you to lose everything. I understand that you don't feel like that about me and probably still hate my guts, but there it is. Even if I never see you again after tomorrow, I'm still going to do this for you."

There was a slow, thick, eddying silence. Evie coloured, seeming to take it in. Eventually, she spoke.

"Thank you."

It was decided that, since the Darcys were going out in the afternoon, it was the ideal time to tackle Honoria's room. In between, they passed time in the drawing room, glancing through the sketches, Evie with her notepad out on her knee in case James or Honoria should come in. After a while and as the morning drew on, the sunshine blazing through the huge windows was too inviting, and they went outside. The green of the grass as it rose up to the edge of the wood was almost blinding, and when Evie looked back at the house, she thought it looked like an animal nestled in the landscape, lying in wait. The bloom of the summer had largely died, and there were some leaves falling and mixing with the freshly mowed grass that collected on the soles of their shoes.

Charlie had been worried that she would never speak to him again after what he had said in the drawing room and that her brittle "thank you" meant that she would speak but only as little as possible. Strangely though, and for reasons that he could not identify, saying it straight out like that had not done them any harm. Far from being angry or cynical or any of the other things he had feared, she seemed relaxed and happy. As they climbed the hill behind the lake, the sun on their faces, they talked and laughed, and he dared to wonder what it meant. At lunchtime, they returned to the house and took sandwiches onto the terrace outside the parlour. Charlie had wondered whether he should suggest they drive into Lambton for a pub lunch, but Honoria had been adamant that they should not fend for themselves. In any case, the beauty and isolation of Pemberley seemed to have cast a spell over Evie, and he did not want to be the one to break it.

She sat forward in her chair on the terrace, blinking into the pale gold of the sunshine and spoke without looking at him.

"I've been thinking, and I've decided I don't buy it."

Charlie looked up, completely confused.

"Don't buy what?"

"About Elizabeth. I don't believe she was having it away with someone else."

He closed his eyes and stretched before answering her.

"Well, that's a nice thought, Evie, but are you sure you aren't being blinded by the romance of the thing or by family feeling? I mean, she was your fifth great grandmother. Of course, you don't want her to be unfaithful to her seemingly doting husband. But the fact is that there was something fishy about Victoria. Darcy's letters prove that there was a secret—a secret Darcy was desperate to keep under wraps. Elizabeth in her dying days asked her maid to destroy some incriminating thing for her. There must have been a reason for that. Victoria Darcy was the only one of the Darcy children not to be born here at Pemberley, and that is really weird too. Why would Darcy have taken his pregnant wife all the way to Ireland? It would have been treacherous. It was madness. A secret must lie behind it. There were rumours about Victoria and—well—come on; there's no smoke without fire."

Her body straightened at that, and he feared he had angered her.

"Oh you can't fall back on that one. Just because people think a thing, it doesn't make it true. You have seen that painting. You can say whatever you like, but I look at her standing there with her daughters around her, and I just know it isn't true. Fitzwilliam commissioned it, Charlie, and he never let it be displayed to the public. Can you imagine keeping an object as wonderful as that private? The whole thing is a celebration of Elizabeth and her daughters. It's an act of worship on canvas. It is not the action of a man whose wife has been giving him the runaround."

"Well, maybe he didn't know. People can be blind to what is right in front of them. Maybe he did know, and he just really, *really* loved her. Maybe he was just a very rich guy who got a kick out of spending a fortune commissioning private works of art from the era's foremost portraitist and then not letting anyone see them."

"But that doesn't square with the trust. If he was like that, he never would have set up the trust because it devalued the overall Darcy estate. If he was that kind of guy, he would have been worried about preserving the wealth for his sons, not the fact that his granddaughters and great granddaughters might need protection one day."

"Evie…" He turned and looked at her face sparking with indignation. "You're imagining a lot about these people. We can't really know what was going on with them. It was too long ago. It's lost. It's gone. Time throws up a lot of dust, and you can't expect to see through it all. We have to deal with the facts that remain, and you just can't get away from the fact that there is a mystery surrounding Victoria Darcy—something that certainly Darcy and probably Elizabeth tried to conceal."

With this, she stood up jerkily and with such speed that he thought she might run away. She didn't run, but she did look away from him as she spoke.

"Well, we'll have to see, won't we? As far as I'm concerned, Elizabeth is innocent until proven guilty, so unless you find that smoking gun…speaking of which, don't you think we should get on with it?"

She was right of course, and Charlie didn't need to be asked twice. He walked around to the front of the house to check that the Darcys' mud splattered Land Rover had not returned unexpectedly. When he saw that it had not, he found Evie and nodded, knowing that they could put the task off no longer. Silently, they padded down the corridors to the mistress's bedroom.

"It's this one," he said as they approached the door.

"Okay." Evie folded her arms across her chest and sprang from foot to foot with nerves.

"You just wait here and watch. You will see anyone coming up the stairs before they turn the corner. If anyone comes, knock twice on the door, and run to your own room. Don't worry about me, I'll get out somehow."

She forced a smile.

"Sure. Be quick." With that, he disappeared behind the great oak door.

Inside the room, he found a vast, floral maze of pastel colours and soft furnishings. An old-fashioned perfume dispenser sat on the dressing table alongside an array of small picture frames with smiling children, wedding parties, and engagement portraits staring back. It was so redolent of age and love that it stopped him in his tracks for a moment. He saw the tweed skirt Honoria had worn to dinner the previous night draped over the end of the bed and felt a surge of guilt. With that, he recalled Evie outside and got on with the job at hand. He made quick work of checking the wooden panels on the walls and around the tall windows. He lifted each of the heavy framed oils, one of a young Honoria, painted—he would guess—at some time in the sixties, feeling the wall behind for a cupboard or compartment. The fireplace was obviously never used, and he wrestled with an oversized display of dried flowers to feel along the tiled surround, finding nothing. He stood in the centre of the room, despairing. If he could not find the damned thing with an opportunity like this, then he knew it was a lost cause. In desperation, he got down on the floor and surveyed the polished surface for kinks and irregularities. He knew almost before he did it that it would be fruitless, and so indeed, it was. Standing and thinking of her jittery body and frowning expression in the corridor, he moved towards the door.

He forced himself to look at her as he spoke.

"I'm sorry, Evie. Nothing doing."

FOR EVIE'S PART, AN UNFAMILIAR FATALISM OVERTOOK HER. THEY HAD tried and failed, and now there was nothing for it than to let the future be the future. She could not fault his thoroughness, and there was no stone within her view that he had left unturned. She thought of Clemmie and Milena at home, the studio, and the fragile green shoot that was her career as an artist. She knew that the whole expensive, imperfect edifice may come crashing down at any point. He walked beside her in the corridor and tension poured off him. The weird thing was that, now that the game was lost, she didn't blame him. The afternoon was slipping into evening, and they said little as they reached their rooms and parted. The Darcys would be home soon, and it had already been arranged that they would dine at eight with drinks at seven in the drawing room.

It was to be her last hour in the presence of *Mrs. Darcy and Her Daughters*, and Evie did not intend to waste it. She closed the door of her enormous bedroom, took off every scrap of clothing without thinking, and walked to the en suite bathroom. The bath was so enormous that she had been shy of using it, but now she surveyed its creamy vastness and thought, "Why not?" There was a tiny, probably ancient bottle of lavender oil on the windowsill, and she dripped some into the steaming water as it thundered out of the taps. She looked at her reflection in the mirror until it clouded in the heat, and then she plunged into the water.

Sometime later, when she got out and padded around the room, pink-footed and wrapped in a slightly too small towel, she willed herself to force away the worry. She leaned against the window and looked out onto the luscious, living green of the estate. Defiance welled inside her, and she dressed in clean, cold clothes for dinner. She had planned poorly, and the only unworn clothes she had left were jeans and a blue T-shirt she had originally envisaged wearing on the journey home. She put them on, and when she looked in the mirror, she thought she looked quite reasonable. Her appearance didn't worry her as it did other girls.

As it was, Evie actually regretted not having dressed up more. Honoria was wearing a dress and a different colour lipstick, and even James looked to be wearing a fresh shirt. Honoria handed out glasses of gin and tonic and stood under the painting, beaming.

"Well, cheers! We shall miss you both. It has been lovely having guests, hasn't it, James?"

"Err, yes…"

"And you must send us a copy of your project, Miss Jones. It shall be most interesting to see what you have made of our little painting here. I'm always telling my son that it is really special."

Charlie caught Evie's eye and moved closer. She got the feeling that he knew she was in no mood to discuss her fictitious PhD.

"It is really special, Mrs. Darcy, and the sketches were a real insight into how Clerkenman built it up into what we see today. It looks as though he had each of the girls sitting separately with their mother. We speculated that they were probably too young to reliably sit all together for a long period, so maybe that is why there are so many separate sketches. Some of them are so good and so detailed; I'm surprised you don't display them."

"I had never thought of that, Mr. Haywood. What a good idea. James, what do you think to that darling?"

"Err, well, yes…"

"Yes, I can imagine it. What a good idea! To be honest, I didn't realise we had so many sketches until I dug them out for you. There is stuff everywhere in this house. You never really know what you've got if you know what I mean. Some of those sketches I found in the old library, some of them in the archive boxes in my husband's study, and then there were some others in a little room at the back of the house that has all sorts of odds and ends. I even found a wedding dress in there! Don't know whose it was. The trouble with a house like this is that nobody has ever really gone through things and put them into any sort of order. It just gets passed on generation to generation, and I'm afraid it doesn't come with an inventory."

"Do you know very much about the Mrs. Darcy in the painting?" asked Evie.

"Not much, I'm afraid, Miss Jones. Only that her name was Elizabeth and she was very good at having daughters!" She laughed and lifted her eyes to the painting. "She is rather lovely, isn't she?"

"She is. Her eyes are wonderful. What a gift Clerkenman had. You can feel them looking at you and laughing. Well, even if you don't know all that much about her, you get a sense of her just by looking at her picture and being in the place she lived. I mean, she sat in this room and walked in that garden and ate in your dining room. That's amazing to think of, isn't it?"

"I suppose it is, Miss Jones. I've never thought of it, but you are right." She gave Evie an appraising look and took a sip of her gin and tonic before continuing. "Of course, the place has changed over the years, probably more than you would think. People imagine that grand houses like this are fixed in aspic, but they're not, you know. This Mrs. Darcy lived in a Pemberley with no electricity, no telephone line, no plumbing system, and far more servants than you can imagine because it was before they all went to the towns to work in the factories. I suspect that we would be shocked if we could go back and spend a night in her shoes, don't you?"

"When you put it like that, maybe we would."

"And of course, speaking of spending the night...this Mrs. Darcy was well before my husband's American grandmother completely relocated and redesigned the family quarters."

"Really?" Charlie's interest perked up like the ears on a dog.

"Oh, yes. It was James's grandfather—married a tea heiress from Boston, didn't he, darling? She got an association with an old family and a rolling estate, and he got a thumping great dowry to shore up the family finances. She was quite a lady as well—I'm given to believe. These days she would be called "high maintenance," but I don't think people were so cheeky then. Had the whole place stripped and redecorated as soon as she arrived. Installed all manner of mod cons. Took one look at the mistress's chamber and wasn't having any of it. According to James's mother, she didn't like the lack of light in the afternoons, and so that was when the family quarters were moved to the other side of the house."

"So the family quarters were moved from where they would have been during Elizabeth Darcy's lifetime?"

"Oh, yes. Goodness me, Miss Jones, did I not say before? They were moved from the current guest wing. Indeed, my dear, the room that *you* are sleeping in was the mistress's chamber then."

An odd, comforting feeling stole over Evie. She recalled how she had wandered around the room only an hour earlier, naked and warm from the bath. She knew on instinct that Elizabeth had done the same. Somewhere on the edge of her consciousness, Honoria continued.

"It is our best guest room *because* it used to be the mistress's chamber. That is why it is so big and has such a super view. The next room was her sitting room and the one on the other side, which is not actually as nice, was the master's chamber. For myself, I have always thought that set of rooms enchanting, but I am not my husband's grandmother, and the thought of rearranging things again—well—I can't be doing with it."

Charlie began to speak to Honoria about which rooms had been changed over the years, and it sounded as though the mistress's chamber had not been the only victim of the American Mrs. Darcy's idea of a well-planned house. When Evie looked at him, his eyes were alive with suppressed excitement. To see him in the warm light of the Pemberley evening, chatting to Honoria and strangely enervated, moved her. She thought that, when his eyes glanced her way, he might be trying to speak. But since there was no way they could have a private discussion with James and Honoria present, she could hardly ask him what he was trying to say.

Honoria had promised them that they would be spoiled on the last night, and so indeed they were. Dinner was delicious, and the four of them chatted happily until the sky was black with night and a chill crept over Evie's bare arms. The soft light from the chandelier above the table fell on their faces, and by the time the plates were cleared away, even James was telling jokes and suggesting that they move on to port in the drawing room. Evie was about to say, "Yes please" when Charlie surprised her.

"That is kind, Mr. Darcy, thank you. But I think I might turn in. We have to get away rather early in the morning…"

He met her eyes, and she somehow understood that she should follow suit. The Darcys looked crestfallen, but she trusted Charlie, and if he didn't want to stay up with them, then there must be a reason. It occurred to her that he might want to search her room now that he knew it used to be Elizabeth's. And so it was that they drank the last of their wine, thanked their hosts, and began to meander their way up the great staircase towards the guest corridor. As they rounded the corner, Charlie turned and, with a quiet, gentle "shh," placed his hands on her goose-pimpled arms.

"What are you doing?"

He lowered his face to hers.

"We need to go back, Evie."

"What? Go back? But there's nothing down there. I thought you might want to search my room—"

"Shh," he commanded swiftly and gently as he pulled them both into the recess at the top of the stairs. Silently, and with Evie's heart thumping in her chest, they watched James and Honoria potter past on the other side of the landing towards their own bedrooms, James muttering about some weeds in the turning circle. After a moment of pulse-quickening quiet, Charlie leaned in to her and spoke again.

"I don't think there is anything in your room. We can look, but I don't think it's there. We need to go back downstairs."

"Why?"

"Because I've had an idea. Do you remember we said that Hannah would have put it somewhere where it would not be disturbed?"

"Yes…"

"Well, think about it. Where in this house is there a place that is completely safe? A place that is going to stay the same over time? A place that isn't going to be changed around and turned upside down on someone's whim?"

She looked at him blankly. She had drunk more wine than she was used to, and the scent of him was stealing around her.

"Where?"

He looked over her shoulder, seemingly distracted, and in a moment had taken her hand in his and was guiding her back down the stairs and into the darkness beneath. Before long, they were moving through the house without light or sound and at a speed that did not seem real. Together they whipped past the drawing room and the dining room into more Spartan corridors with doors on all sides and unprepossessing portraits, not interesting enough for the main rooms, glaring down at them. Although they had been there before, when they reached the great mahogany door, it took her a moment to process where they were.

"The chapel?"

"Yes, the chapel," he whispered, opening the door and ushering her in. He wrestled with the dusty curtains and flicked on the lights.

"I can't believe I didn't think of it before. It is the only sacred space in the house. It is quiet. It is mostly unoccupied. It is not kept locked, and I don't imagine it ever was. You could put something in here, and if you were careful and hid it properly, it might go completely undetected."

"Clever." Evie looked around the cold, empty cavern. "But where? There's nowhere to hide anything in here."

With that, Charlie began to trace his way around the walls, running his hands around the edge of stone reliefs and framed oil paintings. At the altar, he crouched down and examined the underside and the compartments around the small organ at the back. There were only a few wooden pews, some of them pushed against the back wall. Those that remained on each side of the narrow nave were heavier and appeared to be bolted to the floor.

Charlie bent down and began running his hand along the underside. In the final row on the "bride's side," he looked up at Evie.

"There's something here."

Feeling useless, she joined him on the floor and tried to focus on the underside of the pew.

"It's some sort of box."

Evie lay on her back and slid towards him, dust from the floor gathering on her shoulders.

"It's really big, Charlie. Are you sure it's not just part of the pew?"

"No. Look, it's been screwed on, and there's a weird clasp at this end."

He began to jostle with a dirty, metal handle that was fixed over one end of the box, trying to shake it loose and swearing under his breath. Anxiety welled up inside Evie, and she felt her palms becoming sweaty. She sat up and watched him in the harsh light. Suddenly and without preamble, the handle moved, there was a loud clatter, and a heap of leather-bound books landed on Charlie's chest. He did not seem to be fazed by it.

"Okay. Whatever it is, I think we've found it."

"I think *you've* found it."

He jumped to his feet and quickly turned a few pages.

"This looks like it. Female handwriting. Right period. Yes, look. 'Elizabeth Darcy, December 25, 1817,'" he read from the inside cover, and his finger gently stroked the empty space beneath her name.

"Let's go."

"Where are we going?"

He looked back at her with laughing eyes, the books piled up in his arms. "Well, I thought that, after going through all of this, you might like to read them?"

He was, she knew, teasing her, and she smiled back. "Okay. Let's take them to my room."

They nodded to each other, switched off the lights, closed the door on the dusty, old monument, and were gone.

Chapter 21

April 4, 1821, Holyhead, Wales

We have been travelling through Wales for some time, and the road is so narrow and uneven that I can hardly credit it. Lydia has been in slumber for several hours, and I cannot begrudge it to her after the night we all passed at Pemberley before our departure. Fitzwilliam, I know, would never sleep in a carriage and certainly not with Lydia for company, but he is tired to the bone and stares, misty eyed, out of the windows at the damp, vivid beauty of the country beyond. The splendour of the countryside, I must confess, quite passes me by. I cannot turn my mind from my discussion with Lydia last night. Upon Hannah announcing that my sister, quite unaccountably, was installed in the drawing room at such a late hour of the night, I immediately went to her. When I flew into the room, she was sitting on the chaise staring like a statue at the piano. Her hands, which I have never previously seen still for two moments together, were clasped and motionless in her lap. She turned to me, smiled in a resigned manner, and said, "Hello, Lizzy" as if there were nothing unusual about her appearance.

"Lydia, whatever is it? I thought you were with Jane at Bollington! How did you get here?"

"I hired a carriage, Lizzy. I had to. When you know everything, you will understand."

"Hired a carriage? What on earth for, and how did you pay for it?"

"Oh, I had the money to pay, Lizzy. I have been saving some of the funds you send me out of your pin money for some time, so I had enough. When you hear what I must tell you, you shall not be worrying about carriage bills."

She spoke the words with an odd intonation, and a sense of dread came over me. She looked different, but I could not say how. I moved towards her and sat down beside her on the chaise. She began to fiddle with her wedding ring and bit her bottom lip as she looked at me.

"Lydia, what is it? Is everyone in Hertfordshire well?"

"Oh, yes, they are well."

"It is not Mama?"

"No, it is nothing to do with Mama. Although, if she knew what I must tell you, she would die of shame. As things are, I believe she is fine. Jane is fine. Everyone is fine—except me."

"Lydia, whatever is it?"

She let out a quiet sob, and before I knew what she was about, she had taken my hand and placed it flat against the swell of her belly. I know all of my sisters' figures. I know how they walk, how they sit, and how they look in their undergarments. Lydia and I are alike in body, but even if we were not, I would know the uncompromising hardness of a baby in the belly. It is unmistakable. I fought not to shrink back, not to take my hand away in horror. After a moment, I took her hand in mine and stood.

"Come, let us go to my chambers."

Hannah was in the hall outside, and I asked her to bring some tea and toast to us. As she disappeared in the direction of the kitchens, Lydia asked in a whisper, "Can we trust Hannah?"

"Yes," I said without a moment of hesitation.

When we were in the room with the door closed, I allowed myself to breathe.

"Lydia, how can this be true?"

"How, Lizzy? Well, I believe you know that as well as I."

"Do not be impudent. How can you be sure?"

"Because I have not had my courses for five months. I have been poorly for weeks and weeks. My bosom is much increased as you can see, and as for my belly…well, you have touched it yourself."

"Have you spoken to anyone about this?"

"Yes. When I was visiting with Aunt and Uncle Gardiner last month, I took a carriage to the west of Town and asked in the marketplace where I may find a midwife. I gave a false name, and they directed me to a dreadful, old woman who, for a fee, laid me down upon her floor and felt about me. I should not have wasted my money, Lizzy, for she said nothing that I did not already know. It is true. It is real, and I cannot stop it."

"Anyone else?"

"No. No one. I have been wanting to tell Jane and have even rehearsed it a few times, but it is so hard to get her alone, Lizzy. Miss Bingley is always there, and even when she is not…well, Jane is so *good*, is she not? She is too good to hear such a truth as this. Somehow I simply could not say it to her."

The face of my elder sister appeared before me, and although I was boiling with rage at Lydia's situation, I had some sympathy for her inability to confide in Jane. She is my closest sister, and even I do not know how I should face her were I in such a predicament as this.

"Lydia, I have to ask you this. Who is…responsible"—the word seemed to stick in my throat as I spoke—"for your condition?"

With that question, her curly head turned away, and she spoke through a cry.

"Oh, Lizzy, must you?"

"Yes, I must. Lydia, this man should be made to marry you. I am sure that Mr. Darcy will prevail upon him to do so, but you have to tell us who he is."

"Mr. Darcy shall not prevail upon him to marry me, Lizzy."

I knew it would be cruel to mention that it was he who had procured her first marriage, so I remained silent.

"I am sure he shall, Lydia, and all may be well. But we have to move quickly for we have already lost no little time."

"No, you do not understand. Mr. Darcy shall not prevail upon the father of my child to marry me…because he is already married."

With that, she turned and looked me squarely in the face, the light from the candles bouncing on her plump cheeks and lighting sparks in her eyes. I felt a pain creeping into my temples and a sudden urge to sit.

"Married?" The word came out as a croak. "Oh, Lydia."

There was an endless, agonising silence before I mustered the strength to speak again.

"Where did this happen?"

"In Margate when I was staying with Maria. I met him at a dance and then again at a card party. His wife is unwell."

"How unwell?"

"Not as unwell as I should like I am afraid. But she is sickly and does not come out much in company. I saw him a great deal, Lizzy. There were several gatherings, and then there was a picnic, and then a ball on a local estate. I hardly thought that I should ever have such laughs again, but I did, although I wonder at the price of them now. We had a wonderful time and were so merry. I am sure that I do not need to go any further, Lizzy—you know the manner of these things."

I opened my mouth to deny this calumny, and then thought better of it.

"How many times?"

"Just once. Is that not unlucky?"

There was a light tap upon the door, and Hannah entered the room with a tray of toast and sweet tea. When Hannah had retreated, I placed my hand on Lydia's knee.

"You must eat."

"I am not hungry."

"Well, try."

I felt my patience growing short and battled to remain calm. I thought of Fitzwilliam, no doubt sitting in the next room, and wanted to feel his breath on my face.

"Are you going to tell Mr. Darcy?"

"Of course."

She hung her head slightly and sighed. I knew it must be done, however disastrous the news. I recalled the dreadful things that I had said to him, the ill-considered fictions I had accused him of only an hour before, and my insides sank. The sight of my husband surrounded by my family came to me in a flash, and Mama's silliest remarks and loudest shrieks roared through my memory like a fire. They were as nothing compared with this, and I prayed that the scandal and thoughtlessness of it would not break us. Would this outrage push him too far? There was nothing for it but to speak and find out. Fitzwilliam always knew what to do, so I slipped into the next room, and closing the door quietly behind me, I told him.

Was he shocked? I believe he was. He blinked, pursed his lips, and straightened his back with a deep breath. However, just as I anticipated that he would rake his fingers through his hair and turn his back to the room in his accustomed manner, he took me by surprise. Noiselessly, he moved towards me, took me in his arms, and kissed my head. After some time in this unexpectedly calmed state, he began to ask questions. Who was the man, and where did he reside? What was known of his circumstances? Was it known how long Lydia had before the babe was expected? Was she well in body if not in mind? Did anyone else know? I answered him as best I could.

"You say that she came here from Bollington in a hired carriage?"

"Yes."

"And is it still here?"

"No, she said that she paid in advance, and the carriage left directly she alighted. It is probably stopping for the night in Lambton."

"Hmm. Who at Bollington knew she was coming here?"

"Nobody. She left a note for Jane to say that she had been invited to stay with the widow of one of Wickham's fellow officers. Jane must have believed her, or we would have had an express already."

"I see. Forgive me, but I must ask. Is it—is it obvious? Are her circumstances plain to the casual observer?"

"Not quite but they shall be soon. It was plain to me, but that was because I felt about her middle. A person who knows her well may see it—but a stranger? At this moment, I do not believe that she is large enough to be unambiguous."

"Well that is a temporary advantage."

He began to pace the room, his long limbs casting moving shadows on the carpet.

"And what about her journey here? Did she stay at an inn?"

"Yes. She stayed one night at an inn near Grantham, the White Horse. I do not believe we have ever stopped there."

"I have, Elizabeth, before we were married. She could have done worse. It is a reasonably respectable place, and there are many people coming and going—probably too many to notice a young woman who does not wish to be seen. What about here? Who at Pemberley knows she is here?"

"You and I and Hannah. And James. He let her in. I imagine he was just about to retire."

There was a moment of aching silence, and I felt his hand stroke the small of my back with such care I could have wept.

"Would you like me to pour you a whiskey, Fitzwilliam?"

"No, thank you, Elizabeth. I believe that I shall need a clear head for what is before us, and so shall you."

I swallowed hard. "What is in your mind, sir?"

"Well, it seems to me that there is not much time. The babe shall be in the world in a matter of months. The thing is in progress, and he or she shall wait for no man. If Lydia could pass for a maiden today, she shall not be able to do so next week or the week after. It is good fortune that she wears a wedding ring, although of course anyone of your family's acquaintance knows that she is long widowed. Time is extremely short I am afraid."

"Yes." I agreed, but I confess, I knew not where he was leading me.

"We have only one thing on our side, and that is that nobody knows she is here except Hannah, whom we can trust completely. And James. He is a good young man, and if I speak to him personally, I am confident he will be silent."

"But others will realise she is here in the morning. I cannot keep it from the staff for she must sleep somewhere, and she must eat and wash. And Lydia is Lydia; wherever she is, she is known."

"I know. That is why I propose that we escort her somewhere else."

My heart sank. Was it in his mind that my sister be put away somewhere—that she and her shame be hidden in some far-off, half-maintained place where nobody shall know her or her connection to us?

"Do you mean somewhere on the estate?"

"No, Elizabeth. I do not believe there is anywhere she could be accommodated comfortably and properly without causing talk. The people here are very loyal, but if your sister, approaching two years a widow, appears heavy with child with no warning and no husband, it is inevitable that she, and we, shall be the subject of gossip. People are people, and they will make connections that are there to be made. I cannot completely protect her against that. She and the child would be at a great disadvantage."

"Well, what do you propose then? This man is married already, Fitzwilliam, and he cannot have two wives."

"No, he cannot. In any case, even if it were possible, it may not be best. He has a wife already, and yet he has done this. When I paid Wickham to marry her, I took him for a scoundrel, but I credited him with having some affection for her, albeit not enough to have treated her properly. But this is a different matter. We could not in conscience force her into matrimony with a man who could do such a thing."

"Well, what do you suggest? Do you know of some respectable man who would take her in her current condition?"

"I am afraid I do not. If I did, I would be beating a path to his door."

The clock ticked on the mantle, and tension climbed the walls like mist. Fitzwilliam's voice broke through the fog.

"Lydia needs to depart from here as soon as possible, preferably before the household awakes. We cannot send her alone, so I propose, Elizabeth, that you and I go with her."

"But where?"

"Do you recall that I mentioned a problem at Rosschapel?"

"Yes."

"Well, the dispute with the tenant has been going on for some time. I have not bored you with it. You have had much to concern yourself with, and as you know, I do not like to have my time with you sullied with talk of business. That is why I did not tell you about Avery. But the fact is that it has been a thorn in my side for some time, and my steward in Ireland has been requesting that I visit the estate for months. He has written to me this very week to say that he has finally, and at no little expense, evicted the tenant but that the property has been left in a distressed condition by their occupation. The fact is that whatever damage has been done can be repaired before our arrival."

"*Our* arrival?"

"Yes. It is in my mind that we take Lydia to Rosschapel for her to have her child. Nobody there knows her or anything about her. The house is in a secluded part of the country outside Dublin. We can take Hannah. I will write to my Irish steward directly and request that he ready the place. Once we arrive, we can obtain such assistance as Lydia may require. She can have her babe in secrecy and comfort."

"And what then? I am by no means persuaded that Lydia could cope living alone in another land, particularly with a child."

"Neither am I, and I do not suggest it. No. Lydia and the child shall return to Pemberley with us after a suitable period—I would suggest as soon as they are fit to make the journey."

"But then—"

"We cannot send Lydia away from here again. It was remiss of us to let her leave before. The fact that she is…difficult…is not an excuse. She should be here for her own protection. She can live well and safely and be sheltered from the excesses of her own character. You can have the comfort of knowing that she is coming to no harm. As for the child, well, we cannot expose the poor creature. If it is known that it is illegitimate then its life will be blighted by it."

He stopped and looked at me in a searching manner. Words galloped through my overcrowded mind quicker than I could give them voice. He continued, untroubled by confusion.

"If the child is a girl, I suggest that we pass her off as our own, Elizabeth. She can be a sister to the girls. They are four in number already; let them be five. You can say, if anyone is impertinent enough to ask, that you did not realise you were with child until after we departed and that the child came slightly early or some such. I am sure you can somehow dissemble and pass it off creditably."

"And if it is a son?"

"If it is a son...I have said already this night that I have not given up on our having a son of our own, and I am not bequeathing Pemberley to the child of an unknown stranger. If I do not have a son, then the estate will go to Anne. On that, I am implacable. If Lydia's child is a boy, we will have to invent a story."

He paced the room further and brought his hand to his chin in thought. For myself, I felt somewhat lightheaded. Before long, Fitzwilliam continued. "I suggest that we say he is the orphan of some eminent person in Ireland connected to Rosschapel, and for that reason, I felt a sense of obligation towards him. He can live with us and be treated as a member of our family in every particular except that he would not be treated as an heir."

"You would do that—undertake such a thing for my sister?"

"Is *your* sister not also *my* sister, Elizabeth? In any case, you must realise that, as much as I respect your family, I think only of you. If there is a thing in the world I would not do for you, I do not believe I have found it yet."

With that, he looked at me and smiled a subtle smile. I shall keep the memory of it in my heart forever.

Chapter 22

April 7, 1821, Rosschapel, Ireland

We have journeyed three days together to reach this place. The sea crossing from Holyhead stirred my stomach although Lydia and Fitzwilliam appeared to be unaffected by the awful movement of the sea and the rushing sound of the waves about us. The air over the water was chilly indeed, but now that we have the dry land of Ireland under our feet, it is crisp rather than cold. The light—so bright—cracks across the sky, and I have fancied myself in a dream. Odd sounds come from people's mouths, but I fight not to be intimidated by unknown dialects, for we must appear to them to be very strange in our turn. The road from Dublin to Rosschapel has tested our carriage sorely, but it has survived, as have we. Fitzwilliam handed me and then Lydia out of the carriage in front of the house, and I was not entirely surprised to see that he had downplayed its attractions. Lydia and I turned our faces to its mellow, mustard façade as Fitzwilliam motioned for us to follow him in. A faded, wind-battered rose garden surrounded by a low wall and a pile of abandoned wooden beams to the side of the house caught my eye as we advanced towards the front door.

"How pretty this is, Lizzy," said my sister as we were greeted by the small staff and ushered into the hall.

The ceilings here are low, but the rooms are large, and I believe that a great deal of work has gone into preparing for our arrival. I note that there are not many people here: a couple of maids and footmen. When I look around, somebody behind me is sweeping a corner of the room. A young woman places a vase of flowers in the drawing room as I enter it. She curtseys and looks away from me. Lydia plumps down on a seat by the window and gladly accepts the cup of tea that I hand her.

"Is not this nice?" she asks, her pretty face upturned towards me, her slippered feet peeping out from her travelling gown.

For myself, I resolve to conclude that it is nice. The house is unfamiliar but comfortable. And large. While Lydia rests in the afternoon, I have wandered from room to room, and I do not believe that I have found them all yet. Fitzwilliam has taken tea with us and answered some of Lydia's many questions on the neighbourhood, but now he is gone to meet with his Irish steward, and I do not know when he shall return. As he left, he brushed a kiss on the inside of my wrist. I have investigated our chambers and found them to be quite comfortable. I have tucked a rug around Lydia as she sleeps on the chaise and noticed that her poor ankles are awfully swollen. My sister made comfortable, I have busied myself by writing to Mrs. Reynolds and to Nanny as well as Mama and Jane. To Jane, I have confided the partial truth that Lydia is with us, but I have not said why for fear that the letter may fall into the wrong hands. This is a story for the lips and the ears only.

On a short walk in the garden, I noticed that the wooden beams have disappeared from the front of the house, and a young man in a wide-brimmed hat is attending to the poor roses. I smiled and nodded to him and hoped that he understood my gratitude. These tasks complete, I ventured into the kitchen where I found Hannah sitting at the great oak table, conversing, apparently easily with the cook. They were setting about preparing supper. Somewhat unsure of the formality or otherwise of the house, I sat and looked on. I was pleased that I did for, in light conversation of the weather and our journey and the state of our horses, further time was spent. I thought of my children at Pemberley and pushed my distress at our separation as far inside myself as I could reach. Later, when Lydia had retired to bed, I read to Fitzwilliam, and we sat together on the chaise, our arms touching in the flicking light of the fire.

"I am sorry there is no pianoforte, Elizabeth. I will have one delivered from Dublin."

"There is no need for that, Fitzwilliam. It would be too extravagant. I shall improve my singing and manage quite well without your going to the expense of a new instrument. You are too generous with me already."

"I think of myself as well as you." He kissed the top of my head. "If we are to be here, far from home and the children, then I should like things to be as familiar as possible."

"I take it that you are responsible for the wood clearing and gardening that has taken place today?"

"Yes. I had hoped these things would have been attended to before we arrived, but I understand from O'Leary, the steward, the former tenants have caused such trouble in the village that many of the people refused to work here. That is why the staff is so small. I have set about remedying this. The fact is that if people are treated well and paid properly then they shall be loyal and be willing to work."

"I am sure that is right. And in the meantime, we shall manage quite well. Hannah has made a friend of the cook, and the remaining staff appear pleasant."

I returned his kiss, and we sat in companionable silence for some time before we retired.

THE NEXT DAY WAS MUCH THE SAME, AND SO THE DAYS AT ROSSCHAPEL seemed to pass by like clouds—the same, small acts of routine repeated, and the same, small cast of faces for company. Fitzwilliam came and went to meet with his steward and various others. Lydia ate and slept between walks in the garden and reminiscences of Longbourn. Hannah sat in the kitchen, letting out my sister's gowns and gathering local information between attending to us both. I met with each of the maids and the footmen and those working in the garden and thanked them for their assistance. I sat at my desk while Lydia dozed and sought to commit all of their names to memory.

When not many weeks had passed, Lydia did indeed grow to a size and condition that could not be disguised. The narrative spun to outsiders by Fitzwilliam, to the servants by Hannah, and by me to the small number of local ladies who called on me was that my poor sister had been widowed last month and that, for the sake of her health, we took refuge in this quiet place. Hannah made enquiries, and before long, the local midwife visited us. She was a kindly lady who had the air of a woman who knew her business. She spoke quickly and with a thick brogue, but between Hannah and me, we were able to make reasonable sense of her advice. She advised soda bread, and so, soda bread Lydia ate.

"What peculiar foods are favoured here, Lizzy!" she exclaimed as she chewed her way through it, disconsolately.

That night, before I retired, I looked in on Lydia, who had been too tired to stay awake after supper. Pausing in the draughty corridor for a moment, I pushed the great oak door of her chamber, and my eyes struggled to find the outline of her bed in the darkness. I crept across the carpet, straining to hear the rhythm of her breathing, and was surprised by her voice.

"Lizzy, is that you?"

"Yes. I only wished to check on you. You seemed so fatigued at supper; I am surprised that you are awake."

I sat softly on the side of the bed and stroked her blanketed arm as the small light from the passage cast shadows on her pale face.

"You should try to sleep."

She sighed and turned onto her back.

"I know, Lizzy, I try. But I cannot." She sat up, and her long hair hung about her shoulders.

"Are you uncomfortable? Have you tried lying on your side?"

"I am afraid."

I exhaled and straightened the scratchy blanket atop her, thinking.

"Afraid of the birth?"

"Afraid of the birth, of the child, of what we shall do, of everything."

There was a catch in her voice as she spoke, and I wrapped my arms about her and drew her to me.

"Oh, Lydia, you shall do very well, I am sure. Our mama has had five children, has she not? And I have had four, and are we not alike in the body? Please try to rest your mind on it. I shall not leave you, and the midwife will be here and Hannah as well."

"Well, it sounds dreadful to me. When I think of it, I can scarce believe it is even possible."

I smiled in the darkness, for I recalled that feeling myself when I was big with Anne. I was about to stand when I felt the grip of her hand pulling on mine.

"Lizzy?"

"Yes."

"When—when the baby is born, will you promise me that you shall take her directly? That you shall be her mother from the first moment."

"Oh, Lydia, let us leave it undecided. You may not feel the same when the time comes, and your baby may be a boy."

"I am sure she is a girl, Lizzy. And if you are to be her mama, then it should be from the start."

I felt her body shake as she began to sob, and I held her tighter.

Chapter 23

During our months at Rosschapel, time seemed in no great hurry to pass us. We each attended to our tasks, and the household blossomed. Before long, there were several new faces within our doors and out of them, whatever damage had been done by the former tenants seemingly rectified by Fitzwilliam's efforts. A small pianoforte arrived on a cart from Dublin and was a great distraction for me. I wrote often to Pemberley, and my hands shook as I opened letters from Nanny and Mrs. Reynolds. I noticed even my husband hovered about me when he knew I had received word from home, and it was a comfort to know that he missed them as I did. As she grew full large, Lydia lost much of her energy, and apart from short walks upon my arm in the smartened rose garden, she hardly ventured from the drawing room and her chamber. In the evenings before bed, she asked me to brush out her hair as I had when we were girls, and I found this to be a most relaxing occupation. As her body expanded, the dramas of her character seemed to die down, and she grew quiet and oddly restful. Excepting the appalling scandal of her situation, I smiled to think of what our sisters or parents would say if they could see the quiet creature she had become. She did not speak to me again of how we would treat the babe when it was born, and I did not want to distress her by raising the subject. She knew that she and her child would always have a home at Pemberley, and that, I judged, was enough.

We had been at Rosschapel for many weeks when Lydia's time came upon her. It was a Sunday afternoon, and the heat of the day was beginning to ebb. Fitzwilliam was out riding while my sister and I sat in the sunny patch of the drawing room. I had put down my book, and I was thinking of home when Lydia's hand grasped my wrist, and she said in a breathy whisper, "Lizzy, I believe it is happening."

It was happening. We did not retire to her chamber immediately but sat for some time talking gently between pains, I encouraging my sister to breathe easy and lean back into the comfort of the chaise. After a short time, I summoned Hannah, who has of course been present at the birth of all of my own children, to join us. After she, too, had made some enquiries of Lydia, she hurried off to send for the midwife. Later, Hannah and I assisted Lydia up the stairs and into her chamber where we eased her out of her clothes and onto her bed. Gradually, the matter proceeded, and as time passed, the respite between her pains grew shorter. We encouraged my sister into various positions upon the bed, rubbed her back, and spoke softly between her cries. She clasped her sweaty hands about my shoulders, hung her head, and screamed out my name like a woman distracted. With the curtains drawn and the fire blazing, the room was a furnace. Heat seemed to rise all around me, and reds and oranges cast about the walls like so many flags in the wind. Awful noises came from my sister, and her face shimmered with perspiration. For all of this, the midwife appeared reasonably content, and so time passed, the light going out of the sky behind the curtain, the chill of night creeping over the world outside the window. When it came time for the babe to leave her body, Lydia lay back on her many pillows and gripped my hand with great ferocity. Hannah and the midwife attended her at the nether end, and after a period of straining and crying out, the thing took place.

"The baby is coming, Mrs. Wickham. Push one more time," said the midwife, looking up at my sister, Hannah lending her voice to this entreaty from behind. An odd, keening kind of sound broke forth from my sister, and it was followed by a gasp from the other ladies and then an infant's triumphant cry.

"It's a daughter, madam," pronounced the midwife as she swept the child up and, wiping its face, wrapped it in blankets to make a parcel. Lydia had not released my hand, and her eyes flicked to me in confusion and hesitation as the woman advanced towards her, offering her child for an embrace. I knew very well what she wanted.

"Hold her, Lydia. You must do what your heart tells you."

A wide, weary smile spread against her face as the babe, eyes closed and face mottled, was deposited in her arms. After some time looking lovingly and bestowing light kisses on the infant's forehead, she invited me to touch her, which I did. She remarked upon the child's beauty and perfection in a hushed, reverential voice, quite unlike her own. I agreed and swept a damp curl back from Lydia's face.

"Do you have a name for her?"

She looked at me quizzically and hesitated before speaking.

"Yes I do, Lizzy. I would like her to be Victoria. Victoria Darcy. Does that not sound smart?"

The little girl gave a slight twitch of her face, and I could not but laugh.

"It certainly does."

At length, and in the hazy heat of the chamber, I became aware of some activity about me. It was like a bee buzzing just above my head. At the corner of my vision, there was Hannah's gown dashing around, her arms full of linen, her hands moving in great haste and agitation. Then the midwife and other maids were with her, but I knew not what they were about. I have brought four daughters of my own forth, and I know the way of things. Their hurrying about and strained expressions, I could not account for.

"Hannah?" I was deliberately quiet.

Lydia did not hear me and continued to focus on her baby. Hannah's head shot up, and I shall never forget the look of fear upon her face.

"Mrs. Darcy." She inclined her head slightly, and I stood and went to her. I wanted to gasp but forced myself to refrain. Between my sister's legs, there was a lake of blood, red-stained linen piled on the floor beside the end of the bed and more in the making. The midwife's apron was a horrific sight as was Hannah's pinafore. Maids were sent for water and sweet tea and more cloth. Voices were hushed but panicked to the core. I addressed the midwife in a whisper.

"What does this mean?"

A fresh gush came forth, and I reeled back on my heels as the midwife and Hannah tried to stem it. Lydia's face glowed white before me, and each end of her body seemed to be like two different worlds. When the midwife turned back to me, she was frank.

"Madam, this is very bad."

I felt myself begin to shake and clenched my fists to steady myself. Hannah and the midwife exchanged some words that I did not quite hear.

"Hannah? What is being said?"

She blinked as she looked at me, and there was a moment of silence before she spoke in an almost soundless whisper.

"Madam, Mrs. Reidy does not think Mrs. Wickham will live. She says the bleeding is too fierce."

"What can be done? There must be something that can be done. Call for a physician."

I felt my voice climbing like a scale. I looked at the midwife, but she looked back at my sister on the bed.

"The nearest physician be in Dublin. Even if some person in the house rode for him this minute, he would not arrive in time. And it would profit your sister naught. If he was here, he could do nothing. Nothing can be done. This is a bad bleed, madam. She cannot live with this loss. She shall likely pass out before long, so you and Miss Tavener here need to take the baby."

The harshness of her words chilled me, and blood rushed to my ears like a wave in a storm. And yet, I battled to be calm.

"That is as may be. Hannah, please call for the physician anyway. While there is a possibility that he will help, we should summon him. Send Bobby, the groom. He is a young, fast rider."

I returned to Lydia's side and stroking her arm, I kissed her cheek.

"You have done very well, Lydia. What a bonny baby girl!"

She looked towards me and smiled. Her mouth opened slightly as if to reply but she spoke not. The green of her eyes had lost their characteristic expression and her left arm had fallen away from its place under the baby's legs.

"I believe she has your face shape." My voice cracked. "Just like Mama's. And what fine hands she has. Are they not the beginnings of pianist's fingers?"

Lydia's left hand lay palm up on the blanket, and the child slipped slightly against the cushions that Hannah had piled up against her right side. I looked at my sister's face, motionless in the odd light and overwhelming heat, and thought of her laughing louder than she should and careering around the ballroom at Netherfield. I recalled the sight of her parading about Meryton on Wickham's arm and pushing Kitty off the swing in the Longbourn garden. I could not credit that she could be so still now. From somewhere far away, I was brought back to the present by Hannah's voice.

"Madam, shall you take Miss Victoria now?"

Hannah leant over and gently took the child, who had begun to squirm slightly. She jiggled her around for comfort and straightened her shawl before kneeling down before me.

"Madam, do you feel able to take her? I shall attend to Mrs. Wickham."

I nodded, and into my arms she placed the warm, solid babe who was now my daughter in every sense but the biological. My arms tightened around her, and I fought the tears that were welling up in my eyes. Seeing Hannah and Mrs. Reidy hurrying about my sister, my vision blurred. I was silent as Hannah straightened out my sister's body and closed her eyes. Mrs. Reidy left the room with an armful of bloody rags, and in spite of the horror of it, my senses seemed to awaken.

"Hannah?"

"Yes, madam."

"Thank you."

There was a beat of silence before she smiled and looked at her feet.

"Do we have a wet nurse here? I believe this baby shall need feeding shortly."

"Mrs. Reidy says there is a lady in the village. She is on her way."

I touched her hand lightly as she moved out of the room. I know not how long I sat in the dark, hot chamber with my sister and our child, but it was probably for a shorter period than it seemed. After some time had passed, the child began to move around in my arms and grow discontented. I heard steps and voices in the hall beyond, and Hannah returned with a lady from the village who took the baby into the next room to nurse her. I wondered how many hours after my sister's death we could expect the arrival of the physician, who would need to be paid and accommodated for the night. I made a note in my mind to attend to it. Unsteadily, I rose, and before departing the room, I kissed my sister's cheek for the final time. The air in the corridor was icy cold on my face as I closed the door behind me, and my shaky hand struggled to turn the handle.

From some small distance away, Fitzwilliam advanced towards me and said, "I know," as he folded his arms about me.

Chapter 24

We buried Lydia in the village churchyard. Although ladies do not usually attend funerals, on this occasion I did. We were far from home, and matters were far from regular. I wished to attend my sister's burial, and Fitzwilliam did nothing to dissuade me. The sky was grey, and the wind howled mercilessly around us. The words of the liturgy were spoken, but I hardly heard them. After the thing was concluded, his warm hand helped me back into the carriage. As we pulled away from the lychgate, I turned back and saw my sister's burial place vanishing to a pinprick on the horizon.

"Fitzwilliam?"

He turned to me and smiled kindly.

"I believe I should like to go home."

"Then you shall."

Again, a physician was summoned from Dublin, and he pronounced that, provided that she be kept warm, Victoria would be safe to travel to Derbyshire some weeks hence. Hannah attended to the packing of our belongings, and Mr. Darcy's local steward believed that he had found a new tenant for the property. I visited Mrs. Reidy at home to thank her for her services to my sister, but in a bid to fight the melancholy that threatened to consume me, I did not revisit the chamber in which she had died. I had written to Jane with a story that Lydia had died of a local fever. It shamed me to write lies to her, but there it was. She was tasked with telling Mama and Papa and Mary and poor Kitty, a challenge I did not envy. It had always been my plan to inform Jane of the truth in person at some private moment, but

Fitzwilliam was not in favour of this. On our last day at Rosschapel, he and I sat in the drawing room, the late afternoon sun spilling through the leaded windows, a sleeping Victoria in my arms, and he took up the subject.

"If you wish to tell your sister, Elizabeth, then you must, but I would urge you to think on it. Jane will have to tell Bingley. The more people who know, the greater danger there is that one day some unreliable person will discover the truth."

My mind flew to Caroline Bingley chattering away in Jane's wake, feathers bobbing, lurid colours flashing, her eyes primed for the misfortunes of others.

"The truth is that I now regret having told Galbraith. It never occurred to me that we would be returning home without Lydia. I thought that we would need his help with legalities, but now that we have lost our sister, nothing shall be necessary. Fortunately, he is completely trustworthy, and if I instruct him to destroy my letters on the subject, then I know he shall do so. Although it is not necessary for him to know, I do not believe it shall pose a problem."

"Do you suppose Jane a problem, sir?"

"No, of course not. I do not mean that. It is not that I do not trust Jane. I do trust her. It is more that I think the smallest number of people possible should know this truth. We have to think of Victoria. Think of the impact on her were this to be known."

He looked at her tiny form, and a shadow of softness played across his face. She shifted slightly in my arms, and a corner of her blanket fell away.

"Do you think she is warm enough? Shall I call for another shawl?"

"She is fine, Fitzwilliam. But if you wish to hold her yourself to verify this, I shall not betray your secret."

He smiled, knowing a tease, and offered his arms into which I gently transferred Victoria.

"I hope you can accept her, Fitzwilliam, as if she were your daughter…"

"It is not a matter of hoping, Elizabeth. There is nothing for which to hope. I do accept her. I accept her, and I love her. Let us resolve that Victoria is my daughter and yours and say no more about it?"

He looked at me searchingly, and his thumb absently stroked Victoria's plump cheek. I spoke not, and he continued.

"No doubt in the next few days, we will need to discuss matters. We need to agree on how we shall present this when we return to Pemberley. There is the question of dealing with your family and the children. There is also the fact that you have been greatly injured in your feelings. You have lost a sister and gained a child, and you shall need to speak of it if you are to survive the cruelty of the thing. But may I suggest that those discussions being had, we say nothing further, even to each other? If we live it, then it shall become the truth. If we talk of these events beyond the time that it is necessary, then we run all manner of risks. We risk being overheard or raising the suspicions of others. We risk our own feelings. You are one for turning matters over, Elizabeth, but sometimes, it is as well to be silent. Live as if Victoria is your child and mine, and she shall be."

I reached over and kissed him.

September 27, 1821, Dublin, Ireland

THE INN AT WHICH WE ARE SPENDING OUR LAST NIGHT IN IRELAND IS HALF in darkness even with all the candles lit, and the ceilings are so low as to whisper above my head. In the early morning, we shall board the boat to Holyhead and be gone. Hannah is presently in her room with Victoria and the Irish wet nurse we have with us. I hear my dear maid through the wall, sorting and shuffling, no doubt ensuring that all the right things are in the right trunks for the English part of our journey home. It is a journey that cannot be too soon completed. My letters to Mrs. Reynolds and Nanny and Georgiana shall have arrived before us, and my heart sings to think that within days my eyes shall rest on their recipients.

Our rooms here were the best available, but they are rather dark, and noises creep up from below on all sides. I hear the sound of men's voices in the bar, and a dog barks without. The clunking of the great gates opening and a horse's hooves upon the uneven ground of the unmade road outside echo in my ears. I pull my shawl tighter about me and wonder where my husband is and when he shall return. He said he had business in the bar, but I cannot think what it is at this hour when we are to stay in this land for a matter of mere hours. I shiver, close my book that I have long ceased to read, and just as I am about to snuff out the candle, I hear his familiar gait approach. His appearance in the light of the door makes me start forward in our bed.

"Do not disturb yourself, Elizabeth."

"Is all well, sir? You have been below stairs a long while."

He sat on my side of the bed and brushed my arms with his warm hands.

"I am sorry to be so long, but I hope it shall not be wasted time. I have been speaking to an associate of the captain and believe that I have secured us the best cabin for tomorrow's sailing. I am afraid that I cannot predict the weather, but if it is bad, we shall have all the comfort the boat can provide. I know you did not enjoy the sea journey here. Now of course, we also have to think of Victoria."

I pictured my restrained husband in the raucous bar below, bargaining with Irish sailors for a better berth, and I wanted to fold him up in my arms. I held his hand, and our fingers knitted together.

"Thank you. You are too kind to us."

"No, I am not. There is no kindness that you do not earn every moment."

He looked up, and a light in his eyes sparked. The air of the room shifted, and suddenly, something new and familiar was at large. His hand went to my shawl, a mauve affair from Mama, and deftly, he removed it, never taking his eyes from mine. The soft side of his thumb moved over my cheeks and eyelids, and my pulse quickened in a beat. I heard a roar of laughter from the bar below and the muffled sounds of tankards crashing down on wood as his lips found mine in the semi-darkness. He moved to me, and his hands moved down my cotton-clad body in a motion I knew well. He pulled at my nightgown.

"May I?"

When I was a younger woman, learning his touch, I had nodded and shuffled about to allow this custom. As a young bride, I believe I closed my eyes. But now, in my middle years and having seen life break forth and expire, I fixed him with a stare to match his own and spoke clearly. "Yes." My gown removed, he beheld me in the flickering light against the thin pillows and unfamiliar bed linen.

"Beautiful."

I could not but laugh at this.

"Why do you laugh, Elizabeth?"

"Because I love to laugh, and…well, because it is humorous to hear such a word on your lips upon beholding such a sight."

"Humorous?"

"Yes. Once, it was true maybe. But you could not possibly think such a thing now, Mr. Darcy. I am not a girl of one and twenty."

"You are not. You are much more."

"That, I know too well! Much more in terms of years traversed!"

"I did not mean that."

"I have had children. I am far from perfect. I do not expect you to pretend, Fitzwilliam."

"I am not pretending. Every part of you is as I would have it. The changes wrought by the years, they are nothing to me."

With this, his lean body crashed against me, and I felt his lips press upon mine—upon all the parts of my person. Candlelight caught the silvery threads in his hair, and my fingers pressed into the flesh of his arms, his back, his shoulders, his face. The mark of them shall always be there, known only to us. When he said my name, tears sprang from my eyes. Was this relief or grief delayed? Was it the unvarnished joy of loving and being loved in return? To know him so well and still to be touched by him in darkness and light is surely the greatest fortune of all.

Chapter 25

Pemberley, 19 September 2014

Charlie read the last sentence aloud, closed the book, and looked up from his seat by the dressing table. Elizabeth's journals were piled up beside him, dusty and a little worn but essentially well preserved. Evie lay back on the bed, barefoot and in her jeans and T-shirt, trying to digest the words. The black of the night pressed on the windows like thick soup, and she had no idea of the time. He had not read it all; there was so much. He had focussed on the dates around the time that Victoria was conceived and then born. Now that she knew the truth of her descent, she felt unaccountably shocked by it. Charlie's voice broke through the muddy silence.

"So you were right...about Elizabeth, I mean."

She was silent for a moment and rolled over onto her side to face him across the room.

"I was right that she was faithful. But she wasn't my fifth great grandmother—her sister Lydia was. And my fifth great grandfather was a complete unknown. So, it is true that I am not a Darcy at all. Not even a poor and distantly related one."

She smiled, and he smiled back.

"It's okay, Evie, because we have it now. No one need ever know."

"Except you and me."

Charlie inhaled and looked down at his feet before raising his gaze to meet hers.

"Your secret's safe with me. Surely, you know that by now?"

She did know. She focussed on his shadowy figure sitting across the room and felt a slight dizziness. *"The unvarnished joy of loving and being loved in return."* Evie let those words turn around her mind. She sat up on the bed and stretched. The air in the room was crisper than before, and they looked at each other in silence. From somewhere, a question cracked open. It ricocheted around in the space between them like a firecracker. What was this thing, and where had it come from? *"Still to be touched by him in darkness and light."* A voice inside Evie spoke, and she felt bold—bolder than she ever recalled. Knowing that she had to act quickly or not act at all, she stood, walked across the floor, and stopped in front of him. Charlie looked from her bare toes on the carpet to her blonde hair falling across her face, and moved, seemingly on instinct. He stood up and, wrapping his arms around her, kissed her lips. It amazed Evie that she did not feel shyness or embarrassment or any of the other creatures of loneliness and insecurity with which she was so familiar. She did not. She reached her hands up to his stubbly face and kissed him back. His hands roamed around her body from the edge of her breasts, along her slim waist, and around her bottom, and she was on fire. Hurriedly and intertwined, they stumbled towards the high bed where he sat her on the edge and fixed her with a searching, almost unbelieving stare.

"Yes?"

With one movement and without taking her eyes from his face, she peeled up the bottom of her T-shirt and swept it over her head. He observed her perched on the edge of the bed in her bra and jeans, cheeks flushed, hair ruffled by his hands, and she knew she had made herself plain enough. He pushed her back against the covers and the excess of pillows, and in the dim light of Elizabeth's bedroom, he slipped off the rest of her clothes and then his own. The feeling of his naked body above hers and the sound of his voice in her ear electrified her. Afterwards, they lay facing each other in the massive bed, his hand resting on the side of her tummy.

"If I knew it was going to have that effect, I would have read aloud to you before."

She smiled at this and stroked his bare chest.

"You do have a lovely voice."

"Thank you. You have a lovely everything."

She rolled to him and played with the curls in his hair, her breasts squashed against the side of his body. They regarded one another in silence for a moment before she spoke again.

"Now, you are not allowed to avoid answering my questions when you are actually in bed with me."

"Really?" He raised his eyebrows.

"Really. So, I want to know about you. You know everything about me."

He began to kiss her neck and mumbled, "Not enough."

"Stop deflecting me. You do know everything. You mapped out things about me before I even knew your name. You know who my great, great, great, great, great grandparents weren't. You've been to my house. You've met Clemmie. You've even seen me naked, and there aren't many people in the world who've seen me naked."

"You've seen me naked too, Evie."

"I know, and that"—she paused to kiss his cheek—"was its own reward. But, I still think you owe me some information."

"What information do you want?" he asked, stroking her hair. The gentle pressure of his hand soothed her. She knew that he was distracting her, avoiding discussion, and she wasn't going to let him get away with it.

"Just—you know—who you are, what you're about. That kind of thing. How on earth you managed to end up doing what you do."

"Sounds a bit deep. Can't we just enjoy each other?"

"I don't even know how old you are. When is your birthday?" She paused for a moment. "What happened to your dad?"

He rolled onto his back and swept his hair back from his forehead with his hand.

"Now that really is deep. You sure you want to know now?"

She rested her arm across his chest. "Yes."

"Okay. Well, I'm thirty-four. My birthday was the eighth of June."

"Hmm." She planted a soft kiss on his chest.

"My dad was a vicar in an inner-city parish in Hackney. He was an amazing guy. He was kind and intelligent and forgiving, and he always saw the best in people. He was willing to help people the world turned their backs on. He didn't want wealth. He didn't want glory."

"He sounds pretty saintly."

"He *was* pretty saintly. He even forgave me for not being as good as he was."

"Did he get ill?"

"No. He died when a young drug addict he had been trying to help stabbed him outside his church and left him for dead."

There was a moment of silence before Evie found the presence of mind to speak.

"Oh." It sounded inadequate to her ear. "How old were you?"

"Eighteen. Mum had had to give up work a couple of years before because of her legs. It turned out that Dad's church pension wasn't enough to keep a dormouse. And we couldn't stay in the vicarage without a vicar. So…"

She waited, but he said nothing.

"So…?"

"So, I had met this guy who ran a private detective agency. He seemed to do pretty well, and he had given me some holiday work. He had more work than he could cope with, so he offered me a job. I couldn't see any other way out, so I took it. I rented a flat for Mum and me to live in. I told Cambridge I wouldn't be coming. I got down to work. No job was too hard for me; no hours were too long. I just worked. It went well. I earned enough to keep us afloat, and then when I started my own business, the money really started rolling in. I bought my flat and a little house in Berkshire for my mum to be near her sisters. I took on staff. I rented an office. The problem with money is that it makes you need more of the same."

"You don't sound like you love it."

"I don't love it." He looked at her hard, and in the dim light, she tried to read his face, as he seemed able to read hers. "Now," he said, pulling her closer, "don't you think you have had enough confessions out of me for one day?"

She pulled her head back and looked at him questioningly.

"Do you mean what you said to me in the drawing room? Yesterday."

CHARLIE TIGHTENED HIS GRIP ON HER WARM BODY AND HOPED. IT DID not escape him that she had said nothing of how she felt about him. He wanted to ask what it all meant, but he didn't dare. Would they get in the car in a few hours' time and pretend this had never happened? Would he ever even see her again after he dropped her back in Fulham? The thought of her absence made him ache.

"Do you want to know whether I like you back?"

He smiled at the disarming frankness of the question. "Erm. Yes. But only if it's the right answer."

Evie blinked at this and put her finger to his lips. "Well…put it this way: I don't just jump into bed with men willy-nilly."

He laughed quietly, assuming there was a compliment buried in there somewhere. "I hope you didn't do it just out of curiosity."

Evie looked at him strangely and steadily. She started to speak and then did not. In the still of the early morning with the first hints of light creeping against the windows, she sat up and straddled him. Was this her reply? He thought that he would never forget the sight and the feel of her, the happiness in her face, or the bone-shaking, soul-splitting joy of her body collapsing against him afterwards. He understood her suggestion—that she had not slept with many men. He guessed the years since her parents died had not exactly been party time, and although she was beautiful, exquisitely so, she was also shy and reserved. He could tell that there hadn't been many before him. But for all that, there was nothing lacking. By some unknown creature of instinct or intuition, she knew exactly what to do with him.

At some unremembered moment, they must have fallen asleep because, some hours later, Charlie found himself blinking into the daylight and stretching his hand out for her, only to find an empty space. He sat up, stretching, to see her scampering around the room, dressed and stuffing things into her leather holdall. She crouched down and retrieved her knickers from behind the dressing table where he had thrown them.

"Good morning," he said, and she spun around, holdall in one hand, screwed up knickers in the other.

"Good morning."

"You're up early."

"Not really, it's nine o'clock."

James and Honoria ate their breakfast early, and the breakfast things would have been cleared away at some time after eight. They had told their hosts that they would be leaving early, so their non-appearance at breakfast had probably raised eyebrows. Evie looked agitated, and he thought she must be worried about this.

"I'll go and get dressed, and we'll get breakfast at that pub in Lambton. How about that?"

She zipped up her bag and placed it at the end of the bed.

"I think you should definitely go and get dressed, but before we leave, there's something we need to do."

"Of course, we'll say goodbye to the Darcys."

"No, I mean something else. I decided during the night after…when you were sleeping."

"What, Evie?" He hooked his fingers in the belt rings of her jeans and pulled her gently towards him.

"I'm going to put Elizabeth's diaries back in the chapel. I'm not taking them. I'm going to put them back where Hannah hid them and leave them there."

"You're kidding."

"No, I mean it."

"But you would be leaving them for someone else to find. Those books are what we came here for, and they're a smoking gun, Evie. It's all there. Victoria Darcy was not the daughter of Fitzwilliam Darcy. It is in black and white in his wife's own hand. It's enough to see you and Clemmie disinherited from the Darcy Trust. If you take them, you don't have to worry about it. You can get on with your life without looking over your shoulder."

"But it's stealing, Charlie. They're not mine, and I'm not taking them. It's Elizabeth's story, and it belongs here even if nobody knows about it."

He took one hand away from her jeans and raked his fingers through his hair. His mind was racing to catch up with the sheer boldness of it: to come all this way and go through so much, and then to simply turn away from the prize when she actually held it in her hands. It made him dizzy.

"It's a risk."

"I know. My risk."

There was a steeliness and a certainty in her eyes that reminded him of his dad. She was the kind of person who would do what was right rather than what was best for her, and once she was decided, there would be no moving her. He knew it was pointless to try to budge her, and somewhere inside him, he knew that she was right as well. He wrapped his arms around her middle and kissed her head.

"Okay. I'm going to shower and get dressed, and then I'll knock for you, and we'll go down to the chapel together, okay?"

She smiled broadly and playfully.

"Okay. Thank you for not arguing."

Charlie sneaked across the corridor and into his own bedroom. Looking at the made bed, untouched, he thought of how much had changed in the night. He knew that, if the worst came to the worst, he would look after her, and if the price of her love was the uncertainty of leaving Elizabeth's diary behind, then it was worth paying. As he showered, dressed, and threw his things into his case, he decided that, if they could get the books back into the box and close it securely, there was no real reason to think that anyone would ever find them. They had been there for a hundred and sixty years without disturbance, and even if Cressida came here, she would never think to look there. He reassured himself with these thoughts and collected Evie, and together they made their way downstairs to the chapel.

Charlie flicked on the lights and, once inside, slid on his back underneath the pew with Evie kneeling beside him holding the books in her arms like a baby. There was a layer of dust on the floor, and the evidence of what they had done crept about her. It made her all the more certain that she had made the right decision.

"Are you okay? Do you have enough light? I have a torch on my phone…"

She started fumbling in her pocket, but the truth was that Charlie could see perfectly fine.

"No, I don't really need it. I just need to get this catch back in place…" He squinted as he concentrated on the antique fastening, and Evie's heart began to race. She clenched and unclenched her fists and looked around at the yawning emptiness of the chapel before she felt Charlie's hand on her knee.

"Hey, don't worry. I will only be a minute. If you like, wait outside or go and find the Darcys. I'll catch you up when I'm done."

"No, no. I want to stay."

With that, she forced a smile, and he knew he had to speed up. Somehow, by luck or judgment, he managed it. One by one, he squeezed the small leather-bound books full of secrets back into the box, firmly closed the lid, and fastened it. It occurred to him that Hannah had probably been in just as much of a hurry when she had done the job originally in 1853. He prayed that his handiwork would last as long, and as he sat up, he kissed the girl in front of him because he just couldn't resist. It happened so rapidly that it confused all of them. He moved away from her soft face, and over her honey blonde-shrouded shoulder, his eyes rested on another—Honoria Darcy—framed in the doorway. Her face was somehow abashed, and she folded her arms under her bust defensively. Charlie stilled, and his expression must have said it all because Evie spun around and gasped as Honoria spoke.

"You won't find many original Clerkenman's down there, Mr. Hayward."

SOMETIME LATER, JAMES DARCY MOVED A PEN ON HIS DESK AND LOOKED up at them.

"Now, I am going to give you time to speak, but I should tell you right away that I am going to need a very good reason not to telephone the police. My wife tells me that she found you rummaging around in the chapel where you have apparently discovered a number of documents belonging to me which you were in the process of removing."

"Mr. Darcy, I—"

"You will allow me to finish, Mr. Haywood. I have had a brief look at these books, and they appear to be the reminiscences of a relation of mine. I had no idea that they existed or that they were secreted in the way that they were. I cannot imagine what they have to do with either of you, but then I get the impression that I am not in possession of the full facts. It may not surprise you to learn that I am of the old school and not confident with modern technology. However, Mrs. Darcy has spoken on the telephone to our son who has discovered by way of the internet that you, sir, far from being an art historian, are in fact a private detective of some flavour. I do not even begin to address the untruths you spun in order to gain access to my home. What the role of this young lady is, I know not. But it will not surprise you to be told that I am far from happy. And so, I have the disadvantage of limited information which you shall remedy for me now."

"Mr. Darcy, firstly, I should say that everything I am about to say is my responsibility and mine alone. Miss—"

"Pemberton. My name is Evie Pemberton."

"Well, good grief," muttered Honoria from behind James as she turned to the window.

"Evie would not be here if it were not for me, and she would certainly never have deceived you."

"I will be the judge of that. Who are you, both of you, and what are you doing here?"

And so, in the simplest language, Charlie told him. He told him of how Cressida Carter had come to his office and what she had alleged, of how he had found the letters and realised their importance. He described how he had pursued Evie for information. How he had changed tack and encouraged her to come here searching for the lost Elizabeth papers, which they had eventually found and read the previous night. Passionlessly, he summarised the contents of Elizabeth's diary. To boil it down to a series of facts seemed a savage way to treat that story of love and loss and loyalty and secrets, but he had to cut away the emotion. James Darcy raised his eyebrows as Charlie described how he had been in favour of Evie taking the papers and destroying them, but she refused. Honoria had caught them not in the act of stealing but of replacing. To be believed seemed like a forlorn hope.

James straightened his spectacles and stood. He moved slowly but steadily towards the window where he remained with his back to them, his old hands clasping his stick behind his back. Outside, a gardener dragged a rake across the freshly mowed lawn. The silence that followed filled the room, and Evie's hand circled around Charlie's wrist. Breaking the deadlock, Charlie spoke.

"Mr. Darcy, I—"

"Miss Pemberton, it disappoints me greatly that you did not approach me directly with this problem." He turned slowly, leaning on his stick, and Evie detected a new expression in his eyes.

"You see, I do know about the Darcy Trust. There is not a great deal for me to do, but I am the trustee, so I am aware of it. I am told whenever a new beneficiary is born or comes of age. I am also told whenever a beneficiary dies. I was sorry to be notified of your late mother's early death some years ago, and I was aware of the fact that your sister has increased needs."

He lowered his gaze, and Evie flushed. She had not thought that anyone outside of her immediate circle was aware of it or remotely interested. James's words and the heat she felt from Charlie's wrist—which she realised she was still hanging on—made her blink in surprise.

"You see, my understanding is that Fitzwilliam Darcy set up this trust because he thought it possible that, in the future, his female descendants may need it. He didn't know why or how of course, but nobody ever does, do they? It would have been far more conventional for him to leave his entire estate to his only son, who was my third great grandfather. And yet, he did not. He separated out the Rosschapel estate and left it to his daughters and his daughters' daughters and so on. What he did was a very definite thing. It wasn't an accident. It wasn't a coincidence. He set up this trust because he wanted that money to go to those people. Do you agree with me, Miss Pemberton?"

"Yes."

"Now. Whatever the truth of things, when he died, he knew that he was including Victoria in that bequest. He intended that she should be considered as his daughter and not the child of another. If he had wanted to exclude her, he could have done so. But he did not. It seems to me that for her to be excluded now and, through her, you and your sister would be the last thing Fitzwilliam Darcy would have wanted. Do you agree with that?"

"I think so, Mr. Darcy."

"I am going to consider this matter and formulate a response. It may be complex, or it may be simple. I need to think about it. In the meantime, until you hear otherwise, your share of the trust shall remain the same."

"Thank you."

"It will take me time to read the whole of this diary and digest its contents, although I am sure that the salient points as described by you, Mr. Haywood, are correct. I should say at this point that I have no intention whatsoever of destroying these papers."

Evie allowed herself to breathe. She could not understand her relief, but it flooded over her.

"I understand why my third great grandmother and her maid wanted it destroyed, but that was long ago, and I cannot agree that it would be necessary or appropriate now. I hope that does not worry you, Miss Pemberton?"

"No, not at all. I would not destroy it either if I were you."

"No. And you did not destroy it when you had the opportunity, which I acknowledge."

"Mr. Darcy?"

"Yes?"

"Do you know how the rumour started?"

"No, I do not, and I think maybe we will never know. The story as you relate it to me is a complete surprise. I certainly have no reason to believe that Victoria was troubled in her lifetime by the circumstances of her birth. Maybe some people were suspicious. It would have appeared odd that she alone of all her siblings was born away from Pemberley, and of course, her date of birth (which may have been falsified) was rather close to that of the final child, Bennet Darcy. Maybe there was a bit of talk. Who knows? We have all played Chinese whispers. Can you imagine a game that lasts nearly two hundred years? I suspect that is how Miss Carter's Aunt Mary—who, let us not forget, was a very elderly lady and not in good health—came to believe a tale so far from the truth."

Charlie looked down at her figure beside him before he addressed their hosts. "Mr. and Mrs. Darcy, it has been a tumultuous morning, and I am conscious that, in addition to our other offences, we have trespassed on your time and your home far too long. Unless there is anything you want us to stay for, we'll head back to London."

James Darcy nodded. "Very well."

As Charlie ushered her out of the oak-clad room to the doorway, Evie turned and surprised them all.

"I really did love the painting. Thank you for letting us spend so much time with it—with them. I felt as though I knew them."

"Of course, you did, my dear. They are your family."

OUTSIDE ON THE GRAVEL DRIVE, EVIE SANK INTO THE PASSENGER SIDE OF the Porsche while Charlie loaded their bags into the boot. He started the engine and drove slowly up towards the road at the top of the valley, Pemberley diminishing in the rear view mirror. He wondered whether he would ever see it again. If it wasn't for the fact that he never recalled his dreams, he almost might have believed that he had dreamt the whole thing. Evie sat motionless beside him, her hair obscuring her face, and it occurred to him that she might be crying. As they rumbled towards the road at the top of the valley, he reached out his hand to hers. She took it and looked up, dry-eyed.

"Evie?"

"Mmm?"

"I'm sorry, darling."

"Don't be sorry. I'm not sorry about anything that happened—even getting caught. Thank you for calling time on it as well. I like them, and we owed them the truth. But I am so tired, and I just want to go home."

"I'll take you home. You will be back in Fulham in about four hours, tops."

"I might nap. I'm feeling a bit sleepy." She crossed her legs and snuggled down into the seat, gently closing her heavy eyelids.

"What do you want me to do when I get you home?"

She opened her eyes to the pale, gold light shimmering through the window and turned in her seat to face him before answering. "Stay."

Chapter 26

Today, I was looking over my left shoulder at Mr. Clerkenman in the pose that I have held for several days, and I was reminded of the late Sir William Lucas about his garden. The small frame of the artist hunched, and his eyes focussed with formidable concentration. He occasionally lets out a sound I do not believe he is aware of, and altogether, the comparison brings a smile to my lips.

"Mrs. Darcy, you have changed your expression. Please, may I ask you to desist?"

I am startled out of my reflections and immediately comply.

"Of course, Mr. Clerkenman."

I notice Victoria smile out of the corner of my eye and fear that, if I look at her, she shall laugh.

This is the tenth day that this august artist has been at Pemberley, and his direct manner of addressing us has surprised us all, Mr. Darcy in particular, I believe. Nevertheless, it has been a diversion, and every time I look at the underside of the enormous canvas before me, I blush that I shall be at the centre of it. On the first day, after the introductions were made, I sat with all of the girls around me in their various positions. We were told that the artist wished to see us as an ensemble, get a notion of us when we are together. Thereafter, each day has been spent with me and but one of the girls. It was felt that they are too young to be reconciled to more than a few hours of posing, and Mr. Clerkenman has made a number of sketches from which

I assume him to be working.

Today is Victoria's day, and presently she sits on the rug a foot or so from the hem of my gown. From my vantage point, I see her delicate fingers worrying at the ribbon on her dress and the slight twitch of her head of chestnut curls, which speaks of restlessness. If she could tell the time, she would be watching the clock that ticks on the mantle. Alas, she is only five years old and so must amuse herself otherwise. When Mr. Clerkenman indulges us with a short rest, she flings out her arms and breaks into a great smile. I nod to her, and taking my meaning, she thanks the artist before throwing herself at me for an embrace and a request to run to the day nursery to visit Bennet. My son is most put out not to be included in this endeavour, but it is a point on which Fitzwilliam was adamant. There would be, he said, many portraits of Bennet painted in his lifetime, including with his father. This painting, he determined, would feature his wife and daughters and no other. What a thrill I felt when I heard those words!

When Victoria returns from her mercy mission to the nursery, having acquired a small doll that rightly belongs to Beatrice, Mr. Clerkenman is most displeased.

"Miss Darcy's colour is now too high, Mrs. Darcy, and she is too agitated. We shall have to wait yet awhile for her to restore herself."

I looked at her flushed face and loosened hair and could not regret it. Yes, we shall wait for her to restore herself, but Victoria is a character who shall not be stopped from running here and there. She plumps down on the floor, throwing her head back in one last laugh before the silence that must follow, and I think instantly of Lydia.

Does any person suspect? I cannot know, and I dare not ask. I look at her pretty round face and mass of curls and worry myself insensible that it is obvious. Fortunately, there is enough likeness to me to be a diversion from the truth, and although she shows every sign of being tall, I shall be able to pass that off as being due to Fitzwilliam. There have been moments of panic over the years. When Bennet was born nine months after Victoria, I believe my sister Kitty looked at me askance. She and I sat in silence in my drawing room one night, and I was sure that she had words she wished to speak. I know not what I would have said in response, and in the event, she turned her face to the fire and spoke not. Even now, she looks at Victoria and tilts her head, and I wonder about how much she has surmised.

Mrs. Reynolds, I have wondered at as well. She says nothing, but when I stepped out of our carriage upon our return from Rosschapel with Victoria in my arms, she blinked before her curtsey. I thanked her profusely for her letters and her care of the household in my absence. Her loyalty to my husband's family would, I believe, champion over any supposition of her own mind. The discovery, weeks after our return to Pemberley, that I was again with child presented new complications. During one of our morning meetings, I told Mrs. Reynolds that I was expecting again. I had deliberately left it as long as I considered reasonable, knowing it may be necessary later to claim that the babe was before his time. Mrs. Reynolds smiled and congratulated me. Behind those eyes, I saw a question suppressed. I shall not be the one to surface it.

I say "before *his* time" because, in the autumn of 1821, I knew in my bones that I was carrying a son. I knew as well exactly the moment of his creation in the inn by the dock at Dublin. Apart from the occasional necessary remark, Fitzwilliam and I do not speak of the events at Rosschapel. It is part of our story and known to both of us. It is as he suggested to me. We have acted as though Victoria is the child of our bodies; therefore, she is. My eyes move down to her delicate figure on the floor, and I am shocked out of my reverie by her suddenly violent sneeze.

"Miss Darcy!"

"I am sorry, Mr. Clerkenman. *Achoo!*"

The gentleman slams his brush down upon his pallet just as the door creeks open, and Fitzwilliam appears, smiling.

"Papa!" shrieks Victoria, leaping up from her place at my feet and hurling herself into her father's embrace.

"Well, really," mutters Mr. Clerkenman, and he peers over his spectacles at me, standing alone before him.

Fitzwilliam, it appears, is unaffected by his discontented resident portraitist.

"Good afternoon, sir. I am pleased to see that matters are proceeding well. I am not here to disturb your endeavours. I came to tell Mrs. Darcy that Mr. and Mrs. Bingley have been seen on the road and should be here within the hour."

Mr. Clerkenman let out an unfamiliar noise and looked away before saying, "Of course, Mr. Darcy." I fear that the poor man's nerves shall not survive his stay with our family, and when Fitzwilliam has departed,

I encourage Victoria to sit quietly to enable as much painting as possible before our guests arrive.

How busy is this life? Too busy, I find, for writing, for it is a rarity for me to sit down and record my thoughts where once it was commonplace. I know not whether it is the demands of a large household and six children or simply the contentment of both, but I do not feel the urge to write that once I did. Indeed, it occurs to me that it was rash of me to write as freely as I have done on some subjects. My own words in these pages haunt my mind: this is a story for the ears and the lips. Did I not tell myself that once and yet not take heed? Although there were times, not long ago, when my diary gave me great solace, I wonder now whether I have said too much. I believe I have. And so, I have decided, standing in my sitting room with the sun on my back and Mr. Clerkenman painting away in front of me, that there are certain portions of my books that ought to be destroyed. They are quite safe for the moment as I keep them in the cupboard below my vanity. One day, I shall speak to Hannah, and we shall destroy the parts that should not be seen by other eyes. It shall not be today, for I am engaged in this wonderful prison of sitting in silent happiness with my youngest daughter, and in less than an hour, Jane and Mr. Bingley shall be here. Maybe some time hence, when the painting is completed and the Bingleys are away. With this resolved in my mind, I rest my eyes upon the artist and resolve to think on it no longer.

Chapter 27

Pemberley, 14 December 2014

Cressida's eyes widened as she turned her car off the main road and slowly advanced down the gravelly drive. A blanket of bone-chilling cold hung in the air, and there before her was a sight, all at once familiar and completely new: Pemberley. How strange to see it in reality with her own eyes, part of her own story. Her mind flicked to one of many Sunday evenings past, and she recalled Granny getting out her big book of great British houses after supper. The book always fell open to the same page. And there the stories always started, of course: the terribly grand relations just out of reach, the glories of the past remembered. Cressida reflected that the house looked rather different in the bitter December air, framed by leafless trees, than it had in the picture in Granny's book, taken no doubt in the height of summer who knows how many years previously. The memory of it slightly caught her off-guard, and she shook herself to snap out of it. The vast, cold stone of Pemberley was before her, and she was invited, anticipated. She had written, and they had responded. At the edge of the turning circle were parked a mucky, Land Rover and a red sports car. Cressida thought of her battered Golf and parked it a bit to the side. The notion of the Darcys coming out and seeing her sad jalopy next to their terribly smart wheels made her draw in her breath. As if for reassurance, she reached into her open handbag on the passenger seat and felt inside for Honoria's note. It was there. It was real. This was a thing. She was expected for tea.

Soon her reverie was broken by the appearance at the great door of a small and well-presented lady of advancing years, muffled up in a too-large wax jacket, shivering against the season. She hurried down the stone stairs and met Cressida as she was locking up the Golf.

"Miss Carter?"

"Yes." She held out her slim hand and the woman's rings clinked against hers as they greeted one another. Their breath danced in the chill air, and Cressida, who had been warm inside the car, fought the urge to shake with cold.

"I'm Honoria Darcy. Come in. It's perishing out here."

They bundled in through the enormous door, and Honoria thrust it shut with a forbidding sort of clank. Cressida's eyes drifted over the richness and wonder within: the painted faces on the walls, the warm acres of historic luxury. She realised with a start that she had missed what Mrs. Darcy had said to her.

"Sorry? Come again?"

"May I take your coat, Miss Carter?"

"Erm, yes, thank you." She slipped it off and slightly wondered at the lack of home help. Surely, people like the Darcys had somebody to assist with this sort of thing. Who ever imagined Mrs. Darcy hanging up the coats of her guests herself? That was certainly not the sort of life that Granny had said they lived at Pemberley—quite the reverse.

"It's awfully kind of you to have me so close to Christmas, Mrs. Darcy."

Her eye was caught by the half-decorated Christmas tree at the foot of the staircase; a box of tinsel and baubles sat open on the floor.

"You are welcome. And you must call me Honoria. As you can see, I'm afraid we are rather behind with Christmas! But never mind that. I say, 'well done, you' for battling the weather. Our housekeeper, who is attending her granddaughter's Christmas play at the school in the village, says the roads are treacherous with ice. I say you've done awfully well to get here at all. Now, let us warm you up with some tea. Come along."

Cressida nodded and followed Honoria as she clipped across the uneven tiles of the hall floor, past the piercing eyes of her ancestors, and into a drawing room with a blazing fire. This, Cressida thought, as her gaze fell on the flame-brightened walls laden with gilt-framed portraits, was where she belonged. She noticed—a moment too late to be really polite—that an elderly man stood up from a chair by the fire and held out his hand.

"Miss Carter? Welcome to Pemberley. I am James Darcy. I am sorry not to greet you at the door, but as you see, my legs fail me somewhat." In his left hand, he held on to a stick that glistened slightly in the orange light.

"Cressida, please. It's wonderful to be here, Mr. Darcy. I have heard so much about Pemberley over the years—stories and what not. My granny came here once before the war."

"Did she?"

"Yes. Her name was Letitia Blackburn. She was one of the Shropshire Blackburns, not the London lot. She could never abide Town, but she loved it here. She said that I would love it too, and I can see that she was right." Her voice faded in volume, and her eyes took in the room. James smiled, and she felt suddenly light.

"Well, I'm pleased to hear it, although I suspect that I was only a boy when your grandmother came here. Now, we are cousins, aren't we? So firstly, you must stop this 'Mr. Darcy' business and call me James, and secondly, you must sit down and have some tea after such a long journey."

Cressida smiled at this and blushed slightly. "Thank you, James." She moved towards an incidental table on which Honoria had placed a tea tray before leaving the room. Cressida clattered the saucers slightly as she separated them and placed the small teacups ready to pour. She had slightly expected to spend time with Mrs. Darcy as well as her husband, but no matter. After a short interlude, they were each settled with their tea and regarding one another through the wisps of steam that rose from their cups.

"Now, Cressida, I haven't thanked you for your letter, but I ought to do so. I'm sorry that it has taken us so long to arrange this meeting, but I was very glad to hear from you. I'm afraid that we have just had rather a lot on. We had some guests here in the late summer, and there were a lot of matters arising from that visit that took up my time. And then our younger son and his wife came to stay. So it has been, as my wife would say, 'like Piccadilly circus' here. I hope that you don't think we were putting you off."

He tilted his head and fixed her with a flash of his hazel eyes. Taking a sip from her cup, she looked away slightly although she could not say why it was that she felt discomforted.

"No, of course not."

"Good. I also hope that the next time you visit shall be in a more clement season."

Cressida sat up straighter and beamed. She hadn't expected that and didn't quite know how to respond. Of course, she was family, and so, really, it was only right that she be invited back.

"That would be wonderful. It was summer when Granny visited here—1936."

"Well, in that case, she will have seen the gardens at their best although it was, of course, rather an inauspicious year. Tell me a bit about your grandmother, Cressida."

"Well, you know, she was just a county lady really. Married, lived in the country, had children, kept dogs, that sort of thing. Family history was her bag, and she made a great study of the Darcys and Pemberley. When I was growing up, she was full of it, terribly proud to be a member of the family—very well up on things too. She knew all about the Victorian Darcys and the turn of the century and the roaring twenties and all that. I wonder that she should have been a historian. Her mother had married a chap—"

"Was that her father?"

"Yes. But he wasn't quite out of the top drawer if you know what I mean, and I think she felt it rather."

"I see. That is rather a shame, isn't it? I wonder whether she was aware of the fact that we are all of us descended from a remarkably happy but unequal marriage." Cressida held in her breath and looked confused. They peered at one another for a moment before he waved his hand almost imperceptibly and continued. "Go on."

"Well, there isn't much else to say really. She was a passable pianist. Made a good pastry, that sort of thing. I suppose it is hard in this day and age, when one has so many relations, to keep a hold of them."

"We do have rather a lot of cousins drifting about, it has to be said. Having said that, I do recall the name Letitia from my involvement in the Darcy Trust, of which I believe you are also a beneficiary."

"Yes, I am." Cressida almost barked in response.

"I am the trustee."

"I thought that was the solicitors—those people in Fleet Street."

"Well, they act for me, Cressida. Ultimately, the responsibility is mine. So, if one year you get less than you should or you think that there is anything amiss, it is me whom you should approach. I hope, now that we have met, that you will feel confident doing that."

Cressida's mind bolted. In the heady excitement of her invitation, she had nearly lost sight of why she had written to the Darcys in the first place. Her schemes to ransack the house in pursuit of Elizabeth Darcy's lost document had receded, and her imagination had been given over to images of strolling in the gardens and swooping down the staircase in her best dress. Now that she was here, the idea of searching the house for the secret papers seemed an impossibility. It was suddenly ludicrous. The drawing room alone was a cavernous, great place, and heaven knew how many rooms there were altogether. She fiddled with her watch, shifted on the chaise, and considered that her best chance had just presented itself to her of its own volition.

"Goodness. Well, as it happens, I do have a few questions about the trust."

"Go on."

"Well, how can you be sure that all the women who get money from the trust are real Darcys? I mean, if someone was illegitimate or anything like that."

"It wouldn't actually matter whether someone was illegitimate. When Fitzwilliam Darcy settled the trust in 1860, the words he used were 'all of my female descendants.' Now, as far as I am aware, the only children Fitzwilliam Darcy had were the children of his marriage, which I am given to understand was a famously happy one. However, if, for the sake of argument, any of his descendants were born out of wedlock, it wouldn't actually make any difference."

"But it would if they weren't really his."

"Well, yes, but I think that most unlikely."

She felt the familiar stirrings of agitation rising up in her. People were so credulous, so complacent. She had to make him listen to her. When she spoke, the words came out more aggressively than she had intended.

"That isn't what I've heard. I've heard that Fitzwilliam's wife was no better than she ought to be, and one of the daughters was the offspring of God knows who—"

"Cressida, my dear, would you mind turning and looking at the wall behind you?"

Cressida blinked and clanked her cup clumsily against her saucer, but she did as he asked. When she looked upon the painting on the wall, it surprised her that she hadn't noticed it when she walked into the room. It was a huge group portrait of Regency-era women, several of them children, framed in gold. Cressida wasn't much of a one for art, but it was pretty.

"These ladies are the wife and daughters of Fitzwilliam Darcy. The painting was done here at Pemberley at eye-watering expense by an artist named Alfred Clerkenman who was extremely eminent. It is rather momentous, isn't it? I am told that it has some significance for the history of art as well. There are scholars around the world who would like very much to see this for various academic reasons, with which I shall not detain you. However, since its creation, it has been—to some extent rather selfishly—kept here. I have grown up with these ladies looking down on me just as you have grown up with Granny Letitia's stories. Now, in my old age, I am considering loaning the painting to the National Portrait Gallery for a short time in order that people outside of our family circle may see it. But when I look at the painting and think of the trust that was created for these girls, which endures to this day, I am inclined to conclude that Fitzwilliam Darcy had an ardent loyalty to the women in his life."

Cressida's gaze danced over their faces, and she gripped her teacup tightly to stop a shake.

"But what if there were evidence that one of them wasn't his?"

"Oh, but I can't imagine there would be, can you, Cressida? It is very hard to imagine that there is any truth in the rumour that you have heard or that, even if there were, there would be any sort of proof of the same."

"Well..."

"It also occurs to me, that there are some avenues of investigation from which we should all shrink. I believe that there have been certain enquiries made about this subject, and please be clear, I do not intend to tolerate it. Some things in life are for questioning and some are for accepting. I, for example, accept that, over the years, I ought to have made greater efforts to stay in touch with remote relations. I have signed cheques every year, but until now, I have not paid personal attention to the beneficiaries of that money. I hope you understand that I am willing to be a friend to you now, Cressida, but I must ask you to accept that the family in this portrait was, in every sense, a family and say no more about it. After all, you are a Darcy, are you not? I am sure that you are more than able to live up to the examples of generosity and magnanimity that our shared ancestors set us."

She looked from James's face to the light cotton dresses and ringlet-framed faces on the wall and began to feel queasy. This was not how she had imagined things. A clock chimed in another room, and she heard a telephone ring briefly in the distance. The room was closing in around her like a vice.

James leaned forward in his chair. "Are we agreed?"

"Yes, we are agreed."

"Good. Now, let's find Honoria. She will show you around the house if you like, and then I believe that lunch will be about ready."

Cressida swallowed. "Sounds lovely."

Chapter 28

London, the same day,
a little later in the afternoon

Isobel Langley-Jones had been trying to type one of Mr. Samuelson's tapes for the last hour, and she was beginning to wish that she had not given up smoking. He had a habit of bounding about his office while he was dictating and holding the ageing Dictaphone too close to his lips. Each burbled sentence was punctuated by the sound of his cursing as he knocked over a stack of papers or text messages buzzed away on his mobile. One of the other secretaries said you needed a PhD to decipher the babble, and Issy was inclined to agree. She was about to get another biscuit by way of comfort when his light lit up on her phone.

"Yes, Mr. Samuelson."

"Issy, would you mind popping in here a sec?"

He sounded distracted, and she could imagine him already, poised between standing and sitting, sinking behind a mountain of papers. She wandered from the secretaries' bay to his office where she found him exactly thus.

"Ah, Issy, super. Take a seat."

She removed three files and a book about taxes from the chair opposite his desk and gingerly sat, pen poised above notepad.

"I've had a call from James Darcy up in Derbyshire about this bloody Darcy Trust. You might remember that we send out the cheques on the same day each year to a number of beneficiaries. For legal reasons, the dratted thing has to be re-settled every eighty years, but due to my youth"—he laughed at his own joke—"I have never had to deal with that. Apart from the cheques, there is precious little to do on it."

The words "Darcy Trust" rang through Issy's mind like a siren, and she felt suddenly cold. She had hardly thought of Charlie since seeing him in the summer, but suddenly their meeting in Temple Gardens seemed like it was yesterday. She recalled taking the file and copying it before sending it to him and shuddered with guilt and regret. Issy took a deep breath, determined to appear calm even if she didn't feel it. In her panic, she had missed some of Mr. Samuelson's instruction and desperately strained to catch up with him.

"...bit of a strange one. He wants me to draft a slight amendment to the trust document. I've had a look at it, and he is the sole trustee, so there's nothing stopping him, although I can't for the life of me see why."

He leaned over the side of his desk and momentarily disappeared behind a pile of correspondence files, his voice muffled by the sheer volume of paper.

"Ah, here it is. It's very peculiar..." He stood up and handed her a large blue folder. "You will find the trust document here, and the latest version will be on the system. What I need you to do, Issy, is change the wording slightly. It currently reads 'female descendants of Fitzwilliam Darcy.' You need to change it to 'female descendants of Anne Bellamy, nee Darcy; Emma Warburton, nee Darcy; Frances Cathcart, nee Darcy; Beatrice Hopkins, nee Darcy; Victoria Montague, nee Darcy; and Bennet Darcy.' Have you got that?"

He paused just long enough for her to nod, her pencil dancing the shorthand across the paper in front of her. She exhaled—no mention of Charlie or the old file that she had taken from storage and copied and sent to him, no mention of the records, and no mention of the Elizabeth Darcy business that had been spoken of in those old letters. It seemed—she dared herself to conclude—to be about something completely different.

"...got no idea why he wants this. It seems to me that it makes no difference because those women *were* the daughters of Fitzwilliam Darcy, and Bennet Darcy was his son. I've got the family tree here, and it's as plain as the nose on your face. But anyway, there it is; the client is king and all that. You have a go at drafting it and print it out. I'll have a look at it, okay?"

"Yes, Mr. Samuelson. Do you need it today?"

"If you have time, or tomorrow would be fine. It can't be urgent; that bloody trust has been going since 1860."

"I will get on to it as soon as I finish your tape, if that is all right?"

"Yes, that's fine, Issy."

She stood up to leave.

"Here is James Darcy's letter. Can you pop it in the file for me? Oh, and that's the other thing. He makes rather a strange comment. He says that if this firm receives any correspondence from a Miss Cressida Carter, who is one of the beneficiaries, we are to notify him straight away and not communicate with her without his approval. Seems to think that she is a bit of a troublemaker. So it might be worth writing that on the inside cover of the file in case somebody other than you or I need to pick it up. Very strange, but there it is. Ours is not to reason why, that's what I say…"

"Right-o, Mr. Samuelson. Will do."

With that and with a gushing sense of relief, Issy returned to her desk and to the impenetrable tape. She got herself a sweet tea in quiet celebration that she had been called into a partner's office to discuss the Darcy Trust and it had not involved her being handed her P45. The afternoon pushed on in frustration and an excess of caffeine until, at last, the clock above the secretary pool ticked to five thirty and Issy got up to leave. She had managed to finish the tape, she hoped with a reasonable degree of accuracy, and had made a start on amending the Darcy Trust document. The strange coincidence of Charlie's request all those months ago and this change to the trust played around in her head, but she could not explain it. Like much of her work, she understood the edges of it rather than the whole thing, but even so, like Mr. Samuelson, she could not quite see the point in the amendment James Darcy had suggested. She wrapped her pashmina loosely around her neck, fastened her winter coat, said goodbye to Mr. Samuelson's trainee, whom she guessed would be working late, and wandered out.

Darkness had already fallen on the icy street. The walk to the Tube station took its usual four minutes, and on the way, she thought about what she would make for dinner and recalled that she had promised to call her mum that evening. The magazine stall outside the station entrance was teeming with people, muffled up against the pre-Christmas winter, trying to buy a magazine or a newspaper to read for their journey. She picked up a copy of the *Evening Standard* from the stack and, tucking it under her arm, glanced across the road to a sight for which she was quite unprepared. On the other side of the road—silhouetted against the purple pitch of the city at night, the bright lights of the South Bank flickering on the Thames—was Charlie Hayward, walking along with his arm around a girl, laughing.

Finis.

Author Q&A

Why would Fitzwilliam Darcy be so worried for future generations of Darcy women if his own daughters were so well taken care of?

I think Fitzwilliam looks at the example of Lydia and worries about the fate of a woman who doesn't have a protector in a world in which women had no resources of their own. He knows that his own daughters are wealthy women and that they have married men whom he trusts. He is not worrying about them but future generations. His frame of reference is one in which women have very limited rights and may easily lose the benefit of their family's wealth over time. Darcy is relentlessly honourable. His fans would call him a patrician (amongst other things...); his detractors might say he is something of a control freak. I think both of those elements are present in the Fitzwilliam in this story. He is trying to protect future generations of women in a patriarchal world. At the same time, rather than giving resources directly, he is doing so by way of trust in order that his male descendants can retain a level of supervision. His gamble is that they shall remain steadfast to his purpose, which, of course, they do.

Why do you think Charlie, a worldly man, is so flustered by Evie?

I think that Evie speaks to a need for honesty and integrity in Charlie's life. He is successful, but success is not enough for him in ways that he cannot acknowledge until he meets her. She manages to challenge and engage him directly and on her own terms. It works the other way around as well. Evie is quite a naive girl, but although she has a few weak-kneed moments, she is not especially flustered by Charlie. She is more composed than a lot of other women would be in her position. She does not appear to be too interested in him, and that is what he finds surprisingly alluring.

Why did you choose Elizabeth and Darcy's story from Elizabeth's point of view, and yet Charlie and Evie's story from both?

Those who have read *Suddenly Mrs. Darcy* know that I love writing in the first person. Although it has its disadvantages and pitfalls, it affords a closeness between the reader and the subject that really pulls me in. In this particular case, the experiences that Elizabeth has in *The Elizabeth Papers* are so intense and personal that I judged it right to speak them from her point of view. Also, writing as Elizabeth herself fits the plot of *The Elizabeth Papers* because, for the story to work, she has to leave some evidence of her secret behind to be discovered later. Between *Suddenly Mrs. Darcy* and *The Elizabeth Papers*, I am conscious that, although I have included some of his personal correspondence, I have neglected Mr. Darcy, and so maybe there is an idea for a future novel somewhere in there...

As to Charlie and Evie, I felt their story was more effectively told in a traditional third person narrative. They are equal partners in that they each develop as people and in relation to each other—so I tried to treat them even-handedly.

Why does Elizabeth not tell her beloved husband of her fears about not giving him a son?

There are secrets and unspoken fears in the closest and most loving relationships. One of the problems here is that Elizabeth perceives the "problem" of her not producing a son as an open secret, which everybody knows but does not speak of. English history is full of the aching problem of the absent male heir, as Anne Boleyn could testify! There would have been a great deal of pressure on Elizabeth to produce an heir to Pemberley, and Fitzwilliam himself acknowledges this in chapter 1. At first, she takes the view that the issue will resolve itself and, therefore, she does not need to say anything. Jane Austen tells us that Elizabeth is not given to melancholy nor do I think her prone to unnecessary self-analysis. As time goes on, however, she becomes troubled—and then desperate. She thinks of her own Bennet family where a lack of a son has had enormous ramifications. She is torn between the fear that it is her fault and her outrage at being blamed (as she perceives it) for something plainly beyond her control. This, together with pride and her innate English reserve, leads to a policy of non-communication with her husband.

How do you think the rumour about Victoria came about—and stayed around—but never was pursued until the present day?

My idea is that there must have been significant suspicion at the time amongst family and friends and amongst the staff at Pemberley. For Elizabeth to have travelled with Darcy to Ireland, not known to be expecting, and to have returned five months later with a baby would have appeared odd. At least one member of staff knows that they departed with Lydia and returned without her, and maybe he was not as discreet as he intended to be. Elizabeth tells us that she feared Mrs. Reynolds and Kitty suspected her. Rumours likely started—as most rumours do—when independent parties start joining up the dots. So, behind the scenes of the story, I imagine James the footman keeps the secret about Lydia for many years until he lets on to a maid whom he is sweet on. She is called to Mrs. Reynolds's office about something and, for some reason, imparts what she knows. That strikes a note in Mrs. Reynolds's mind because, of course, she has always had her questions about Victoria. Mrs. Reynolds and the maid are overheard speaking by another servant, and the matter becomes a well-known trope below stairs. Many years later, it is imparted to the ladies' maid of a member of the family, and so it spreads wider and deeper. Over time, the suspicion that Victoria is not Elizabeth's child becomes the suspicion that she is not Fitzwilliam's child. I think it most unlikely that, in Elizabeth's lifetime or during the lifetime of her children, anyone would question her fidelity. But as time moves on and memories cloud, the more salacious explanation appears to be the most satisfactory, and somewhere along the line, it takes hold. Or something like…

This is two stories woven to tell one. How did the change in eras affect how you thought of writing each story?

The Regency chapters alternate with the modern chapters, with Fitzwilliam's letters dotted around. I forced myself to write the chapters in the order that they appear now rather than to write one story, then the other, and then interlace them. I wanted the discipline of relating the stories to each other, but there were times when I was so mentally enmeshed in each story that, in my heart, I just wanted to focus on one and not the other. The fact that the two halves of the narrative are in completely different periods, one of which is my own time and place, had a huge impact on how I thought about them. When I was writing about the Regency, I made a conscious effort to push my mind back to that period, and I found writing the modern story somewhat more relaxed. I try to think about the variances in dress and comforts such as heat and electricity and how this would have made the world "feel" different—I hope that those differences are reflected in the two halves of the story. Since this was my first attempt at writing a contemporary love story, I was surprised by how much I enjoyed slipping in things that are exclusively of our own time like email and text messages.

I held my breath the entire time Charlie and Evie were searching Pemberley. Why do you think Evie did not explain the circumstances to the Darcys after their discovery? And what made you give Evie a change of heart, especially after all the trouble and stress they put themselves through?

It would be Evie's natural inclination to tell the truth, but she is wrong-footed by the plot. They make their discovery at night when the Darcys have gone to bed. Evie then discovered a truth that she was unprepared for, and she found herself unexpectedly emotionally moved by Elizabeth's words. She is emboldened by the discovery to act on her feelings for Charlie, and so that is her initial response to it. The decision not to remove the papers from Pemberley is another consequence of her reaction to reading them. Evie respects Elizabeth too much to effectively steal her story from its hiding place within her home. **Why does Evie not suggest that they take the story to the Darcys and explain?** The answer to this also lies in her response to Elizabeth's words. Evie feels that the most respectful treatment of Elizabeth's diary is to put it back where it had been hidden for nearly two centuries rather than invite further prying eyes (albeit they are family eyes).

Do you think there would be grounds for a real lawsuit if this were a true story? Do you think Cressida would have a chance to change the trust?

Although it is possible to set up trusts of this sort in English law, it is a challenge to keep them going over long periods of time, and in chapter 24, I have had to do some explaining that the lawyers amongst you may appreciate. The reality is that, to some extent because of the period of time, the trust is something of a flight of fancy. However, it is certainly true that, if a class of beneficiaries were to be the descendants of "person x" and somebody had evidence that a person involved was not so descended, they would have a case to challenge that person receiving anything from the trust. The key would be finding the evidence, which in the circumstances would be remarkably, probably prohibitively, difficult. In other words, the advice that Cressida says her solicitors have given her is bang on: you've got a case, but you'll never prove it!

The group portrait *Mrs. Darcy and Her Daughters* plays a major role in this story. What is the inspiration behind it?

The group painting of Elizabeth and her daughters that features in the story is the product of my imagination and not based on any particular work of art. However, it is inspired by the fashion for domestic group portraits in late eighteenth and nineteenth century European houses. These paintings were used to celebrate the particular family's wealth and power but also to memorialise family relationships. Often—because of the cost involved—the whole family would be included. In this case, I deliberately had Fitzwilliam subverting the genre by making it a female-only painting.

In terms of the artist, Mr. Clerkenman is also fictional. However, in imagining his work, I think of the nineteenth-century painters John Prescott Knight, Richard Rothwell, and the Royal portraitist Sir George Hayter. The style of the painting I imagine to be soft and not excessively formal, a sort of pre-cursor to the work, some decades later, of John Singer Sergeant.

The image on the front cover is taken from *Mother with Her Young Daughter* by Belgian artist, Gustave Leonard de Jonghe. It was painted in 1865, and readers will no doubt note that the fashions are slightly late for the period of this story. Despite this, something about the softness and intimacy of it really touched me. However, it is not intended to be a detail from *Mrs. Darcy and Her Daughters*. In my mind, I think of it as being Elizabeth and Victoria relaxing between sittings rather than in their formal poses.

You have chosen to end the modern story in an unusual way with Charlie and Evie being glimpsed in the street, laughing, by a third party. There is no explanation and no real "happily ever after" as in typical romance stories. What is your reader to make of this?

Well, I think it is just the beginning for Charlie and Evie. The reader can assume that they are together, and they are happy in that particular moment. You will have to judge for yourself whether they are well suited to one another, but I think they are. What happens next belongs to another story.

Acknowledgements

Thank you to Michele and all of the Meryton Press family for taking me in and being lovely.

To the inestimable Christina: speed editor, scene tweaker, character masseur, error corrector, US/UK diplomatic language envoy, head-hopping trouble shooter, big picture observer, social media coordinator, confidence builder, idea believer, friend; thank you.

Ellen, where would my grammar be without you? The Chicago Manual of Style also has a lot to answer for. ☺ Your corrections were all improvements, and your comments always make me smile; thank you.

Zuki, for another beautiful cover, fusing so cleverly the historical and the modern, and for all the colouring against the clock. It's lovely; thank you.

Jakki, for organising another blog tour and for doing so much behind the scenes to promote this and other stories. Thank you for the many bloggers who have supported and encouraged me.

Thank you to my fantastic beta readers, Chanda and Beau, who gave up time to read this story pre-edit.

Adam and Sophie, for their support and medical advice, and to Liz, for her obstetrics expertise. All errors and omissions are mine, of course. ▶

Thank you to my brilliant, nurturing, observant Mum.

To my children, who are the bees' knees.

Thank you to my husband Marc, who is an unfailing enthusiast, believer in unlikely plans, and general all-round top person.

Lastly, thank you to all the readers and reviewers of *Suddenly Mrs. Darcy* and anyone who reads this book. I love to hear from you, so please message me. I am on twitter @JenettaJames, and my Facebook page can be found at: https://www.facebook.com/jenettajameswriter/

Author Biography

J enetta James is a mother, lawyer, writer, and taker-on of too much. She grew up in Cambridge and read history at Oxford University where she was a scholar and president of the Oxford University History Society. After graduating, she took to the law and now practises full-time as a barrister. Over the years, she has lived in France, Hungary, and Trinidad as well as her native England. Jenetta currently lives in London with her husband and children where she enjoys reading, laughing, and playing with Lego. She is the author of *Suddenly Mrs. Darcy*, which was published by Meryton Press in April 2015. *The Elizabeth Papers* is her second novel.

JUL -- 2016
3497559

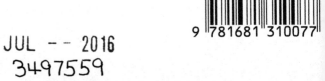